D1214794

ERYNN MANGUM

Paige Torn

A PAIGE ALDER NOVEL

TH1NK, an
Imprint of
NavPress

Discipleship Inside Out®

NavPress is the publishing ministry of The Navigators, an international Christian organization and leader in personal spiritual development. NavPress is committed to helping people grow spiritually and enjoy lives of meaning and hope through personal and group resources that are biblically rooted, culturally relevant, and highly practical.

For a free catalog go to www.NavPress.com
or call 1.800.366.7788 in the United States or 1.800.839.4769 in Canada.

© 2013 by Erynn Mangum O'Brien

ISBN-13: 978-1-61291-298-1

Cover design by Studiogearbox
Cover images by Thinkstock, Shutterstock, and CSA Images

Some of the anecdotal illustrations in this book are true to life and are included with the permission of the persons involved. All other illustrations are composites of real situations, and any resemblance to people living or dead is coincidental.

Scripture quotations in this publication are taken from the *Holy Bible, New International Version®* (NIV®). Copyright © 1973, 1978, 1984 by Biblica, used by permission of Zondervan. All rights reserved. Other versions used include: the New American Standard Bible® (NASB), Copyright © 1960, 1962, 1963, 1968, 1971, 1972, 1973, 1975, 1977, 1995 by The Lockman Foundation. Used by permission.

Mangum, Erynn, 1985-
  Paige torn / Erynn Mangum.
     pages cm. — (A Paige Alder novel ; book 1)
  Summary: "When Paige meets Tyler — a fun-seeking, Jesus-loving, easy-going guy who thinks it's crazy that she is so busy all the time — will Paige see that staying busy for God is not the same thing as spending time with Him?" — Provided by publisher.
  ISBN 978-1-61291-298-1
  [1. Christian life — Fiction. 2. Responsibility — Fiction. 3. Dating (Social customs) — Fiction.] I. Title.
  PZ7.M31266532Pai 2013
  [Fic] — dc23
                                    2012038386

OTHER NOVELS BY ERYNN MANGUM

LAUREN HOLBROOK SERIES:

Miss Match

Rematch

Match Point

MAYA DAVIS SERIES:

Cool Beans

Latte Daze

Double Shot

For my grandmother Eloise Terry —
I am so blessed to be the granddaughter of a woman
who loves the Lord so much. What an amazing legacy I
have been given! I love you so much, Nama.

Acknowledgments

To my Lord—thank You will never be enough. May every breath I breathe serve to give You glory, even in the midst of pain and questions. I love You, Jesus.

To my little family—Jon and Nathan—I love you both more than words can say. Jon, you are my best friend. I love how you make me laugh and hold me when I'm crying. Nathan, sweetheart, you are the light of my day, and being your mommy is the biggest honor God has given me.

To my family—Mom, Dad, Bryant, Caleb, and Cayce—God blessed me beyond comprehension when He put me in this family. I don't think I even realize how blessed I am that my parents and siblings are some of my closest friends. I love you all.

To my in-law and extended family—Nama, Greg and Connie, Allen and Vicky, Tommy, my aunts and uncles, and my dear cousins—thank you for being there for me during this last year. Your prayers and love kept me going! I love you.

To my dear friends — Leigh Ann Trebesh, Eryn Beechem, Melanie Larson, Jamie Poore, Thalia Chan, Shannon Layer, and Kaitlin Bar — I love you with all my heart. I can't imagine a sweeter circle of friends. Thank you for everything.

To my incredible NavPress team and my agent, Tamela Hancock Murray — I am so grateful to each of you for making this book a reality! Thank you for pushing me outside my comfort zone and making Paige a real character.

To *you*, my dear reader, I pray daily that God will bless you with His presence and that He will flood you with His love. May we both "grow in the grace and knowledge of our Lord and Savior Jesus Christ" (2 Peter 3:18).

Chapter
1

Living in Texas can be awesome. Or awful.

Like during the winter. I turn off the car and sigh at the blinking bank billboard across the street from the Starbucks parking lot that keeps repeating: *5:34 p.m. . . . 74° . . . 5:34 p.m. . . . 74°.*

So I am late, and snow is nowhere near in the immediate future. It's January, for goodness' sake. I climb out of my used Camry that I've scrimped and saved for two years to buy and trudge into the Starbucks where my best friend, Layla Prestwick, is waiting for me.

She has an enormous smile on her face, and she doesn't even bother with a greeting or volume control when she sees me. *"Paige! I am getting married!"* she screeches, grabbing me in a hug so tight I can't even choke out a congratulations.

I grin just the same. I knew it was coming. I had an idea after reading her text that brought me here today.

YOU MUST MEET WITH ME @ STARBUCKS ASAP! HERE IS A CLUE: <>O

An inkling, anyway.

"I'm so excited for you!" I say when she loosens her grip a little bit. "Macchiato is on me today." I order us both caramel macchiatos while Layla talks a hundred miles a minute about how her used-to-be-boyfriend-now-fiancé, Peter, proposed.

"So we were just sitting there on his couch watching a movie like we always do on Sunday nights and he is like hey Layla I love you and I am like yeah Peter I love you too and then he suddenly is handing me a ring and it is soooo special and I couldn't believe it so I started screaming and I am pretty sure I woke up his entire apartment complex and then the cops showed up because his downstairs neighbors thought Peter had gone postal or something but they were really nice and then told me congratulations and here's the ring!"

She shoves her left hand over to me—a solitaire, spar-kling in the lights.

For all the zero-breaths-taken during Layla's engagement story, I'm not about to confess to her that I think Peter's way of proposing is pretty lame.

The couch?

Compared to all of Layla's passion and exuberance and romance, Peter is about the dullest person on the planet, maybe right behind that *Thinker* statue everyone is so enam-ored with. I just don't see what Layla sees in him. And I really don't get the fascination with *The Thinker* either.

He is thinking. Got it.

It's about the same reaction I have to Peter. For all intents and purposes, Peter will make a great groom. He is male, he will show up to the wedding, and he will have no opinions about the ceremony or reception. He is like a Ken doll with dark hair but minus the great facial bone structure. I've compared him to a head of lettuce before. Obviously, I've never told Layla that, but I did tell my mom.

She didn't think it was very nice of me to compare one of God's creatures to a head of lettuce. Until I pointed out that a head of lettuce was created by God too.

"Paige, he's a person for goodness' sake. You can't just arbitrarily decide you don't like someone."

I've known Peter for almost four years. I am pretty certain I'm not being arbitrarial, or however you say that grammatically correct.

You know how there's always that one person you just don't like, and you don't really know why?

Mine is Peter.

All that aside, I'm happy for Layla. She's been wanting to get married since she was a flower girl in her cousin's wedding when she was eight.

She's still talking. "We've already set a date." She grins around her Starbucks paper cup. "It's going to be this fall. October 25. And it's going to be outside at that park with the gazebo at sunset. And then we're going to have the reception somewhere where we can dance. And you *have* to be my maid of honor."

I nod, because of course I will be her maid of honor. We decided this years ago.

I take a sip of my macchiato and pull my planner out of my purse. The cover is denim that I've sewn and decorated with daisy embroidery.

"Better use a pen to write that one down." Layla giggles. "Because you are not rescheduling my wedding!"

Layla knows my habits well. I roll my eyes and dig in my purse until I find a black Bic pen and start writing.

Layla's Wedding.

It looks weird writing it down. Weird and final.

Like when I finally paid attention to the expiration date on the milk in my fridge and realized I'd been drinking milk a week past due.

Layla is getting married. *Married.* Like a grown-up does. And instead of being overwhelmingly happy like I always thought I'd be, I suddenly just feel overwhelmed. And maybe a little sad. I am going to be twenty-three in three months. And while my mom likes to remind me that she had been married a year by the time she was my age, I am not ready.

I don't really know what I'm not ready for, but I'm not ready. For any of it. A wedding sounds fun, but a marriage sounds terrifying.

Layla suddenly seems about twenty years older than me. *God, don't let this be one of those typical friendships where one girl gets married and they stop being friends.*

Layla is still talking. "I'm going to have the colors be cream and blue with pops of pink, I think. I want it to be all vintage and shabby chic."

Layla is my stylish friend. Even now she looks like she's just walked out of a campaign for Forever 21. Her shoulder-length brown hair curls around a headband decorated with a flower right by her ear. I've always envied Layla's ability to wear accessories like that without looking completely ridiculous, like I do.

I nod at the right parts in her wedding detail monologue. I've known this girl for thirteen years. She went through puberty with me. Any friend who sticks by you through acne, braces, PMSing for the first time, and growth spurts that send you flying above every other head in the ninth-grade class—including every male—deserves to be your friend for life.

Thankfully, I haven't grown another inch since the ninth grade. At five foot eight, I usually feel uncomfortably tall at least once a day. Mostly because the man I work for, Mr. Lawman, is only about half an inch taller than me.

Add any shoe at all, and I am immediately taller.

It is frustrating. And a good reason to wear ballet flats every day.

"What do you think?" Layla asks, and I realize I never heard the question.

I blink at her. "I'm so sorry, Layla, I am—"

"I knew you weren't listening." She smiles though, so apparently it's okay. "I was telling you why we're putting it off for ten months."

That is a good question. "Why are you putting it off?" I ask. Layla doesn't wait ten months for anything.

"My parents' twenty-fifth anniversary is February 22. Remember? We're planning a surprise party for them." Layla waves a hand. "There's no way I'll be able to plan that and a wedding. Will you help me with it?"

"With the party or the wedding?"

"Both. You're super crafty, Paige. And have you seen my apartment?"

She has a point. Her apartment is white. White walls. Tan carpet. Nothing decorative anywhere. Any style sense Layla has goes right to her outfits.

At six thirty, Layla looks at her white watch and declares that she has to go because she is supposed to meet Peter and his equally boring parents for dinner. She doesn't say the equally boring part; I add that in.

The apple does not fall far from the tree.

Or trees, in this case.

If nothing else, at least Layla will add some color to their black-and-white family.

We walk out to the parking lot together and she gives me another hug. "I can't believe it!" she squeals, getting all giddy again. "I'm so excited!"

Whether she means the wedding or the marriage or the anniversary party we haven't even begun to plan, I'm not sure. But I hug her back. She climbs in her brand-new Jetta that her dad bought her last year when she graduated college and drives away with a wave that sends sparkling rainbows from the new diamond bouncing off the window.

I look at my planner again. Today is Wednesday. Which means I have thirty minutes to run home and change out of my office clothes, eat dinner, and get to church for youth group. I teach the ninth-grade girls.

There is a special place in my heart for acne-stricken faces, thanks to one too many taunts back in the day from the awful kids at my school. Though the girls I am currently working with seem to be drinking some kind of wonder water, because rarely is a zit present in the room. I remember feeling a lot uglier and way more awkward than any of these girls look or act.

I drive to my tiny one-bedroom apartment. I live alone. I don't even have a plant, and while sometimes the silence gets to me, most of the time, I'm not there to listen to it. Before I graduated, it was close to school. Now, it is close to work. And it is well within my price range.

And the management has overlooked a glue-gun-accidentally-burning-the-carpet incident with barely a slap on my wrist. So it is all good.

I change into jeans and a T-shirt, yank on a pair of sneakers, run for the door, and grab a cheese stick on my way out. For tonight, it will have to be dinner. I glance at my hair and makeup but decide there is nothing I can do about my hair. It is way too long. It's time for a drastic haircut, but I haven't had a chance to schedule an appointment yet. I attempt to use a comb on it, which just makes things worse. I always wanted hair that fits into a mold. Brown and curly. Blonde and straight. Black and wavy. Whatever.

Mine is brownish-reddish-blondish and some weird disaster of curly, wavy, and straight.

Maybe a dye job is in the works too.

I give up on styling my hair and head out the door.

I drive straight to church and park in the already-crowded parking lot. The youth pastor, Rick, is standing by the door, joking around with the kids and greeting people who are coming in. He sees me and shakes his head.

"You missed the leaders' meeting, Paige."

"What leaders' meeting?"

"The one I told you about last week. I want all the small-group leaders to start meeting before the kids show up so we can pray."

Oops.

Now I remember. I rub my forehead. "Sorry, Rick."

He sighs soberly. "I'll have to dock your pay."

"You're finally going to start paying me?" I wave at one of my girls, Tasha, who just walked in.

Rick grins. Rick is a great youth pastor. He is a big man

with a bald head and probably the cutest little wife ever. She is about three weeks away from having their first baby, so Rick bounces between being so excited he can't sit still to being so panicked about Natalie being in labor and him being a father that he just sits in a chair after teaching Sunday school and stares at the empty stage.

I alternate between being excited with him and being scared for him. And I am more than a little worried about tiny Natalie giving birth to huge Rick's most likely large child.

"Since you missed the leaders' meeting, you missed meeting the new guy in charge of the ninth-grade boys." Rick waves over a tall, curly-blond-haired guy who is leaning against one of the walls by the door to the youth room, talking to a few pimply faced boys who tend to squeak like a vacuum cleaner needing a new belt when they laugh.

If I am honest, it is one of my favorite reasons to talk to those particular boys. I love the squeak. On the boys. Not necessarily on vacuum cleaners.

"Paige, this is Tyler Jennings. Tyler, Paige Alder." Rick makes the introductions and Tyler shakes my hand. "Paige is in charge of the ninth-grade girls."

"Oh, you're the one who missed the meeting," Tyler says, but then he grins and I sigh. I have to tip my head up to meet his eyes, which are crinkled up in a smile.

It's nice. I don't get to feel short often. And Tyler's smile is friendly, if not a little mischievous, like a little kid planning a way to break into his mother's cookie jar.

"I forgot, I forgot," I say. "So, how long have you been coming to Grace Church?" Our church is huge, so there is a good chance he's been here since the first grade and I just never met him. Those are always awkward conversations. "Oh, you mean I should have known you my whole life?" Very awkward.

"Almost a year," Tyler says. He has pretty blue eyes. "I moved here from Austin about two years ago, and it took me a few months to find a church I liked." He shrugs, and I notice his shoulders look like they are made to haul logs around. "Time to start getting involved in something other than passing the offering plate to the person beside me."

I smile. I'm sure Rick is relieved. He's been looking for someone to teach the ninth-grade boys for a few months now. The guy who used to teach them, Jason Waters, up and moved to some fancy new job three states away. Rick grumbled for weeks about how money was too big of a factor for some people.

Really, I think Jason did the right thing. And really, Rick isn't mad about Jason taking a higher-paying job. He's just sad that he had to find a new leader for the boys. Tyler has big shoes to fill.

I watch Tyler as he grins at the kids filling the hallway, and I get a good feeling about him deep inside. I usually can trust that feeling. It has only screwed up on two occasions.

Granted, those results were disastrous, but I have finally moved on.

I am pretty sure, anyway.

Rick lets out a loud whistle and the hallway quiets. "Everyone get to your groups!"

The hallway turns into a frenzied movement of people finding the right room. I wave at a still-smiling Tyler, follow red-haired Megan to the preschool Sunday school classroom our small group meets in, and close the door after all ten of my girls are inside.

"Hi, guys." I turn to face them as they all settle onto the carpet, Bibles in their laps. This is our eighth weekly meeting. The routine has been set.

I take prayer requests and pray, and then we start our lesson. We are slowly going through 1 John, and I've been enjoying the study on God's love. I have Olivia pray for us in closing, and then we join the other small groups for snacks and music.

I make a beeline to the snacks but get waylaid by Rick. "So, Natalie is two centimeters dilated," he tells me, standing right between me and the quickly disappearing Oreos. High school boys equal snacks that don't last very long. Except for the time when Natalie brought organic peanut butter on celery sticks. She had plenty of leftovers that night.

"Fine," Natalie grumbled, packing up more than half of what she brought. "Rot your teeth out. I don't even care anymore."

I think some early pregnancy hormones had been causing a little of that rage.

"Where is Natalie?" I ask.

"Dilated. Didn't you hear me?"

"I heard you." Two more Oreos make their way from the package into someone's digestive tract. My stomach is grumbling in protest.

"So she can't be out around teenagers when she's dilated."

I frown and look at Rick. "Why?" Obviously, I don't have a lot of firsthand knowledge about babies and dilation and things that go along with that, but I am fairly certain that teens will not scare the baby out into the loud, scary world. If anything, they'd convince the kid to stay in there longer.

There are still a few ninth-grade boys who haven't quite gotten the hang of putting on deodorant every day. Some weeks, it is enough to scare me away.

A wave of pity for Tyler and his sinus areas washes over me.

Rick grabs a couple of Oreos and waves his other hand. "Germs," he declares. "They're swimming in them."

Justin, one of my favorite boys who I've seen grow up at this church and is now, in my opinion, one of the funniest guys in the youth group, rolls his eyes. "Speak for yourself, dude."

I have to give Justin the upper hand in this debate. I have been around Rick on retreats when he hasn't showered the entire time we were there.

Youth pastors are a strange breed of human.

If Rick can grab Oreos while talking to me, I can too. I reach around him and yank four from the package, hungrily devouring them.

"Sheesh, Paige. Eat much?"

"I had a cheese stick for dinner." I try my best not to spew Oreo crumbs as I speak. "Give me a break."

"All the more reason to get married. Marriage equals home-cooked meals and clean laundry."

"Yes, but Rick, who makes these home-cooked meals and does your laundry?"

"My smoking-hot wife."

Justin gags and walks away. I nod. "See? I don't have the time to do my own laundry, much less someone else's."

Rick makes a face, then leans over and sniffs my shoulder.

"Uh, what are you doing?" I scoot away from him.

"Is that a clean T-shirt?"

I sigh. "My last one." There is a middle-of-the-night trip to the apartment complex Laundromat in my near future, and I am not looking forward to it.

Rick shrugs. "I'd offer the services of Natalie, but like I said she's two centimeters dilated. I've been doing all the cooking and cleaning lately, and I'm about 98 percent certain you don't want me doing your laundry."

I am more certain than that.

"And considering Natalie got all grossed out because I made Beanee Weenees for dinner, you probably don't want me cooking, either."

I finish my last Oreo and nod. No wonder Natalie does the laundry and the cooking. I need to add *high-class chef* to the list of qualities I want in a far-off, distant future husband. "Well, laundry awaits me."

"Eat dinner," Rick says, walking away.

I wave at a few of my girls who are standing around waiting for their parents to show up, and then I drive back to my apartment. I sort out my dirty clothes and then head to the Laundromat.

It is almost ten at night. I have to be at work by eight the next day.

And I still haven't eaten anything other than a cheese stick and some Oreos.

I shove my first load into the washer and mash quarters into the machine. "God, please give me more hours in my day tomorrow." As the washer starts humming, I lean against the machine and close my eyes.

And please let those hours count somewhere.

Chapter 2

I work at the Lawman Adoption Agency. Mark Lawman, my boss, is an attorney who specializes in family law. There are two family counselors—Peggy Foreman and Candace Mitchell—who also work there. Both of them are in their late forties with grown kids of their own.

Which makes me the junior member. Basically, I run the office side of things, and when the caseload is extremely high, I get to take on a few clients and actually use my degree. I majored in child learning and development. I've spent half my life waiting to make a difference in people's lives.

It's never actually happened that I've gotten to take on clients, though I'm told it's a possibility. The longer I work here, the more I think that word *possibility* is just a proverbial carrot to get me to stay. In this economy, any job is a good job, but I still get a sinking feeling in my gut every time I think about being just a secretary.

I get to work at eight and flip on the lights in the tiny front office/waiting room. There are two sides to any adoption—the adoptive parents and the birth parents.

Usually it's just the birth mom as opposed to both the birth mom and dad we have contact with, but there are exceptions.

Thursdays are generally filled with adoptive parents. New parents come in for their initial interview and to set up a time for Peggy or Candace to do a home study.

Mark gets there about eight thirty, right after I've finished turning on the computer, copier, and fax machine and writing up all of the voice-mail messages we received after hours.

"Morning, Paige," he says, smiling. Mark Lawman is an average-height, balding man who just turned forty-nine, so he bought a motorcycle. At least, he calls it a motorcycle. It has three wheels, so to me that makes it a tricycle.

But I humor him. I need the paycheck to continue to eat my cheese-stick dinners.

"Morning, Mr. Lawman."

"You've really got to stop calling me that, Paige. You're making me feel older than I am," he says, frowning.

"Good morning, *Mark*."

"Thank you. Any messages for me?"

I hand him a stack of message slips, and he goes down the short hallway into his office, mumbling to himself.

That may be a sign of old age. Right behind getting a motorized tricycle.

Peggy and Candace come in the door together, talking recipes. "And then I just added a can of pineapple juice, and it was about the moistest chicken I've ever tasted," Candace says.

"Wait, pineapple juice?" Peggy asks.

"Right. And a can of Coke. In the slow cooker for six hours."

Whenever Candace is making a point, she stops talking in complete sentences. What would take the normal person two or three sentences at the most to say takes Candace forty-seven fragments.

It makes transcribing her home studies a joy.

"Morning, Paige." Peggy smiles sweetly at me. I love Peggy to death. Since my mom lives two hundred miles away, Peggy is basically my second mother.

"Hi, Paige." Candace waves. "Any messages?"

I hand them both their stacks of voice-mail slips and tell them good morning.

"I don't know, it sounds awfully sweet," Peggy says to Candace as they walk down the hall.

"Oh, but it's so good. And I just scooped a little of the broth into a pan and thickened it up with cornstarch for some sauce."

"I've never had good luck with cornstarch," Peggy says.

"The trick is to put the cornstarch into hot water. It has to be hot. Boiling hot. Like lava. Except water."

Like I said. Home studies are a joy.

I spend a good chunk of the morning responding to e-mails. Tuesdays and Thursdays are my e-mailing days. We get e-mails from people all over the world, thanks to Mark's nephew who decided to create a website for the agency. It was for one of his computer classes at school, and he did a great job making it all fancy and professional. He just failed to mention that we can only do home studies for people in Texas, preferably in the Dallas area.

I'm sorry, we are not currently staffed to perform your home study in Canada, I write in an e-mail.

I really need to get ahold of Mark's nephew and ask him to show me how to add a sentence in the "About Us" section.

The other thing I need to do is go to the grocery store after work today. My lunch break will be spent driving to Sonic for a quick hamburger or something, because I looked in my freezer for a Lean Cuisine or something to eat today and came up with nothing, except a frozen-solid bag of green beans.

And while that sounds nutritious, it doesn't really sound tasty.

"Hey, I'm going to Sonic for lunch," I say a little while later, poking my head into Mark's office. "Want anything?" It's a dumb question. Mark is a Sonic freak. He thinks their tater tots will be served in heaven alongside a Route 44 Coca-Cola.

He looks up at me from his desk. "Sure, let me get you some cash." He digs out his wallet and passes over a ten dollar bill. "Can I get the number two with tots?"

"Coke?"

"Diet." He nods.

Mark's funny that way. He will order the most calorie-packed meal in the restaurant and then a Diet Coke. At that point, it would be better to just go ahead and get the Coke and only eat carrot sticks the rest of the day.

"Oh and Paige?" he says as I leave his office. I stop and poke my head back in. "How are things coming on the banquet?"

Every year, our agency throws a huge banquet as a fundraiser to help some of our clients who can't afford the legal bills. It really is a great thing we do and one of the biggest reasons I wanted to work here.

It is scheduled for the end of February. "So far so good. I've got three speakers lined up, and a news team from KNJO is coming to do a special on it."

"Music?"

"I'm going to be listening to three different bands this week," I tell him. Two I have already picked out as potentials for the banquet. One is a band that Layla wants to go listen to and see if they will be a good choice for her parents' anniversary party. But after listening to a few samples on their website, I think they might be good for the banquet as well.

Two birds and one stone. Or two Oreos and one cup of milk. Or three Oreos. Or whatever the preferred idiom is.

"Great, great," Mark says, turning back to his desk. "Thanks for heading that up, Paige."

I ask Peggy and Candace if they want anything from Sonic and they decline, telling me how they are on days twelve and fourteen of their new diets. If they eat something now, they won't be able to splurge at Christmas this coming year.

"And, Paige, I am eating my pecan pie," Peggy declares, then swallows her Special K shake and reaches for a Ziploc bag of raw almonds.

"It's January," I say.

"Regardless." Peggy waves a hand.

I drive to Sonic and yawn while sitting in the drive-through line. I was up until one doing laundry. I hadn't done it in almost three weeks, and that meant I had three loads. And with the ancient dryers in the apartment Laundromat, it takes an hour each load.

I'm pretty sure I fell asleep for a few minutes on one of the folding chairs in there, but it didn't last long. Thankfully.

I think our Laundromat is creepy, and it creeps me out worse that I actually fell asleep there.

My phone buzzes right as I get to the speaker to order. It is Layla, so I answer and yell at her to hang on.

"Sure, just let me know when you're ready, ma'am," the voice over the speaker says.

"Oh, not you, my friend on the phone. I know what I want." I tell the speaker my order and get a staticky total back.

"What's up?" I say to Layla, tucking my phone between my shoulder and my ear while counting change from my wallet.

"I hope the chicken sandwich is yours," she says.

"Yeah, why?"

"Because," she says in a *duh* tone of voice. "You have to fit into a bridesmaid dress in nearly ten months."

"Oh gosh. Please don't tell me you are going to be one of *those* brides," I tell her, because it is Layla and I can.

She laughs. "Only a little. So here's the thing. I am thinking we could do this whole girls' night thing tonight, and you can help me pick out invitations for my parents' anniversary."

"I thought you were going to send an e-vite?"

"Or we could do that, too."

I sigh, away from the phone's speaker, and hand a woman who looks about as tired as I feel my cash and accept the bag and two drinks from her. "Thank you," I say.

"For asking? Sure, no problem," Layla says.

It seems pointless to correct her. "When should I be at your apartment?" I ask instead, mentally calculating how much money it will cost to eat out every meal since I still haven't made it to the grocery store.

"Just come after work. And bring those gross black heels of yours."

"Why?" Layla has made no secret about her hatred for those shoes. At one point, I think she even composed a ballad about how she would rather walk across hot coals in Crocs than wear my heels to a concert benefiting research for some horrible intestinal disease.

I think she was kidding, but I have been very careful to avoid wearing those shoes around her ever since. They aren't bad shoes. They just apparently look like something her great-aunt has been seen wearing.

That makes them awful.

"Because they're your only heels."

I know that already. I am five foot eight. She is lucky I own even one pair of heels.

"And they just might be nice to have with us in case we happen to come across any wedding dress shops and want to look at bridesmaid dresses. You know. For the length."

"Okay, first, your wedding is almost ten months away. We are seriously going to already start looking at dresses?"

"I didn't say we were going right now. I just said to have them with you in case we come across a shop. The practical bride is always prepared," she says an octave higher than her regular voice.

"Where did you read that?"

"*How to Be a Bride.*"

"Okay, whatever. Second, you're really going to make me wear heels to your wedding?"

"Yep!" she says, cheerfully.

I sigh. Loudly and into the phone this time. Layla is a reasonable five foot four. She can wear heels around anyone

and still be shorter than the average male. She has no idea
how awkward it is to tower over men.

And Peter is not what I would call tall. Actually, he's not
what any person would call tall. Quiet, yes. Withdrawn, yes.
Tall, no.

It looks like I'll be praying for a tall best man.

I pull back into the adoption agency's parking lot as
Layla chatters happily about possible venues for her parents'
anniversary party. "I think we should look into something
exotic, like a yacht or something."

I think Layla sometimes forgets that we live in landlocked
Dallas.

I don't mention it, though. "Mmm, listen, I'm back at
work, so I've got to go. I'll text when I'm on my way tonight."

"Okay. Hope you get a few kids adopted."

She hangs up and I push the button on my phone,
shaking my head. I've been working here for a year, and Layla
still has no idea how the adoption process works. In her
mind, women set babies and children right outside the door,
and then I have to take care of them until we finally find a
nice couple to adopt them.

That isn't exactly how it works.

She even told me one time how envious she is that I have
a job that lets me work with children.

If by children she means their legal papers, then yes,
I work with children.

Layla is one of those people who, if I didn't love her as
much as I do, I would have stopped being friends with years
ago.

I walk back inside, give Mark his hamburger, tater tots,
and Diet Coke, and settle back at my desk with my chicken

sandwich and cherry limeade. Since I've spent my allotted thirty minutes driving, waiting in line at Sonic, and driving again, I will now have to work while I eat lunch.

I work on tax reports in between phone calls from prospective adoptive parents wanting to know everything there is to know about the adoption process. From the very beginning of working here, I've always had a special spot in my heart for these people who walk through our door wanting nothing more than to love on a baby. Mostly because they come in looking like little lost puppies and leave months later absolutely and fantastically overjoyed.

Mark says my compassion comes through in my voice, and that's why my phone conversations with them last over an hour. I think he'd be frustrated except for the fact that 90 percent of the people who call end up coming in and using our agency.

"And tomorrow is Friday!" Candace sings as she comes down the hallway at five o'clock, wearing a coat that she doesn't need. Candace is from Vermont and likes to believe that winters should be cold.

I rub my head. I just hung up the phone after an hour-long conversation, not with an adoptive mom but with a copier repair technician. Our copier has been on the fritz for almost a week, and the company who sold it to us still hasn't sent someone out to fix it. I've tried fixing it six times, and all I ever get is a headache and ink stains on my favorite shirt.

"Did you check the power cord?" the repairman asked me. "Are you sure it's plugged in?"

I hate when people just assume you're incapable.

"Yay for Friday," I say to Candace, turning off the computer monitor and grabbing my jacket and purse. I follow her out, wave good-bye in the parking lot, and then drive quickly to my apartment to grab my black heels before heading over to Layla's.

Layla lives in, seriously, some of the creepier apartments on this side of town. Her apartment is all the way in the back, so you have to park and walk about five minutes on a dark, winding sidewalk before you reach her stairs. It scares me every time. Layla thinks it's great, though. She says it's romantic.

"Then you can wind down as you're coming home," she told me one time. "It's like forced exercise."

I still disagree.

I climb her staircase and knock on her door. Layla opens it a second later. "Let me just grab my jacket." She runs back into her living room. "You can come in, but it's a disaster."

I peek in and nod. It is. "I thought we were going to look at invitations here?"

"I've been planning all week." She waves her hand in an excuse for her house as she pulls on her jacket. She grabs her purse off the table and closes the door behind us, locking it. She looks at me. "We have to find a place for the party before we can decide on invitations."

Apparently that is on the agenda for tonight.

I follow her down the steps. "How come Peter isn't helping with this?"

She shrugs. "He said they were my parents. He just said to let him know and he'll show up wherever I want him to."

I could have pretty much scripted that answer from Peter.

"So, I called the city about that park with the gazebo," she says as we climb into my car. I have an unspoken rule of never letting Layla drive. The two times I've ridden in the car with her, we almost died like fourteen times. She is the most distracted driver I've ever met. It's amazing that she's never been in a wreck. She did hit a squirrel one time though and pretty much went into mourning for a week. I pray every night for her to pay attention while she's driving and stay alive another day.

"What did they say?" I can see that being a nice place for an anniversary party. Especially if it's in February. Nothing outside can ever be done in Dallas past the first week of May. It is too hot.

"They said that it was on a first-come, first-served basis. I couldn't reserve it. So basically, if that ends up being where we decide to have the party, we'll have to camp out at the park the night before just to make sure we're the first ones there."

Suddenly, Layla's apartment complex doesn't seem creepy at all when compared to the idea of camping out in an unlit park all night.

"What about that church Mallory and Thomas got married in?" I suggest. "They used that big auditorium thing for their reception. That could be nice too." A church is always a safe option.

"That's so been done before, Paige. I want to be different." Layla sighs out the passenger window. "I really want it to be outside. Mom and Dad got married outside, you know. I think it would be really neat if the party is like their wedding. I even found a picture of their wedding cake, and I'm going to take it to someone and see if they can re-create it."

It is a sweet thought. I, meanwhile, am trying to figure out what to do with a three-tiered cake that could become a puddling swamp of icing from the potential pouring-down rain.

Lord, please let there be sunshine on February 22!

Chapter 3

It is Saturday, and instead of my normal Saturday-morning routine of sleeping until nine before I go for my morning run, I am up at seven, back from my run, showered, and ready to go at eight forty-five. The youth group is having a service day at a food bank today, and Rick asked me to chaperone.

Last night.

Rick is not the most organized.

"We really need some female help," he said on the phone last night. "Kevin Waterson's mom was going to come, but she had to cancel. Can you do it?"

The food-bank project is at nine. I planned on spending the day working on a new wreath for my front door, but it can wait, I guess.

"Sure," I told him. "How's Natalie?"

"Still pregnant."

Yikes.

"I'm scared," Rick whispered into the phone. "She's getting mean."

I laughed. "Hang in there. She can't stay dilated forever." That I know of, anyway. Like I said, my experience with dilation or anything regarding pregnancy is zilch.

However, over Christmas break at my parents' house, I saw a few episodes of that show about the women who don't know they are pregnant until they are delivering a baby.

I'm pretty sure I'm scarred worse than those women are.

I drive to the church and park beside the blue youth van the kids lovingly named Alice. Alice has more personality than three of our tenth graders combined.

Hopefully today is one of her good days.

Rick and a small swarm of kids are standing on the sidewalk, squinting in the winter sun. "Good morning!" Rick yells.

"Hey, guys." I pocket my keys and walk over.

A few of my ninth-grade girls are here and a couple of senior girls. It never ceases to amaze me how much the senior girls dress up for these events. One girl is even wearing a skirt, for goodness' sake.

I went for my typical service-project outfit—ratty jeans, a gray FCA T-shirt from high school, a black zip-up hoodie, and my sneakers.

Tyler Jennings pulls up in a blue truck a few minutes later. The three ninth-grade guys who came make a beeline straight to him.

I grin. It looks like he is a hit.

At nine fifteen, Rick claps his hands together. "Okay, guys, I think we've got everyone. Let's hit the road."

"Shotgun!" Justin immediately yells.

I climb into the back of the van with three other girls, and we all squish around until all of our seat belts click. Tyler and the three guys are right in front of us, two sophomores and two juniors get in the row in front of him, and four seniors take the front row.

Rick turns the radio to his favorite country station, and six of the kids in the van groan. "Really?" one of the guys says. "Couldn't we listen to something else?"

"What do you want to listen to?" Rick asks.

"I don't know. Anything other than this."

So Rick tunes it to the classical station, and then everyone starts complaining. Me included. People talk about how classical music can raise your intellect, calm you down, help a headache, whatever. It doesn't work for me. If anything, it makes my headaches worse.

"Happier with country?" Rick grins.

"Yes," almost everyone in the car says.

Keith Urban starts crooning some song about how the sun turned his girl's hair to gold.

Maybe it's just me, but whoever writes Keith Urban's songs seems to have a love of clichés.

Rick starts singing along at the top of his lungs, which just makes it worse. Then Tyler joins in, trying to harmonize with Rick's very off-key voice.

"And if you ever get looooonely, you can just call me on the phooooone," Tyler belts out, eyes closed, head thrown back. The boys beside him snicker.

"Mental note. Next time, we take my car," I tell the girls I am sitting next to.

"Please." Megan nods and rolls her eyes.

Tyler slings his arm over the back of the seat and turns to look at me. "I think I'm offended."

"You probably should be." I smile.

He grins at me. "So what would you rather be listening to?"

"Elvis."

"The King, huh?" Tyler starts nodding. "Very nice taste you have there, Miss Alder. Ever been to Graceland?"

"No, but it would pretty much be the pinnacle of my life, so I figure I should probably wait and experience that when I'm old and have nothing else to live for."

He laughs. "Uh, okay."

"My grandmother got to meet Elvis. She waited on his table one time at a barbecue place in Memphis."

"So, your grandma was a waitress, huh?"

I shake my head. "She is just a big fan."

Tyler drops his jaw. "Wait, so your grandma faked being a waitress so she could meet Elvis?"

"Even brought him a glass of sweet tea."

"No way. That's awesome!"

I agree. I have the autographed napkin in my little fire safe at my parents' house to prove it. I'm pretty sure I got my love for Elvis from hearing Nana sing "Love Me Tender" to me every night that she watched me while my parents went out on dates.

Rick pulls into the parking lot at the food bank and turns to face all of us in the back. "Okay, ground rules. We're here to help, so a help we will be."

I sort of want to start singing the "tee-dum, tee-dee" song from the Lost Boys in *Peter Pan* right there, but I refrain. Barely.

"We're going to be sorting a bunch of the canned goods people donated to them over the Christmas break. I want you guys to listen to Mrs. Campbell and pay attention to how she tells you to sort them."

Tyler raises his hand.

"Yes, Tyler?"

"Mrs. Campbell?" He is incredulous.

Rick nods. "Word."

I roll my eyes. "So ten years ago, Rick."

"Right. Stay together, don't get lost, the van doors will be locked, and if anyone comes up to you and asks you for a key to the van, *Greg*, just assume they are not with us."

Greg sighs. "Seriously, dude? That was like two years ago."

"To borrow a phrase from my favorite movie, 'Legends never die,'" Rick says.

I've only seen *The Sandlot* once, but I can quote half the scenes just from being around Rick and Natalie so much.

Greg had apparently been approached by a man two years ago while we were here who told him that he needed to get into the van and asked if Greg had the keys. Apparently, Greg was so focused on stacking the cans of corn and pinto beans that he didn't even bother to look up and notice the man wasn't with our group. So Greg just told him he didn't think the van was even locked.

Two stolen iPods later and I think Greg learned to look before he speaks. It made a great sermon illustration. Rick uses it often.

"And thank you, Greg, for running the sound today," Rick opened his group lesson on Wednesday night. "And speaking of not paying attention, let's talk about spiritual blindness."

Poor Greg.

We all pile out and walk into the huge warehouse that is

one of the food banks in town. It is a neat place. The front is split into two rooms; one side is set up like a mini grocery store, and then you walk through a little door and find a room filled with cots and mats in between cubicle walls that businesses around town have donated.

The rest of the warehouse is totally for sorting and stocking, which is where we are going to be. Fifteen cardboard boxes probably six feet across, six feet in length, and about three feet in height are staggered around the warehouse, piled high with cans. I see Mrs. Campbell right when we walk in.

"Hi, guys." She walks over to us, clipboard in hand. I've been to this food bank at least a dozen times by now, and I've never seen Mrs. Campbell without a clipboard.

"Put us to work, ma'am," Rick says.

She does a quick count. "Eighteen of you? Okay. Split into teams of two and then follow me."

The kids all graft to their best friends, and Justin latches on to Rick. I look around and the only person needing a partner is Tyler.

At least I'll get to know this guy a little better. Since I missed the leaders' meeting when he introduced himself and all.

"All right, so I want each team to take a box and get the cans sorted into fruits, vegetables, soups, and miscellaneous. There are plastic tubs to sort them into. Please check the expiration dates on the cans as well, and any expired cans we'll throw away." She smiles at us. "And thank you, guys."

"All right, team, move out!" Rick yells.

"You've always wanted to say that, huh?" I ask him.

He nods. "Always."

I shrug at Tyler, and we walk over to one of the huge

boxes. A stack of plastic tubs, each one with a different label on the front, is right outside the box.

"So, Paige, how long have you been working with the youth?" Tyler asks while we both lean over and start pulling out cans. He pushes the miscellaneous and soup tubs in front of him and hands me the fruit and vegetable tubs.

"Almost five years." I drop three cans of pears into the fruit tub.

"Wow. So, you must have started right when you got out of high school then."

I nod. I moved to Dallas to go to college, found Grace Church, and met Natalie that first Sunday. She was a beaming newlywed at the time, and she and Rick pretty much adopted me as their little sister. They invited me over to dinner that week and talked me into teaching the ninth-grade girls by the time I left that night.

"The first group I ever worked with graduated last year," I tell Tyler. "That was a little weird."

"I bet."

"Did you grow up in Dallas?" I ask him.

He shakes his head. "No, I grew up in San Antonio, but then my dad got transferred to San Diego, and I lived there until I came out here for grad school. I ended up getting a job offer from a company just down the street from where I live, so I just decided to stay."

That makes Tyler a few years older than me. "What's your degree in?"

"Computer sciences. I do a lot with software development."

I hand him four cans of beef broth. He doesn't look like a nerd. He's wearing tan work boots, straight-cut jeans with worn patches in the knees, a blue shirt with a brown plaid flannel shirt over it, and a thick, warm-looking vest.

If anything, he looks more like a lumberjack. Tyler is built like an upside-down triangle. Wide, wide shoulders, thick arms, and a much smaller waist.

It's hard to picture him staring at a computer all day.

"Huh," I say because I don't want to tell him I think he should maybe look into a career cutting down trees instead of developing software.

"What's your degree in?" he asks me.

"Child learning and development. I work at an adoption agency."

"That's awesome. My mom worked as a paralegal for a family law attorney before I was born and after my sister and I went to school."

"Older or younger sister?" I ask him.

"Younger. By three years. She's twenty-two."

"Same age as me."

He grins. "You have any siblings?"

"A sister."

"Younger or older?"

"Younger." Preslee is yet another testament to my grandmother's love of Elvis. She'd been voting for both of us to be boys so one of us could be named after the King. So when my sister was born and my parents told Nana they were done with kids, she convinced them what a wonderful name Preslee was.

Preslee, though, has not fallen in love with Elvis's music like I have. In fact, she's gone the opposite direction. She joined a punk rock band, got a tattoo, which broke my mom's heart, and moved in with her boyfriend, which broke my dad's heart. The last time I talked to my sister was several years ago. She didn't even come home for Christmas the last couple of years.

She is a sore subject.

"Does she live in Dallas too?" Tyler asks.

I purse my lips. "No." Honestly, I'm not sure where Preslee is living now. Last time she talked to Mom, she was touring with her band somewhere in Ohio. A long, long way from home in Austin.

Tyler must have picked up on my I-don't-want-to-talk-about-her vibe, because he stops asking me about Preslee and starts talking about how much he loves Pork and Beans. "I mean, they even stick a cube of bacon in there. If that's not a quality food, then I don't know what is."

I shake my head. "You are quite the gourmet."

"I try. Sometimes, I'll even add freshly chopped scallions on top."

Chapter 4

"Earth to Paige! Earth to Paige!"

I blink and look up. I am sitting in the back row of the singles' Sunday school class. Tim Miller led the class today and spent the entire time talking about the verse on how man was not supposed to be alone, which led into how much he missed his ex-girlfriend.

It's been rough since the pastor in charge of singles, Pastor Dan, left on his sabbatical three weeks ago. So far we've heard lessons on why we should all convert to being vegan from Dave Rightfield, who looked exceptionally slender that day, a look at the genealogy of Abraham from Cal Hanson, and then today's lesson from Tim.

Pastor Dan can't get home soon enough.

Layla elbows me. "Paige?"

I blink at her in the chair next to me. "Sorry. Guess I zoned out."

"Dude, we all did." Layla lowers her voice. "If Pastor Dan isn't back next week, I swear I'm going to strangle someone. And these guys wonder why they are all still single."

Peter walks over carrying a donut that someone brought. "I got you one with sprinkles, Layla." He sits on the other side of her.

"Thanks, baby." She takes the donut and looks back at me. "So, are we going to look at invitations for Mom and Dad today?"

"I thought we still needed to nail down a venue."

Layla waves a hand. "We're camping out at the park. I want to have it at the gazebo. Peter even said he'd sleep there so we don't have to." She sends a brilliant smile toward him. "Right, sweetie?"

"Hmm? Oh. Sure."

Somehow, I know that isn't going to stick come the night before the party. I might as well start looking into how much a warm sleeping bag will cost. And maybe take a few lessons in a self-defense class.

"Okay," I say slowly. "So, invitations."

"Right. You've got the best handwriting I've ever seen, so I want you to address them, if you don't mind. And I am even thinking handwritten invitations will be really pretty. What do you think?"

I think it sounds painful. And I still like the e-vite option the best. But I don't say that. Layla is doing a very sweet thing for her parents. I rub my right hand, wincing. "How many people are you inviting?"

"Oh, just a small, intimate crowd," Layla says, offhand. "Only Mom and Dad's best friends. And then we'll have dinner and dancing and celebrate until dark. Mom and Dad are really into dancing. They won the county dance-off back when they were dating." She sighs sweetly.

Layla is a romantic. Romantics don't often think with all of their brains.

"What time do you want to have the party again?" I ask, because a few nights ago on our fruitless search for a venue that ended with us having coffee at Starbucks and me listening to Layla's ideal party setup, it seemed that she wants the party to be at dusk.

If that is the case, the celebration will only last about twenty minutes. And knowing Layla, that's not going to be the case.

"Oh, around seven or so." Layla waves her donut casually.

I pull my phone out. Last year, the wireless service salesman talked me into getting a smartphone, though goodness knows I don't use it to nearly its full capacity. I still like the feeling of a real Bic pen and a real piece of paper. I click over to Google and find the sunset time for February.

"So, your whole party is only going to be an hour?"

Layla shrugs. "I figure the toasting will be around forty minutes to an hour. I'm having an open mic. And some of Mom and Dad's friends are a little long-winded, but I figure they will like hearing nice things about themselves. Most people do."

I open my mouth and then stop. That is another argument for another day. "Okay," I say slowly. "I meant, the *whole* party—toasts and all."

"Oh goodness no. We need to have time to dance."

"Then you might want to move the time up. Sunset is about six thirty."

Layla purses her lips. "What if we brought in lighting?"

"How much are you willing to pay for this?" I ask, which

is probably where I should have started the conversation last week.

"Oh," Layla says, waving her hand. "Daddy just gave me a huge check for Christmas that I'm going to use to pay for this. And I have some saved up already."

Figures. Layla's father is not the wealthiest man I've ever met, but he is pretty darn close. And while he is stingy on things I thought mattered — like safe, noncreepy apartments for his daughter — he is nothing but extravagant on things I'm not sure matter that much. Like brand-new Jettas for graduation and a flat-screen TV always tuned to Fox News in her parents' guest bathroom.

It is a little weird. I like Shepard Smith okay, but I don't like him so much that I want to listen to him while I'm taking care of business.

I've only been to Layla's parents' house three times, and the second and third time, I just held it.

I pull my planner out of my purse and turn to the back where the notebook part of the planner is. It is January. I don't have a lot of notes in there yet, other than *Go to the grocery store today* written in bold letters across the top.

I do need to do that.

"Okay." I write *Prestwicks' Anniversary* across the top of a page and draw a line under it. "What all do we need to do?"

Layla almost jumps up and down. "Oh thank you thank you, Paige! You know how awful I am at organizing stuff like this. You are the best friend I could ever ask for!"

I start making a list of everything I can think of from the two anniversary parties I've been to — my aunt and uncle's and my grandparents'. By the time I finish just the preliminary stuff, Layla looks sick and Peter has gone to stand in the corner with his other barely talking friends.

"Wow, Paige. That's a lot of stuff to think about."

"Don't freak out. We'll take it one thing at a time. First things first, you need to come up with an exact starting time so we can send the e-vites. And quick. You probably should have already e-mailed those."

"Invitations. I still think the handwritten way is classier. And Mom and Dad are classy people."

Well. She doesn't lie.

Twenty minutes later, I walk out to my car with the start of a headache. More because I don't have any coffee in the apartment, I think, than planning the anniversary party with Layla.

I think.

"Hey, Paige!"

I look over and see Tyler walking through the parking lot as well. He waves and I wave back.

"Hi, Tyler."

"Coming or going?" He catches up to me, Bible under his arm.

"Going. You?" Our church has three morning services. Every other week I teach the two-year-old Sunday school class during the first service and then go to the singles' class.

"Going as well," he says, smiling easily.

"So do you go to second service?"

He nods.

"You should start coming to the singles' Sunday school class then."

He shrugs it off. "Nah, I'm not really a single-y type of guy."

I frown and sneak a quick look at his left hand. Surely I haven't missed something so huge in his life. His hand is bare, though. I look back up at him. "Oh, you're engaged then? Congratulations!" I am always happy to see people get married, especially when I know I'm not going to be called on to help pull off the wedding.

He laughs. "No, I'm not engaged. I'm single, I'm just not really a 'Sunday school' type of guy," he says, using his fingers to make air quotes.

I hate when people do that.

When I was a little kid, I had a teacher who used air quotes every time she said the word "friends." For the longest time, I thought she was half deaf and couldn't really hear the word *friends* and decided to make up her own sign language for it.

Once I figured out that meant air quotes, I wasn't sure if my teacher was trying to say she had no true friends or she was just lonely.

"Why not?" I ask Tyler.

He grins at me, blue eyes sparkling. "I like you, Paige. You don't beat around the bush." Then he shrugs. "Too regimented. I like studying God's Word when I don't have to sit in a folding chair for an hour."

"You go to church, though," I point out.

"I sit in a pew there. And we stand to sing." Tyler shrugs again. "It's just not for me. And trust me. I've tried a lot of Sunday school classes."

He isn't missing out on too much. Not while Pastor Dan is on sabbatical.

"What are you doing now?" he asks me, squinting in the sunlight.

"Going to the grocery store. Then I'm going home for a few minutes." And working on the wreath before Layla calls to tell me she is done having lunch with her parents and Peter.

"I can show you all the invitations I've been collecting that I really like," she said all bubbly when I left a few minutes ago.

I am excited for Layla's parents. And it is really kind of her to throw this party for them. And I don't even mind helping with the party. I just wish someone else was helping who knows more about what to do. It is sort of like handing a person who's only watched monkeys swing through the trees a Tarzan rope and telling them to hang ten.

Or whatever you say to Tarzan before he leaps through the trees. I'm not really a Tarzan buff.

No pun intended.

I blink and rub my head. I need some sleep. Or some caffeine.

Tyler is still there and now he's grinning at me. "Hey, I've got a better idea. Let's go get lunch."

"Let's?"

"Yeah, let's. You and me."

I shake my head. "I'd like to, really, but I *have* to go to the grocery store. If I don't go today, then I have to eat Sonic for the whole next week, and I'm already into March's eating-out budget." Not to mention the awful, greasy feeling my face had after I'd eaten Sonic three days in a row.

"Oh, okay. Some other time then."

"Yes, I'd like that." I don't want to be mean. I just have to go to the store before Layla calls me, because there is no telling how long I will be at her apartment this afternoon. I look at Tyler, feeling bad. "I'm sorry."

"Why are you apologizing?" He shrugs. "You've got plans. It just means I'll have to plan further ahead or find a better day next time."

I nod. Planning ahead is always a good thing.

"Paige! Paige, wait up!" Rick comes running across the parking lot. He stops in front of us, breathing hard. "Whew! I haven't run like that in . . ." He heaves his breath, locking his hands behind his head. "Dude, I can't even remember."

"You can't remember why you ran over here like that?" I ask.

"No, I can't remember how long it's been since I ran like that. Look, Paige, I wanted to ask you. There's a girl who came into youth group this morning who is really going through a rough patch. Her parents just got divorced and she just moved here with her mom. Usually I would give this over to Natalie, but . . ." He shrugs, looking at me.

I nod. "Dilated?"

"Still. I moved a cot into my office here."

I grin.

"Anyway, I am hoping maybe you could find a time to meet her for coffee or something this week and just talk to her and make her feel welcome?"

I pull my planner out of my purse. "Sure, I can meet with her on Thursday." I can skip my Pilates class this week for a girl in need.

"Perfect." Rick smiles at the two of us, all cheekily. "Sorry if I interrupted anything."

I narrow my eyes at him. Natalie has been trying to set me up with someone since I met her. The first guy was a wannabe youth pastor from Corpus Christi who made my name into a six-syllable word.

Needless to say, it did not work out. I have all these expectations of what my future husband will be like, and while most of them have been formed from watching *Pride and Prejudice* too many times, one of the bigger ones is that I like how he says my name.

I'll be listening to him say it for the rest of my life. I figure I should enjoy it.

Besides, I'm pretty sure no one in history has ever said "Lizzy" as wonderfully as Mr. Darcy.

It's important.

"No." Tyler shrugs to Rick's question. "Just chatting. Well, you have a great time at the grocery store, Paige, and I'll see you both on Wednesday night."

I wave. "Bye, Tyler."

"Yeah, see ya," Rick says.

Tyler walks across the parking lot to his truck and climbs in.

"So," Rick says, drawing the word out. "Tyler."

"So," I mimic. "I'm leaving."

"Clean laundry and a hot meal!" he yells as I climb into my car.

I shake my head for his benefit as I start my car, but I can't help the grin.

* * * * *

The grocery store may be my least favorite place on the planet. Because not only do I have to face the fact of just how much of my paycheck I'm eating every week, but the things I'm craving most for dinners are inevitably not on sale. Ever. My appetite has never lined up with the sale ad.

All those budget experts who say you should scour the sales ad before you go to the store and stick to the perimeter of the store while you're shopping obviously never had the sudden and very strong desire for chips, queso, and Oreos.

If I have these cravings now, I will be about the worst pregnant woman in all of history, someday, far down the road.

I push my cart down one of the freezer aisles and pause in front of the frozen pizza section. At least once a week I eat frozen pizza. It's easy and relatively cheap when you consider it feeds me for about three days.

My phone buzzes as I decide on a Canadian bacon and pineapple pizza. And bonus! It even comes with half a dozen presliced cookie dough cookies.

"Hi, Mom," I answer the phone.

"Hi, honey. How's your Sunday going?"

I talk to my mom probably three or four times a week, but she always, without fail, calls me on Sunday afternoon to catch up.

"Good. Just trying to get some grocery shopping done before I meet Layla."

"More party planning?" Mom knows all about the Prestwicks' anniversary party. As far as I know, they are planning to come. They've hung out with Layla's parents a few times over the years and get along pretty well.

"We're picking out invitations."

Mom pauses. "You know, seeing as how Layla and Peter just got engaged, you'd think he would have more of a hand in planning his future in-laws' party."

"Peter is Peter," I tell my mom.

She laughs. "Well, your dad and I are just sitting here very lonely from you leaving after Christmas and—"

That is when I hear my dad in the background. "We are not lonely, Paige!"

"Lyle, for the love of—" Mom hisses at him. Then she turns on her sweet voice for me again. "And we were just wondering when you thought you would be back down here."

"I don't know, Mom. Sounds like Dad's not too anxious for me to come back." I grin at the frozen peas.

Dad, for all the love he has for me, has very much been enjoying these years of having my mom all to himself again. Mom is a different story.

"Of course he wants you to come home again, sweetheart," Mom says, and I hear Dad chuckling.

I pull my planner out of my purse. I have a long weekend coming up in March. In a twist of fate that has brought me joy without fail for the year that I've worked there, Mark and Peggy had both gotten married on the same day.

To different people.

But it means they are easily swayed by Candace and me to just close the agency for the day. Last year, I'd gotten a wonderful Thursday off. And this year, I am very excited about my long weekend.

"March 14 then?" I ask Mom.

"Oh, that will be perfect!" Mom squeals. "I'll make all of your favorite meals. You just e-mail me a list of anything you want to eat. Okay, honey?"

"Sounds good, Mom." I am already imagining a huge spiral-sliced honey ham, sweet potatoes, and my mom's famous spinach casserole. Then we can end the evening with peanut butter chocolate bars, plenty of hot coffee, and card games until late at night.

"All right then. Happy shopping!" Mom says.

I hang up and grab a few bags of the microwave-steamable vegetables. Some days, they are my dinner.

I look in my cart. Suddenly I feel very homesick.

Chapter
5

Monday and Tuesday pass in a blur of working and then spending the entire evening looking up anniversary decoration ideas on the Internet. I love making crafts, and the idea of decorating for a party that isn't my own is starting to sound more fun.

Probably because it isn't my own, I have less of a personal stake in it.

Wednesday morning, I walk into work carrying my lunch cooler. I bought a few packaged salads at the grocery store on Sunday. They probably cost more than making the salad from scratch myself, but they don't take as much time, so packaged salad it is.

Mark is already there when I walk in.

"Morning, Paige. Hey, do you know what I did with the case file for the Wittles? I can't find it in my office."

I swallow my laugh, which then gets me coughing. "Uh, yes sir. You mean the Waughtels? I have it right here, sir." Candace just completed their home study, and I just finished transcribing it. "The home study is all printed up." I set my purse and cooler on the desk and pull the file from my Stuff I'm Working On stack.

Amazing how high that stack tends to get throughout the day.

Mark grins. "Wow, thanks, Paige. Waughtel. That's right." He chuckles. "You realize you can never leave this job, right? The agency wouldn't survive. How's the banquet coming?"

"Good. We're looking at the bands this week, and then I need to talk to the florist next week," I say, doing my best to ignore his first statement. Still, a part of me holds out hope that Mark will come to me one day and offer me a job as a partner.

"Florist?"

"For the table centerpieces."

He nods. "Right. I trust you'll make it beautiful." He sends me another smile before heading back to his office, Waughtel file in hand.

Apparently, the Waughtels' house is so clean that Candace was afraid to walk inside.

"I don't know about you, but I prefer homes where I feel like a kid could be allowed to make messes. It's important for kids to make messes," she told me afterward while she leaned against my desk eating a celery stick.

Candace is one of those women who isn't necessarily skinny but isn't necessarily overweight either. Which means she is also one of those women who goes on a diet about twenty-three times a year.

Or anytime she needs to fit into what she calls her "wear-all" dress.

"If I've got a funeral, it's appropriate. If I've got a

wedding, it's appropriate. Need a dress for a baby shower?" she told me another time. "Got it. It's like the million-wear dress."

Candace always makes me laugh.

I set my purse under the desk and turn on the computer. The message light is blinking, and I pull over the voice-mail message book to start writing them down.

"Yeah, hi, my name is Flynn Anderson, I'm with Office Plus. Just calling to see if there is a good time today to swing by and check out your copier. Give me a call." He rattles off his number, and I breathe a sigh of relief.

Finally.

A few messages are for Mark, several are for Peggy, and Candace got one from a former client about her child's upcoming birthday party.

I call the copier guy back as soon as I finish getting all the messages. A man answers on the third ring. "This is Flynn."

I bite my lip, trying to get the image of the lead male character from *Tangled* out of my head. "Hi, Flynn. My name's Paige Alder. I work at Lawman Adoption Agency, and you called us earlier this morning?"

"Oh, yes, ma'am. I've got a report here that says you need a technician to come look at your copier."

"Yes, please." Like two weeks ago, but I don't complain and I try to keep my voice sweet. My grandmother always told me you could attract more bees with honey than with vinegar. Considering I was six, it was no wonder I smelled like dill pickles for the rest of the summer.

I hate bees.

"All righty, ma'am. I'm on my way to another job, but it shouldn't take too long. Can I be there around three or four?"

I look at the clock. It is barely nine. Suddenly, I understand a little better why it has taken them two weeks to get back to me if a six-hour job is considered a short one.

"Uh, sure," I say.

"Great. I'll see you this afternoon, Paige."

I hang up and spend the rest of the day answering the phone and getting all of the information we need to do paychecks on Friday. We get paid the first and third Fridays of every month. This week is the third week in January, and I always hate doing paychecks for the third week because it is depressing to think this is the last time I am getting paid this month.

I rip open my salad bag at noon and Peggy comes down the hall, holding a fresh-from-the-microwave Lean Cuisine. "Need to work through lunch?" she asks me.

I shake my head. I got the time cards all put into the program, and I almost have the checks ready for Mark to sign.

Mark does everything old school. There are ways to give each person an account on their own computer that will track when they get in and when they leave, but Mark still wants handwritten time cards. Except for him and Peggy. Both of them are on salary. Mark keeps wanting to put Candace and me on salary, but I think that's just another way of asking us to be here longer without getting paid for it.

And Candace agrees, so I don't feel completely bad about it.

"No, I was just going to read some blogs." I have an idea for the head table at Layla's party, and I think I remember seeing something similar to it on one of the blogs I read last night.

"Well, Candace and I are going to eat at the back table if you want to join us." Peggy smiles.

I pick up my bag of salad and my fork and follow Peggy down the hall. The blogs can wait until later. The back table is in the playroom. It's a place where kids can hang out while their parents are in meetings with Peggy, Candace, or Mark. All adoptions require many hours of evaluations, so if you already have kids, it gets expensive fast to hire a babysitter for all those hours. Or if the adoption is for an older child, it's where Candace can do their counseling session.

But the playroom only adds to Layla's confusion about my job. She came by for lunch one day when Peggy was meeting with a couple who adopted two kids previously through our agency. The kids were busy playing, and Layla walked in and told them she hoped we found them a nice family someday.

I think the kids were almost as confused as Layla.

Candace is already sitting at the table with a container of celery sticks, carrot sticks, and cucumber slices. And she has a smaller dish with peanut butter next to it.

"What's the occasion this time?" I nod to her vegetation.

"My niece is getting married."

"The one who just had a baby?" Peggy asks.

Candace shakes her head, mouth filled with cucumber. "No, different niece."

"Oh! The one who just backpacked across Europe?" I ask.

Candace shakes her head again. "Nope. Still a different niece."

"Which one is this, then?" I ask.

"She's the one who wants to be an interior designer," Candace says.

I can't remember any stories about her. Judging by the look on Peggy's face, she can't either. "Is she the one who adopted that Lab puppy without talking to her parents?"

Candace sighs at Peggy's question. "No, still a different one. My brother really obeyed that command God gave Adam and Noah, huh?"

"Which one?" Peggy asks.

"You know. He leaved, cleaved, and reproduced. Go forth and multiply? Replenish the earth?" Candace says, waving her hand around.

I grin.

Peggy shrugs. "My husband just tells me to replenish the earth whenever I forget to run the sprinklers before I leave for work." She looks up at Candace with a frown. "And is *leaved* a word?"

Candace shrugs. "I don't know. It rhymed."

Peggy looks over at me. "So, when are you going to do that?"

"Rhyme?" I finish chewing my bite of salad. "I rhymed earlier today. I told Mark I was going to have to learn how to fix our website before someone came and buy-ent his clients."

Both women just look at me.

I sigh. "And he had about the same reaction."

"Not rhyme," Peggy says. "Because you should definitely never do that again. No, when are you going to get married?"

Here we go again. How is it that every time the M-word comes up, everyone has to swarm the one single person in the room and demand when it will be her turn?

I roll a shoulder. "I'm nowhere near ready. And good grief, you guys. I'm twenty-two."

Peggy concedes. "True."

Candace doesn't. "You are almost twenty-three." She rolls her eyes. "I was nineteen when I got married. Bob was twenty. We look like elementary school kids in our wedding pictures. I'm pretty sure he didn't have to shave every day until we'd been married for over six years."

I laugh.

"I'm pretty sure you haven't dated anyone seriously in about two years either," Peggy says offhandedly, chewing a bite of some sort of Asian chicken.

"Nope, she hasn't," Candace agrees. "Not since Luke."

Luke. There is someone I haven't thought of in a while.

My chest gets all tight just thinking about his name, and there is probably a good reason I haven't thought of him in a while. Luke is tall, he is smart, and he has these chocolate brown eyes that made me follow him around like a lost puppy way back in the fifth grade.

Luke is also Layla's older brother.

There is a sad, convoluted story behind that one. Not one I necessarily want to relive today. Luke moved to California two years ago, and after he moved, Layla and I slipped into this unspoken rule about never mentioning him.

I am better off without him.

I am.

* * * * *

This time I go straight to youth group from work so I can attend the leaders' meeting Rick enforced. He even texted me a reminder this afternoon while I was watching Flynn Anderson—who had no similarity to Flynn Rider from *Tangled*—wrestle with our copier.

It was fairly entertaining. Candace even came out of her office to watch for a few minutes.

"It's like watching that show on the Discovery Channel," she whispered to me at one point as Flynn grunted loudly and flipped the copier over on its side. The copier groaned.

"What show?" I whispered back.

"*Hog Brawl? Swine Struggle? Pig Grappling?*" She shrugged. "I actually don't remember. I wasn't really watching it. Bob was while I checked my e-mail. He watches the weirdest shows."

I grinned and looked down at the text Rick sent.

LEADERS MEETING. 5:30. TARDINESS WILL NOT BE TOLERATED AND LATECOMERS WILL BE SHOT ON ARRIVAL.

Two years ago, Rick somehow managed to get a marshmallow gun from one of the junior high kids for Christmas, and it is his most prized possession. I have definitely seen him walking around the church with the bright-red gun holstered to his hip on more than one occasion.

I swear that some men just never grow up.

So, I make sure I am there plenty early for the meeting. As much as I like getting shot in the head with a marshmallow, I can think of a few other things that are more fun.

Like not getting shot in the head with a marshmallow.

Rick and Trisha, the leader of the junior and senior girls, are in the high school room when I walk in. "Hey, Paige," Rick says. He is sitting backward on a folding chair, arms over the top of it, dangling his marshmallow gun by the trigger. He looks at his watch. "It's 5:23," he announces.

"You'll notice I am still in my work clothes." I point to my dress, leggings, and boots. You have to take advantage of semicold weather when you get it in Dallas and wear leggings and boots whenever slightly possible.

The dress, however, will make it hard to sit cross-legged on the floor like I usually do while teaching my small group. I grab a folding chair for myself and set it up beside Trisha.

"And you look very office professional, casual, whatever the current thing to look like is," Rick says.

Sam Kelson, the leader of the junior and senior guys, walks in then. Sam is probably about thirty or thirty-five, married, and has the cutest little two-year-old twin girls I've ever seen.

"It's 5:27," Rick tells him when he walks in.

"Not only on time but early." Sam drags a folding chair over for himself. He sits down and waves at me and Trisha. "Evening, ladies."

"Hi, Sam."

"Hey, Sam."

Julie, who leads the sophomore girls, and Trevor, who leads the sophomore guys, come in next. Julie and Trevor have been married for a few years but still act like they are newlyweds. Maybe because they don't have any kids. Whatever the reason, they dangle somewhere between very cute and gag-inducing.

"Hi, everyone," Julie singsongs when she walks in.

"Hey, guys." Trevor waves with the hand not holding Julie's.

"It's 5:29," Rick says. "I should give you a single shot just for shaving it so close, but I will refrain."

Julie rolls her eyes while Trevor gets them both chairs. "Whatever. We are clearly within the time frame you gave us."

Rick is just staring at his watch now, his finger tightening on the trigger as excitement over Tyler's lateness starts to set in. "He's so going to be late," Rick says under his breath. "And, three . . . two . . . one . . ." He looks up at us, grinning. "Happy marshmallow time, everyone."

I immediately stand, pick up my chair from where I am sitting sort of near the door, and move to the far side of the room by Sam. Rick is not the best shot in the world.

"Wimp," Rick mutters. He lays his arms across the back of his chair, sets his right wrist on top of his left arm, and takes aim at the open doorway, peering through the sighting with one eye closed.

Tyler comes walking in at 5:32. "Hey, guys, I'm—"

"*Tardy!*" Rick opens fire.

"Augh!" Tyler covers his head with his arms and launches himself into the room.

He lands sort of near my feet, and I look up at Sam, who is shaking his head. Tyler army crawls over to the stack of folding chairs, grabs one off the stack, and scurries around behind it while a stream of miniature pastel-colored marshmallows plasters him in the head, neck, and back.

"Uncle! Uncle!" Tyler yells.

Rick ceases fire. "Lateness will not be tolerated," he says in a very serious voice.

I bite my lip hard to keep from snorting.

Tyler stands, unfolding the chair and brushing marshmallows out of his ears, collar, and shirt. "Dude, these are like rock hard. When did you buy them? Three years ago?"

"Stale ones are the best to use." Rick shrugs. "Leaves more of a sting than just a squish. Okay. Let's pray."

I can't help it. I start laughing right at the same time as Trisha. Tyler is grinning, and Julie and Trevor exchange lovey laughs with each other.

Rick salutes. "Welcome to the youth ministry, Tyler."

Later that night, after small groups, I am once again trying to make up for the lack of dinner by scrounging around the snack table. Someone brought some type of caramel-apple bars, and there is a bag of pita chips I guess the kids deemed too healthy.

I pour some into a bowl and set a caramel-apple bar on a napkin.

"Hey," Tyler says, coming over.

"Hi, Tyler. Sorry about the marshmallows."

He shrugs, grinning. "It is kind of fun, actually. I might have to be late again next week and bring my own gun so at least it's a fair fight."

"You have a marshmallow gun?" I ask.

"Sure. Doesn't everyone?" He reaches around me and grabs a pita chip. "I had to stop and get something for dinner and change clothes before I came tonight. I had a good excuse."

I point to my dress, which forced me to sit in one of those little Sunday school chairs only meant for a child younger than four. "I didn't have time to go change. And this is my dinner." I eat another pita chip.

Tyler shakes his head. "Pita chips are not dinner. They're a snack. And not even a good one at that."

I wave my caramel-apple bar in his face. "Well, this is my snack tonight."

He sighs. "That's it. Let's go."

"Go where?" I ask, crunching another chip.

"I'm taking you to dinner. This is ridiculous."

I shake my head. I have to go home as soon as I'm done eating the pita chips and start planning my lesson for Sunday. If I don't do it tonight, I won't have time the rest of this week. I am meeting Nichole, the girl whose parents are divorced, tomorrow right after work and then Layla right after her. And Friday night, Geraldine, our church's secretary, called me and asked if I could help with childcare for a dinner the church is putting on for families who live under the poverty level.

I'm pretty sure if I'd said no to that, I would have been labeled "Scrooge" for the rest of my life.

"I have to go plan my Sunday school lesson," I tell Tyler.

He looks at me. "What age do you teach?"

"Two-year-olds."

"Do you like it?"

Kind of a weird question. "Yeah," I say slowly. "Should I not?"

He shrugs again. "I'm sure it's fun. You stay pretty busy, don't you, Paige?"

I think about it. I didn't used to be this busy, even just a few months ago. Maybe things are busy right now, but I'm sure they will calm down before too long. "Yeah, I guess so," I say.

"How long does it take you to write a lesson plan?"

"I don't know. An hour or so?"

He looks at his watch. "It's eight o'clock. If I have you home by nine, you can work on it until ten and still have most of your evening left."

I think about it, looking at my pita chips. On the one hand, they aren't super filling. On the other hand, they have to be healthier and are definitely less expensive than eating out.

Like I said, I've blown that budget until March.

"I'm buying," Tyler says.

I purse my lips and then look up at him and nod. "Okay. Where do you want to go?"

He grins at me. "Cracker Barrel? It's open late and they have cobbler."

I laugh. "Fine."

I follow Tyler to Cracker Barrel, and he holds the door for me as we walk in. I inhale deeply and smell bacon.

That is why this restaurant has done so well. Any place that pumps the smell of bacon into the entrance is destined to be a success.

"Good evening. Two tonight?" the hostess asks once we make our way through the country store part of the restaurant.

"Yes, ma'am," Tyler says.

"Right this way."

She leads us over to a table near the windows and sets our silverware wrapped in napkins and our menus on the table. "Your server will be right with you."

Tyler waits until I sit down to seat himself, and I hide a smile. Polite. I like that.

"So," Tyler says, not even looking at the menu. "I know what I'm getting."

"Come here that often?"

"Paige. They have cheesy potatoes. They have bacon all day long. And they serve root beer in a frosted glass." He ticks the points off on his fingers. "I mean, if you could describe heaven, it wouldn't be too different."

"Cheesy potatoes, bacon, and root beer," I repeat, trying hard not to make a face. I am not being very successful at that, apparently, because Tyler grins at me.

"Must be a dude thing."

"Why do you guys say that?"

"Say what?" He unwraps his silverware and puts his napkin in his lap.

"*Dude*. I mean, I hear the word like ninety times whenever I'm around Rick and the youth kids."

Tyler shrugs. "What would you prefer we say?"

"The person's name? 'Hey, pal'?" I shake my head. "I don't know."

"Hey, pal?" he copies, his smile stretching farther across his face. "Hey, pal. Hey! Pal!"

"Okay," I say, holding my hands up. "I didn't mean say it continuously."

"Pal. You know, I once knew a dog named Pal. She was one of those Lassie dogs, with the long hair."

"They named a girl dog Pal?"

"Girls can be pals," Tyler says. "Are you saying you don't have any pals?"

I sigh and close my eyes. "I'm sorry I brought it up."

He laughs.

The waitress comes over then, and I order a honey ham sandwich with fried okra on the side. Tyler orders the pancakes with a side of bacon and cheesy potatoes. And a root beer. By the time he finishes ordering, I am feeling a little nauseous.

"I'll have that right out," the waitress says sweetly.

"So, I know we haven't known each other very long, and I think we're probably still in the coddle-each-other stage of a friendship, but Tyler . . . ew," I say, making a face.

He grins. "I knew we were going to be great friends, Paige."

"So. You said you moved here from Austin? Is your family in Austin?"

He shakes his head. "My mom and stepdad live in Missouri. My dad is in Arizona."

Broken home. I immediately feel bad for him. "I'm sorry."

"It's not your fault. As crappy as divorce is, my parents aren't Christians and have no reason to act like they are, so . . ." He shrugs. "It is what it is."

"Siblings?" I remember we talked about this while we did the service project. I just can't remember his answer now. Hunger tends to make me a little forgetful.

"A little sister. She's married now. Pregnant." He smiles all sappy at me. "I'm pretty stoked about being an uncle."

"Is she a Christian?"

He nods. "I became a Christian at UT, and when I got back home for Christmas totally on fire for Christ, I found out that one of Stephanie's friends from high school had dragged her kicking and screaming to this big Christian concert they were having and Stef got saved there." His expression is full of joy. "So God got both of the Jennings kids in one month."

"Wow! That's really cool."

"It's really great. Especially considering my parents are still nowhere close to Jesus. It's nice to have company at the Thanksgiving table." He leans back in his chair. "I end up seeing them only twice a year anyway. Stef lives in Austin now, so I go see her once a month or so. She actually ended up marrying one of the guys I roomed with in college." He smiles at me. "So. Your turn."

"Oh, my story is pretty boring."

"That's how it should be." Tyler nods. "Stef told me she's been praying from the day she found out she was pregnant for her baby to have the most boring testimony in the whole world."

"I guess that's true. My parents actually live in Austin, too. It's where I grew up. Both of them are Christians; I've been raised in the church my whole life. See? Boring."

"How did you end up in Dallas?"

"I came to TCU for school, and then I ended up finding out through Natalie that the adoption agency I work at was hiring." The waitress sets our drinks in front of us and we thank her. "So, I just ended up staying," I say after she leaves. "I was really close with Rick and Natalie by then, and my best friend Layla moved here, and I found a good church . . ."

Tyler nods. "Despite the marshmallow gun, Rick seems like a good guy."

"He's great. He's like the big brother I never had. And you'll love Natalie. She's just awesome. She's about a week overdue with their first child though, so I recommend meeting her after the baby comes."

I'd texted Natalie earlier in the day. How ARE YOU FEELING, NAT?

She wrote back not even thirty seconds later. ENORMOUS. THIS KID BETTER COME BEFORE THIS WEEKEND OR I'M GOING TO POP LIKE A BALLOON IN THE HANDS OF A TWO-YEAR-OLD.

That was not a good mental image.

Tyler laughs. "Noted. I'll wait to meet her. So, you aren't adopted."

It is a weird statement. I frown. "Should I be?"

"No, I just meant, you work at an adoption agency. What made you want to work there?"

I shrug. "I just want to have a job that makes a difference. You know?"

His gaze warms as he smiles at me. "And do you?"

"Do I what?"

"Have a job that makes a difference?"

Our food comes then and saves me from having to answer that question. It sticks in the back of my brain, though, and pokes at me all night until I shush it with the fried okra. We make small talk over our dinners. He makes me try a bite of his cheesy potatoes, and they are pretty good.

"See? Told you. I mean, really, you have to look at this meal like a balanced breakfast. Pancakes. Hash browns. Bacon."

"Root beer," I add.

"Exactly."

I laugh.

* * * * *

I climb into bed at ten thirty that night and pull my Bible over into my lap. I flip it open to the first psalm I see. It is Psalm 34, which doesn't surprise me. I've read this psalm so many times that my Bible is probably creased there. Verse 14 catches my eye.

"Turn from evil and do good; seek peace and pursue it."

I frown and close my Bible, then turn off the light. How

do you even pursue peace? Isn't the whole connotation of pursuit sort of antipeace? And where does peace fit in when everything is so busy all the time?

I drift off while thinking about it.

Chapter
6

I end up leaving work late on Thursday, so I don't even get to Nichole's apartment to pick her up until well past five thirty. "I'm so sorry," I say when she comes to the door. "I got stuck at work."

Nichole is fairly short with short blonde hair and sad blue eyes. She just smiles. "It's fine, really. Let me tell my mom I'm leaving."

We end up going to a Starbucks just a couple of blocks from her apartment, and she tells me about how she ended up in Dallas. "So then my mom found out my dad has been cheating on her with his secretary for almost six years."

My heart hurts. Little girls should never have to deal with news like that about their daddies. And I feel woefully inadequate to be talking to her about this when my wonderful, amazing father has always been the first person there whenever I needed anything, and he would never hurt my mom like that.

"I'm so sorry, Nichole," I say, at a loss for words, trying to dig up something from my classes in psychology from the recesses of my brain.

"Me too," she says, obviously trying not to cry while she takes a sip of her vanilla bean latte. I'll need to remember that she apparently doesn't like coffee.

"How's your mom doing?" I abandon the psych stuff and try to tune in to the Holy Spirit.

"She's okay. My grandparents live here, so they've been helping us a lot. She's trying to find a job right now."

"What does she do?"

"She worked as a vet assistant in college. I guess she's thinking about something along those lines, but it just doesn't pay very much. I've been applying around to see if I can find some part-time work after school too."

I nod. "If I hear of something, I'll let you know."

"Thanks, Paige."

I take her back home a little over an hour later and ask if I can meet with her again next Thursday. It is the first time she really smiles at me. "That would be awesome."

I smile back. "Great. I'll see you then. Have a good night, Nichole."

I drive away, shaking my head. *Lord, how much I take for granted in the face of others' problems.*

I pull into Layla's apartment complex and climb out of my car, walking the long, creepy sidewalk to her apartment. I knock and Layla opens the door a second later.

"Come in, come in. Oh, Paige, wait until you see what I just found!" She dances through the apartment over to her computer and points excitedly at it. "Look!"

I drop my purse and the folder of ideas I've been printing

off the Internet on her sofa and walk over to her computer on the kitchen table.

"Is that not the most beautiful centerpiece you've ever seen?" she squeals.

It is beautiful. Yellow roses are everywhere and the whole thing is lit in candlelight.

"I'm going to order these tonight!" She jumps up and down, clapping her hands. "Won't they look spectacular on the tables around the dance floor?"

"Layla, how much are they?"

She waves a hand. "I haven't checked yet."

"They're probably around two hundred dollars."

She gasps. "No way."

"Way. We can totally make these on our own for way, way less than they're going to charge you." I am pretty certain I've never used the word *way* so often in such a short amount of time.

"Are you sure?" she asks, looking doubtful. "I mean, I can trim the cost in other ways."

"Where?"

"Well, the park is free."

"But you want to serve steak, chicken, and shrimp for dinner."

She gets all dreamy-eyed again. "With the Burgundy sauce," she says, in a hushed, reverent voice. "Don't forget the sauce. It's exactly the same menu Mom and Dad had for their wedding. I've heard about that sauce since the day I was born."

"With Burgundy sauce," I add.

"We're not cutting the meal." She squints at me. "We can cut the cost of the invitations. I can hand deliver some of them."

"That would probably save you about fifteen dollars."

She snaps her fingers. "Shoot." She looks at the picture again. "You really think we can make this?"

"Look, print a picture of it, I'll work on a mock-up over the weekend, and then you can see what you think. If you don't like it, you still have plenty of time to order them before the party."

She sighs. "Okay. Are you sure? I mean, I want it to be nice."

"Positive." I've been itching to get my glue gun out anyway.

"Well. Okay. I guess we can try it." She closes her computer and looks up at me. "I'm going to make spaghetti for dinner. Want some?"

"With your mom's homemade meatballs?" My mouth starts watering just thinking about it.

"Yeah. She sent me home with three huge gallon Ziplocs filled with them at Christmas." Layla walks over and opens her freezer door just to prove her point. All that's in her freezer are the meatballs and a frozen pizza.

"What can I do?"

"You can sit. You've been doing a lot for me, and I want to make dinner for you," she says. "So, I was thinking about going to look for a wedding dress this weekend."

I sit on one of the bar stools at her tall counter that overlooks the sink. "Oh yeah? Don't you think it's a little bit early?" The wedding is a little over nine months away, after all.

If there's one thing I am dreading about Layla's wedding, it is looking at bridesmaid dresses. Not only are they incredibly expensive for something I will wear only once, but they always look so uncomfortable. I've never been a bridesmaid before, but it just doesn't seem like a lot of fun to me.

But I am Layla's best friend, and of course I will wear whatever dress she picks for me.

"Well, true . . ." she says sadly. Then she grins and starts bubbling about the kind of wedding dress she is searching for. "I want strapless but not skanky and lace but not overdone, and I really like the Cinderella style but I don't want to seem like I'm playing dress up." She dumps about twenty meatballs in a dish and sticks it in the microwave while she pulls a jar of spaghetti sauce and a box of noodles from the pantry.

Layla is not really a homemade kind of person. Which is just funny because her mom is about the most crazy-talented cook in the whole world.

Layla told me once that she just felt like it was a lot to live up to, and she decided one day that she was going to be totally different and not cook at all. She said that lasted until she gained ten pounds eating out all the time.

A copy of a magazine called *Wedded Bliss* is lying on the counter in front of me, so I thumb through it while Layla gets water boiling for the noodles. "Here's one." I hold up a page with the most awful dress I've ever seen in my whole life.

Layla glances over at it. "That's not too bad."

"The wedding dress, Layla."

She squints at the picture again. "Ew. That looks like moss grew on that girl."

"The dress is white."

"It has a greenish tint to it. Pass."

"I was joking, anyway."

"I would hope so. Just think about all the ideas this is probably giving you for your wedding someday, Paige!"

"Mmm." I shrug. Layla and I have such different tastes in everything that our weddings will probably be like night and day.

In ten or so years, when I get old enough to be married.

Never mind that Layla and I are the same age.

"So, we have a big problem." Layla takes the meatballs out of the microwave.

"Not with the meatballs." I hold back a shudder at the thought.

"No. With the flower girl."

"What's wrong with her?"

"She doesn't exist," Layla says sadly. "I don't have any little cousins, and Peter doesn't know any girls under the age of six——"

"Does he know any over the age of six?" I cut in.

Layla purses her lips in thought. "He knows you. And me."

"So two."

"He's a quiet sort."

"Layla," I say, deciding to just voice my concerns while there is still plenty of time to call the whole thing off. "Are you really sure you want to marry Peter?"

She gives me a funny look and dumps the sauce from the jar into a skillet. "Uh, yes, Paige. That's why I said yes when he asked me."

"I mean, he's nice," I concede. Most people would argue that it is hard to be mean when you just kind of stand there unmoving like a rusted-open barn door all the time.

"He is, isn't he?" Layla sighs.

"But he's not very . . . um . . ." I struggle to find a word that doesn't have a nasty connotation to it. "Animated?"

"Of course he's not, and I wouldn't want him to be." Layla spoons the meatballs into the sauce carefully so it won't splash. "He's a very real person. He doesn't try to pretend."

Animated is not the right word.

"He's just not who I always envisioned you with," I say slowly.

She looks over at me with a smile. "I know. I just figured out one day that Gilbert Blythe probably wouldn't be knocking at my door anytime soon."

We both have a moment of sighing silence for sweet Gilbert who stole Anne of Green Gables' heart.

She goes back to stirring the sauce. "Peter's a good guy, Paige. You can stop worrying."

I won't, so I don't promise anything. "If you're certain, Layla. All I'm saying is, you're going to be with him the rest of your life, and I just want you to be 100 percent certain."

She pulls a colander out of the cabinet. "I'm 200 percent certain. Stop worrying about me. You've done that since we were kids."

"You needed worrying about back then." She still does now. She just obviously can't see it.

She waves a hand. "Please. I was fine. You were the one running around during finals like you and six of your rodent friends had to make a ball gown by midnight."

I laugh. "What?"

"Like it?" She grins. "I just came up with it by myself."

"You are so weird."

She pours the spaghetti noodles and the boiling water into the colander and nods. "And yet, somehow, I am still loveable."

* * * * *

"Thank God it is Friday night," Peggy gripes as she comes down the hall, putting on her jacket. "I am not going to have to look at one more birth father who is contesting the adoption or one more adoptive parent who needs to learn some patience, kindness, and gentleness toward their case manager. I am going to sleep in tomorrow morning. I am going to sit at my breakfast table with my husband and drink my green tea while we work crossword puzzles together."

I grin at her while I stack up the papers strewn all over my desk. "Sounds like good, clean fun." I slide them all into a stack to work on come Monday.

"Watch it, Paige. You're going to get old one day too." She finishes pulling her jacket on and waves a finger at me. "And then see how you feel about the antioxidants in green tea helping to prevent the sag under your chin and the chance to exercise your aging brain doing a crossword puzzle."

"I think I'll have to take my chances with my macchiato."

"Suit yourself." Peggy shrugs. "I plan on dying beautiful."

I laugh and stand, grabbing my jacket and purse and turning off the lamp on my desk. My desk is so bare compared to everyone else's here. Peggy has pictures of her husband and kids and new grandbaby, Candace has pictures of her family, and Mark has pictures and a baseball that his kids signed that says, "Warld's Bist DAd."

My desk has a lamp on it. And a pack of gum. And all the files I am working on. And a mock-up of the floral centerpieces for the banquet. But I am pretending it is a bouquet of flowers for me from a secret admirer. Even though I have no time for an admirer, secret or otherwise. Still. The thought of a guy sending flowers is nice.

I wave at Peggy and climb into my car. Time to run home and change into jeans before I go to help with childcare at the church dinner tonight. I yawn, pulling out into traffic. I am tired. And really wanting to just stay on my couch eating chocolate-covered popcorn and watching *Emma* tonight.

The good version with Gwyneth Paltrow.

I hurry up the stairs to my apartment, change out my black skirt for jeans and my ballet flats for sneakers, and throw on a hoodie over my cami. I grab a cheese stick and run back down the stairs to my car.

Cheese sticks should never be dinner as often as they are mine.

Which sounds something like a song by Taylor Swift, but I rip open the package and inhale it on the way to church anyway.

I get to church right at six and the dinner starts at six thirty. Geraldine, the church secretary who is in charge of the event, finds me right when I walk in.

"Paige!" she says. "Oh good. Okay, I've got you guys set up in the nursery. I think there are only going to be six or eight kids here tonight, all ages five and younger. And Madalyn Louis is going to be helping you."

Madalyn is in the fifth grade and is our senior pastor's oldest daughter. She is a sweet girl, but I'm really not sure how much help she will be when she is only eleven.

"Great," I say, faking a genuine smile.

"Thanks so much for doing this, honey. I just love how willingly you serve all the time," Geraldine says.

I am single and live alone. Maybe this is what God has planned for these years of my life. "Sure."

"All right. I need to go talk to someone about the music. You're good?"

"I'm good."

She hurries away and I walk down the hallway to the nursery. Nine kids under the age of twelve.

And me.

Emma is sounding better and better, but I feel horribly guilty even thinking that.

* * * * *

Later that night, I climb into bed exhausted. Two infants screamed the entire night, another one cried red-faced until he finally spit up in my hair and on my shirt. A two-year-old dumped animal crackers all over the floor and then stomped them into the carpet while a three-year-old girl asked nine hundred times if we could go outside and play on the playground in the pitch dark.

And Madalyn just sat there staring at her iPod the whole time.

After all of the parents collected their children and I mopped off my hair and shoulder, Geraldine came by to give Madalyn and me Starbucks gift cards and tell us thank you.

"And, Paige, honey, you'll want to spray that shirt with stain remover before you launder it. Spit-up tends to stain," Geraldine said.

It was a rough night. And now my car smells like spit-up too.

I took a shower the second I got home and immediately sprayed my sweatshirt and took a small load down to the Laundromat.

There is no better birth control than church nurseries. I am to the point that I'm not even sure I want kids anymore, ever.

I look at my Bible and then sigh and turn off my lamp. I am so tired I can barely keep my eyes open. I'll read twice as much tomorrow.

Besides, I've spent the whole night serving. Maybe that counts for my Bible reading today.

Chapter 7

I have every intention of sleeping in the next morning. Sleep in, maybe watch a movie, make myself French toast, and work on the wreath that is still half finished in my closet.

My phone buzzes at seven.

I force my eyes open and look at it. It's a text from Rick.

CLAIRE ELISE. BORN AT 2:13AM, 8 LBS 6 OZ, 22 IN LONG. Then he sends a picture of the new baby.

I can't really be mad about getting a text of a brand-new baby. I roll back over in bed and look at the picture of Rick and Natalie's new daughter.

She looks like every other newborn I've ever seen, and while I haven't seen too many, I do notice that all of them have the same characteristics. Red, splotchy face, eyes squinched shut, mouth tight. She is wearing a striped hat on her head, so I can't see if she has any hair.

I text back. CONGRATS YOU GUYS! SHE'S BEAUTIFUL! CAN'T WAIT TO MEET HER!

I set my phone back on my nightstand, yawn, and

snuggle back under the sheets. I close my eyes and burrow into the pillow.

And lay there.

I try flipping over to my back and putting my arms out to the side.

Nothing.

I moan. Seriously? I am just going to be up now? I roll back over and look at the clock. Seven fifteen.

After lying in bed for another thirty minutes, I finally give up and just get up. I pull on my robe and pad out to the kitchen to start the coffeepot.

Getting up early on a Saturday when there is absolutely no reason to is just depressing. My grandmother used to tell me about how she would wake up at six every single morning just out of habit. "It's the most annoying thing," she always said. "But I just can't help it."

Heaven forbid that is already happening to me.

The coffeepot starts gurgling, and I sit at the kitchen table with a bowl of Honey Nut Cheerios. I don't even like Cheerios very much, but they were on sale and I'm getting low in my grocery budget for the week.

So, Cheerios it is.

I get up and pour myself a cup of coffee, add cream and sugar, and right when I am about to sit down again at the table, my phone buzzes again.

It's a number I don't recognize, but I answer it anyway. "Hello?"

"Hi there, Auntie Paige," Rick says. "I'm calling from the hospital room phone."

I grin. That answers my question. "Hi, new dad. How's the daughter?"

"Perfect in every way imaginable." Rick is obviously gushing. "Oh, Paige, it's the most amazing thing. You can't even imagine what it feels like."

Considering the closest I've ever come to parenthood is being sort of responsible for taking care of the family dog when I was in the eighth grade, nope. I probably cannot imagine what it feels like.

"Anyway. I'm calling for a couple of reasons. The nurses say Nat can have caffeine now since her milk hasn't come in yet. And she really wants to see you."

I grin. I knew it was going to be like this. Not even a month ago, I was over at Rick and Natalie's house for dinner, and they went on and on about how they didn't want any visitors in the hospital after the baby was born. They wanted to just have time to bond as a new family. Neither Rick's nor Natalie's parents live in town, but I think both of them are planning to come after Natalie is released from the hospital.

I look at the clock on the wall. Well, the no-company thing has lasted for about six hours.

Rick and Natalie are too social to go too long without seeing anyone.

"Starbucks then?" I ask Rick.

"Please. I'll reimburse you when you get here." His voice gets muffled. "Sweetie, you know what you want?"

"A grande nonfat caramel latte," I say along with Rick.

"Wow. You're good," he says.

"No, she's just predictable. Anything for you?"

"I'm pretty sure any caffeine would send me right over the edge into Wonderland, so I'm fine. But get something for yourself. On me. And thank you, thank you. When do you think you can be here?"

Considering I am still in my robe . . . "Forty-five minutes?"

"Sounds great. Thanks so much, Paige!"

I hang up, look at my half-eaten bowl of Cheerios and barely sipped coffee, and sigh. Oh well. I'll get a macchiato at Starbucks and consider that breakfast.

I hurry into the shower, skip washing my hair for the day, and am out, dressed, and ready to go in twenty minutes. A new record, I'm pretty sure.

I grab my purse and jacket and head down the stairs to my car. My usual Starbucks is only ten minutes from the hospital.

I walk in and recognize the barista working. Mostly because he is the same guy I dated for about four months sophomore year at TCU.

"Paige?" He smiles at me as I walk up to the counter.

"Nick." I smile back at him. "When did you start working here?"

"About a month ago. Wow, you look great! Have you been well?"

Nick Trayton is about the nicest guy I've ever met. We got to know each other through an on-campus Bible study and started dating. I can't remember now why we decided to break up.

"Thanks, yeah, I've been good," I tell him. "How about you?"

"I'm good." He nods. "I'm back getting my master's and working here to help pay the student loans." He grins.

He looks great. He was tall and on the painfully skinny side when we dated, but he's filled out a little bit. He has a five o'clock shadow thing going on and dark sticky-up hair.

"Well," he says after a few seconds of awkward silence. "What can I get you?"

"A grande nonfat caramel latte and a venti caramel macchiato please." I dig in my purse for my wallet, trying to come up with something to say. It is so weird seeing someone years later that I used to date. Nick and I were more friends than anything else.

Maybe that was why we broke up. You can't force chemistry.

"Sure thing." He tells me the total and passes the cups over to the barista making the coffee. "So, are you still friends with Layla?"

I nod. "She's getting married in October."

"No way! To who? Steve? Stephen? What is his name?"

"Peter." Layla and Peter have been together a long time.

"Very cool. What are you up to now? Counseling?"

I shake my head, stomach twisting. "I'm working at an adoption agency, but I'm just doing receptionist stuff."

"Awesome."

We both just look around for a minute or two, and he finally smiles. "Well, it's great to see you, Paige. Glad you're doing well."

"Yeah, you too."

"Caramel latte and caramel macchiato!" the other barista yells and sets my drinks on the counter.

"Okay, well, have a good day." I pick up my drinks.

"You too, Paige."

I leave, set one drink on top of the car, open the car door, and then put both inside in the cup holders. Why *did* Nick and I break up?

I drive toward the hospital. I remember thinking he was

really cute before we started dating, and then once we did, it was a lot like I imagined being around a brother. We joked around . . . we watched movies. We rarely held hands and he never kissed me.

It just seemed too weird. Then I went home for Christmas and I think we both kind of started our good-byes with, "So . . ."

And it ended from there.

I pull into the underground parking structure at the hospital and slow down to a crawl as I drive through it, searching for a parking space that isn't too far back in the boonies. Parking garages creep me out big time. I've seen a few too many episodes of *NCIS*.

I finally find one sort of near the elevators, grab my coffees, and pretty much jog through the structure to the even creepier elevator and push the button for the hospital lobby.

I walk over to a map, follow a blue painted line on the walls to another elevator, and push the button for the fourth floor. Rick texted me and told me they are in room 412.

I find it a few minutes later. I knock on the door with my foot and Rick opens it a few seconds later, looking worse than I've ever seen him look.

"Well, aren't you just the picture of sunshine?" I say.

"You try staying up for thirty-seven hours and see how you look." Then he grins. "Want to see my baby girl?"

I smile back and follow him farther into the room. Natalie is lying on the bed, a tiny little bundle in a pink blanket next to her. "Thank God," she says when she sees me.

"I'm going to pretend that is excitement over seeing me." I hand her the latte.

"Of course, of course." She grins. Natalie, compared to Rick, looks wonderful. She is smiling, her hair is parted on the side and back in a loose ponytail at her neck. She is wearing a navy pajama shirt and gray sweatpants.

I get a little closer so I can see little Claire.

"Want to hold her?" Natalie asks.

"You should definitely hold her," Rick says.

"Who are you guys?"

Rick clears his throat. "Oh, pardon, we're not so good on manners after being up the whole night. I'm Rick and this is my wife, Natalie."

"Nice to meet you," Natalie says.

"Guys," I say. "You ask me to come to the hospital, you're offering to let me hold your baby . . . I'm just waiting for you to ask me to stay the rest of the day."

"Can you?" Rick asks. "Then maybe I can get a nap without worrying about leaving Natalie alone with Claire and the nurse from down south of the heavenly border, if you know what I'm saying."

"Seriously," I say. "Remember the whole thing I had to listen to for the last nine months about not wanting anyone at the hospital?"

Natalie shrugs. "We changed our minds."

"It's boring here," Rick says. "I can only take artificial lighting for so long."

"You have a window." I point out to the view of the parking lot.

"The sun doesn't even hit this wing after about eleven in the morning," Rick says.

"Come on," Natalie says. "Wash your hands and come hold this precious girl."

I set my macchiato on the table and go over to the in-room sink and scrub all the way up to my elbows.

Natalie picks up the baby and sets her straight in my arms. I hold her and my breath, worried I am going to crush her.

"She's a big girl, huh?" Natalie smiles.

I look down at the tiniest baby I've ever held and shake my head. "She's so little."

"She's really not," Rick says. "The kid next door is like six pounds. He's a scrawny little thing next to her. I saw him in the nursery when Claire was getting her heel pricked."

"They pricked her heel?" I frown.

Natalie nods, making a sad face. "But I guess she did great. I couldn't go watch."

"I did." Rick nods. "She did fine."

All of the youth group kids had this running bet that if the baby ended up being a girl, Rick would become the softest, squishiest guy on the planet. And I always told them there was no way. Even if he had a girl, Rick would always be Rick.

I guess his statement right there just proved my point.

"My girl," Rick says proudly. "This is only step one, you see."

"Step one?" I repeat. "Of what?"

"Learning how to beat up any boy who tries to mess with her."

"What's step two?" I ask.

"Tackling drills."

I look down at the tiny little face in my arms and just sigh. "I'm sorry, little one," I whisper. "You can come see your Auntie Paige whenever you want."

A nurse walks in and doesn't even blink in my direction. "Time to try nursing again."

I give Claire back to Natalie. "Well, I'm going to go."

"Are you sure?" Natalie asks, messing around with her pajama shirt. "Don't feel like you have to."

"Um, yeah, I'm just going to head out. But text me when you get back to your house and I'll bring you dinner."

"Remember what I told you before," the nurse says to Natalie. "Grasp yourself with your right hand and guide the baby's head with your left."

Past time to go.

I wave at Rick and hurry out of the room. Too many mysteries are being answered in there. I'm sure it will be different if I ever have my own kids, but I don't need to know about breast-feeding issues right now.

I find my car in the creepy parking garage, drive back to my apartment, and climb the stairs. It is ten o'clock, and I have the whole rest of the day to myself. I can't even remember the last time that happened.

I pull my half-finished wreath from the closet, plug in my glue gun, and lay a plastic-backed, paint-flecked tablecloth over my kitchen table just in case any glue drips down. I am going to finish this wreath and then start working on those centerpiece mockups that I've promised Layla.

I turn on Michael Bublé, and right then my phone buzzes again. I almost ignore it, staring at my heated-up glue gun, but I bite my lip, dig it out of my purse, and answer it.

"Hey, Paige, it's Geraldine from church. How are you, dear?"

"Good, thanks. How are you?"

"Not so good, I'm afraid. I was trying to help my husband

by cleaning out the garage while he was still asleep this morning, and I'm pretty sure I dislocated my shoulder. We're at the emergency room right now getting it checked out."

I can hear people talking in the background. "Oh, I'm so sorry," I say, honestly feeling bad for her. Geraldine is one of the nicest ladies at the church. But I am also a little confused. She's nice and we talk occasionally, but it's not like we're the best of friends or anything.

"I'll be fine. But listen, I was planning on going into the office today and finishing the bulletin for tomorrow's service, and it doesn't look like I'll get to do that now. Do you still have that spare church key?"

I look at my glue gun again and bite back a sigh. "Yeah, I do."

"Would you mind, honey? It would help me out a ton."

How can I say no to that? I walk over and unplug my glue gun. "No, I'll head over there right now."

"Thanks so much, Paige. I have everything all ready to go on my desk. Thank you again."

I hear someone call for Geraldine.

"I've got to go," she says.

"Hope the shoulder feels better," I tell her.

"Thanks, sweetie. Bye."

I pick up my keys again. Maybe this is God's way of telling me I do not need a wreath for my door. Maybe there is going to be a horrific windstorm in the next few weeks and it would have blown the wreath off the door and crashed it straight into me and killed me with its grapevine pokiness.

Maybe.

Chapter 8

*C*hurches are eerie when you're the only one there. I unlock the door by the offices, punch in the alarm code, and turn on the lights. The silence is deafening.

Geraldine's desk is stacked high with the unfolded bulletins. I've seen her folding the endless papers before and always feel very sorry for her. The church has a folding machine but it's loud and cantankerous, so Geraldine prefers to fold all 2,500 bulletins by hand.

I am not going to be so picky.

I find the folding machine in one of the closets in the copy room and drag it over to Geraldine's desk. Twenty minutes of fooling with the machine and I finally get it to fold a piece of scrap paper into a trifold correctly.

Carefully, I set a stack of the bulletins in the machine, line up all the edges, and press the button.

The first eighty or so look perfect. Then the machine starts spitting out two at a time, then three at a time, and finally it gets in such a paper jam that it takes me another twenty minutes to get all the papers straightened back out and start over again.

Eighty seems to be the magic number, though. Every time it reaches almost a hundred bulletins, the machine fritzes out and causes a paper jam.

So I sit there, frantically counting the folded bulletins as they spit out at me, and every time I reach seventy-nine, I quickly stop the machine, turn it off, let it cool down for a few minutes, and then start it up again.

This thing has more personality than Peter and his parents combined.

I really need to stop giving him a hard time. Even if it is only in my head.

"Hi, Paige," someone says behind me and scares the daylights out of me. I jump at least six feet off the chair and turn to see Pastor Louis, our senior pastor, walking past the desk.

"Didn't mean to scare you," he says, smiling.

Pastor Louis looks like a pastor. I sometimes wonder if when he was born, his mother named him "Pastor Louis" because he just is a pastor in every sense of the word. He's a great teacher, a great listener, and one of those guys who goes and visits every person from his church who is in the hospital.

"No, no. It's fine. I just didn't hear you come in." My heart is beating so hard I think I might break my bra strap.

"Pulled out the old folding machine, huh?" Pastor Louis watches the machine spit out bulletins.

"Yes, sir." And I've lost my count. I have to turn it off early just to be sure it doesn't jam up again. "Did Geraldine tell you what happened?"

He nods. "I actually was at the hospital visiting Mrs. McCreary when she called to tell me, so I just stopped by the waiting room there. Her shoulder doesn't look so good." He smiles pastorally at me. "Thanks for helping her out like this, Paige."

"Sure." I stop the folding machine, turn it off, and set the timer on my phone for three minutes.

"Learning the tricks?"

"Yes, sir."

"You'll have to teach Geraldine. I've told her for years that she's going to end up with arthritis in both arms because of folding all those bulletins every week. Well, I'm going to go study up for tomorrow. Have a nice day, Paige. Thanks again." He waves and disappears down the hall to his office.

I end up leaving at four o'clock. I will have to rush to get the anniversary party arrangement done for Layla. And I still haven't eaten lunch.

I stop by a floral shop and pick up a dozen yellow roses, some baby's breath, and some filler greenery. Then I go by a local craft store and buy a vase, floral tape, and some white twinkle lights. I save the receipts. Layla is going to pay me back.

I get home, eat a small can of Mandarin oranges, and put the wreath back in the closet. The way things are going, I'll have to use it for next winter's wreath.

Layla printed out a picture of the way she wants the flower arrangement to look. I turn on the TV to HGTV and start cutting the flowers.

Two cousins are just about done demolishing a kitchen when I finish with the arrangement. It looks almost exactly like the picture, at least in my opinion. I text Layla.

IT'S DONE WHENEVER YOU WANT TO COME SEE IT.

She writes me back not even thirty seconds later. ON MY WAY. STOPPING BY PANDA EXPRESS. MANDARIN CHICKEN AND CHOW MEIN?

YES PLEASE. AND THANK YOU. Apparently my Mandarin oranges have been a good appetizer for tonight's dinner. I unlock the door for her and sit back down to put a few finishing touches on the arrangement.

Layla gets to my apartment around six. "That weird guy was there again." She comes in with the bag of aromatic Chinese goodness.

"Weird guy?" I look up from my table with a frown. "Did you lock the door behind you?"

She sets the bag on the kitchen counter and goes back to lock the door. "The guy who always asks me what kind of dipping sauce I want." She nods to the TV where the cousins are chatting up the camera about some rare form of mold they've found in the walls. "Great show, by the way. Makes me wish Peter was the carpenter type."

"You mean one of the cooks?"

"Yeah." She fakes a shudder. "He's weird."

"It's his job to ask you that, isn't it?"

"Well, he doesn't have to do it all scarylike."

This coming from the woman who has to walk through Murder Alley to get to her front door.

"What kind of sauce did you get?" I ask.

"Mandarin and sweet and sour."

My stomach starts growling.

She looks over at the table and gasps. "Paige!" she squeals and then jumps up and down. "Oh my gosh! That's incredible! It's beautiful! It's more than I could ever have imagined!"

I grin. "It's just flowers, Layla." If she gets this excited about an individual centerpiece, I don't want to be around when she starts picking things out for her wedding.

Layla is very exuberant.

She goes on and on about the centerpiece until the cousins finish the kitchen and Layla's orange chicken is completely cold. I've already interrupted her long enough to pray and start eating mine before my stomach decides to just bust out of my skin and grab the Styrofoam to-go box itself.

Which would have been just a little disgusting.

"Seriously, Paige. It's amazing. You're like a crafting genius or something." She finally picks up her fork and stabs a piece of orange chicken.

"Thank you," I say for the sixty-eighth time.

"You know what else is amazing?" she says after she swallows.

"What?"

"Orange chicken. I mean, really. How do they get the exact mix of sweetness, spiciness, and orangeyness all in one bite?" She stabs another one and holds it up to her eye level. "Maybe they feed the chickens orange peels."

"I'm pretty sure chickens only eat like bird-seed stuff."

Any knowledge I have of chickens comes purely from Disney movies, and considering the thirty seconds of screen time they get in *Cinderella*, I'm not really a chicken expert.

But I swear Cinderella fed them bird seed.

Layla shakes her head, waves her fork, and swallows. "Not true. My cousin's best friend's mom raises chickens, and she said one time she was eating lunch out in the backyard and had this jar of that premade queso out there and the phone rang inside. When she got back outside to finish her lunch, the chickens had eaten all the queso." Layla sighs. "Apparently, she found three of her chickens dead the next day. Which is a great reason not to eat premade queso, in my opinion. Apparently there is something toxic to life forms in it."

"Why was she eating lunch with her chickens in the first place?" I ask.

"Maybe they're like dogs to her."

"Dogs that lay eggs?"

Layla shrugs. "I don't claim to understand her. Or chickens, for that matter. I mean, if I were the first person to ever own a chicken, I'm pretty sure it would never be known that eggs could be eaten. The thought of picking up something that your animal pooped out, cooking it, and eating it is a little weird, if you ask me."

I laugh at Layla. "You're disgusting."

"And I also just went vegan." She makes a face and pushes her dinner away.

"What about the steak, chicken, and shrimp gourmet dinner in the Burgundy sauce?" I ask, grinning.

"No chicken. Maybe steak. At least it's not called the same thing as the animal it came from."

I finish my dinner and close the Styrofoam container. "So, what are you up to tonight?"

"I don't know. What are you up to tonight?"

I shrug. "At some point before February, I'd like to finish my January wreath for the door."

She waves her hand. "Eh. You live in an apartment complex. As far as I'm concerned, that's excuse enough not to put up wreaths, a welcome mat, or Christmas lights."

"Scrooge," I accuse her.

"Call me all the bad names you want." She falls onto the couch. A show about backyards is starting. "I'm an apartment dweller and proud of it. Hey, do you have any peanut butter?"

I find some in my pantry. "Why?"

"I saw a recipe for this amazing peanut butter and pretzel and chocolate dessert thing online."

"I don't have pretzels," I say.

"Oh, well. Want to watch a movie?"

"Only if I can work on my wreath while we're watching it."

She shrugs. "Fine by me. What sounds good for a movie?" She gets up and digs through my DVDs. "Oh! How about *Clueless*?"

I nod. I've seen it a million times, so it is a good movie to watch while I am going to be distracted. But I am going to finish that wreath before February. Even if I don't sleep from now until then to make it happen.

My phone rings right as the glue gun gets hot enough to actually melt the glue and right as we're introduced to Cher's amazing life. I take a deep, calming breath. It's like my phone has it in for this wreath.

"Want me to pause it?" Layla calls from the couch.

"No, I'll be back in a second." I go into my bedroom so the background volume isn't so loud. "Hello?"

"Hey, Paige. Hi, it's Tyler."

"Tyler."

"From church? Rick gave me your number."

Of course he did.

"Hi." Tyler seems like a great guy. A really great guy, actually. But I just don't have the time for anything right now.

Not if it has taken me three weeks to glue twelve flowers

onto a wreath. Even if a relationship is something I want, it just isn't fair to the guy to be so preoccupied with everything else going on.

"Hey. Listen, since Rick and Natalie are a little preoccupied with their new baby right now, Rick asked me to take the new lesson plans for the youth group to everyone."

"Okay. I'll be at church tomorrow. I can pick it up from you then."

"Right. He wanted us to get a chance to look over them before the leaders' meeting."

"What leaders' meeting?"

"The one after second service tomorrow?" Tyler says, sounding apologetic.

Rick never tells me anything.

"I didn't know there was one," I say.

"Yeah, I kind of got that. Sorry. I hope that works. I know you're pretty busy."

I hold in a sigh. "No, yeah, it's fine," I lie. "I don't have any plans tomorrow." Which was the blessed truth five minutes ago. Now I do.

My apartment hasn't even been vacuumed in like two months. Which I guess isn't a big deal since I am usually only here to sleep.

"So, anyway, do you mind if I drop this off?"

"Right now?" I ask.

"In like fifteen minutes, if that's okay."

I shut my eyes, trying to remember what my living room looks like. "Uh, sure." I tell him my address.

"Thanks. See you in a bit, Paige."

I hang up and walk back out to the living room. Layla is helping herself to an unopened bag of gummy bears that has been in my pantry since last Valentine's Day. "Good luck with those."

"Why? Are they mean bears? They look so tame." She grins at me.

"They're probably hard as rocks."

She bites into one and shakes her head. "Tastes fine to me. Thank God for preservatives. Everything okay?"

"Tyler's going to come by and drop something off for youth group in a few minutes."

"Who's Tyler?" Layla asks, now rooting around in my fridge. "Goodness. Being a vegan is not fun. I'm starving all the time."

"You've only been a vegan for about an hour, Layla."

"I'm still starving." She pulls out a container of strawberry yogurt. "Is yogurt vegan?"

"I don't know."

"I'm saying that it is. Can I have this?"

I look at her and laugh. "Sure. Take whatever you want."

"In that case, I might have a few of those corn chips you've got in the pantry too."

"Also probably stale."

"You need to go grocery shopping."

More than that, I need to clean out my pantry, but that will have to wait for another night.

I straighten up a few things around the living room while Layla sits back down on the couch. "So you didn't answer my question." She crosses her legs underneath her.

"What question?" I toss the throw pillows back on the chair, picking them up from where I had tossed them on the floor.

"Who's Tyler?"

"Oh. You haven't met him?"

"No. Is he cute?"

I think about it. This is Layla asking. She isn't going to be happy with anything except the truth. And seeing how she is about to meet him, I can't lie. "In a flannel-shirt kind of way, sure."

"Like those logger guys on TV?" Layla pops a gummy bear into her mouth. "Because those guys are not very cute at all. No offense to the loggers."

"No." I rub my head. "I don't know. He'll be here in a few minutes. You decide if he's cute or not."

"I will."

"Good."

"But may I remind you that I'm engaged, and since I'm engaged, I'm automatically obligated to set you up with any cute, single Christian guy we meet so you can also share in my Forever Happiness," she says, watching the movie during her entire speech.

I sigh. "Yes, ma'am."

"So if he's cute, I'm getting his number."

"You don't think Peter will have a problem with that?"

She shakes her head. "Peter is just as concerned with your Forever Happiness as I am."

I have my doubts about that one, but I'm not going to argue with her.

Tyler knocks a few minutes later. I open the door. "Hi, Tyler. Come on in."

"Hey, Paige." He comes in, looking . . . well, flannel-y. He has on faded jeans that are shredded at the hem, work boots, a blue-plaid flannel shirt, and a red puffy vest. He has a Bass Pro Shop hat smashed down over his wavy hair.

Layla waves from the couch. "I'm Layla. Nice to meet you, Tyler."

He smiles at her. "Nice to meet you, too." He looks at me apologetically and hands me a stack of twenty or so papers stapled together. "Didn't mean to interrupt girls' night. Sorry."

"Well, we—" I start.

"We're just hanging out," Layla interrupts. "Not an official girls' night by any means because, you'll notice, I'm eating gummy bears and not Oreos." She points to the bowl. "Actually, are Oreos even vegan?"

"Layla's a recent convert," I tell Tyler. "Going on an hour and a half."

"Change has to start sometime, somewhere," Layla says seriously.

"Nice campaign speech," I say.

"Vote for vegetables! Just say no to lamb chops!"

Tyler laughs. "Are you sure those are just gummy bears?"

"Oh yes. That's just Layla."

She grins at him. "Come in. Take off your shoes and sit down for a bit. Ever seen *Clueless*?"

"No, but I've seen *Clue*." Tyler sits in the chair.

"The game?" Layla asks.

"The movie."

"*Ack*," she groans.

"Ugh, really?" I protest, sitting down next to Layla.

"What? I thought it was kind of funny."

"I hate to inform you of this, Tyler, but it is not a funny movie," Layla says.

"At all," I add.

He holds his hands up, surrender-style. "My apologies. I didn't realize I was with the movie police."

I swipe one of Layla's gummy bears, and she shoots me a dirty look. "Excuse me, do you mind? Famished vegan over here."

I point. "My sofa, my gummy bears."

"Fine." She sighs, closing her eyes. "You may have three."

Tyler grins at us.

Layla finishes chewing a gummy bear, studying him. "So, Tyler. What is your last name?"

"Jennings."

"What does your mother call you?"

"Um. Tyler."

"What is a childhood secret that you've never told anyone before?"

I elbow Layla.

"Ow!" she yells.

"Leave him alone. He barely walked in the door," I say.

"It's okay, it's okay. I'll answer the question. When I was in the third grade, I found what I thought was a dinosaur bone in the sandbox at school. But this kid, Arnold, came and stole it and told everyone it was his." Tyler's face gets very sad. "He even took it to Show and Tell."

"So you were a suffering silent one," Layla says.

"Well, I beat him up on the playground after Show and Tell."

"So you were the vengeful, angry one." Layla nods. "I see."

"All before my conversion," Tyler says.

"You don't eat meat either?"

"Are you kidding? That's all I eat. No, I meant before I became a Christian."

Layla sighs sadly. "We can't all be helping protect Bambi.

I guess some of you have to be out there shooting his mother. There are no heroes without villains."

I laugh.

"For such a recent vegan, you sure have a lot of passion for it," Tyler tells her.

"Tyler, meet Layla," I say.

He grins. "So. When did you guys become friends?"

I look at Layla. "Fourth grade?"

"Fifth. Remember? You got assigned to the desk next to mine."

"Oh. That's right. Mr. Hillerman."

She nods solemnly. "Yeah."

Tyler looks at us. "What was wrong with Mr. Hillerman?"

"Nothing. Except he almost destroyed *this*." Layla waves her finger back and forth between me and her.

"He made us switch to desks on opposite sides of the room the second week in the school year," I tell Tyler. "Layla was making me laugh too much in class."

"She still can't laugh silently," Layla says.

"I can too!"

"No, sweetie. You can't." She pats my knee. "But don't worry. It's a learned skill. Mr. Hillerman just didn't give you enough practice time. Just think, if it weren't for him, we wouldn't have had that whole Spelling Bee Horrificalness."

I sober. "Mr. Hillerman," I whisper darkly.

"That's right, Paige. Let it out."

"What is the Spelling Bee Horrificalness?" Tyler asks me. "And y'all realize that's not a word, right?"

"Sure it is," Layla says matter-of-factly. "*B-E-E*. You know, buzz? The thing that stings you?"

"No, I meant—"

"It was freshman year," Layla interrupts. "Our first year in high school and we were not really making strides up the social ladder, if you know what I mean. I had this huge puffy hair and Paige had glasses and braces and, well, neither of us had gotten the whole eyeliner thing down. And there was this schoolwide assembly for a spelling bee about, oh, maybe right around Christmas that year."

"I was a pretty good speller," I say. "I couldn't figure out that stirrup pants had been out of style for like fifteen years by then, but I could spell."

"Read geek," Layla tells Tyler.

"Hey!"

"Loveable geek," Layla says.

"Anyway. I got beaten out of representing our grade by Anthony Lakerson, because the day of the semifinal, I had a sinus infection and I could barely breathe," I tell Tyler.

"Anthony was an even huger dweeb than Paige, if you can believe that," Layla adds.

Tyler raises an eyebrow. "I'm not sure that's a word either, but go on."

"D-W-E-E-B," Layla spouts off.

"No, I meant—"

"So anyway," Layla interrupts again. "Weeks go by and there we all were in the gym. They'd built this little stage with the two podiums on it for the people in the spelling bee and then all of the rest of the students sat on the bleachers. And our gym was really . . ." She looks at me, frowning.

"Echo-y," I say.

"Right. Very echo-y. During basketball games, I had to leave because of how loud the squeaks from the players' shoes were." She shudders. "I still can't watch basketball. Peter spends a lot of time alone in March."

"Peter?"

"My fiancé. Keep up, Tyler," Layla says.

"Anyway," I say, setting a calming hand on Layla's arm, "Anthony was up against another student at the school, and in the first round, he got the word *robust*."

"Okay," Tyler says.

"So, Anthony spells it *R-O-B-O-O-S-T*," Layla says.

"Roboost?"

"Exactly." I nod at Tyler. "And that's when it happened."

"What happened?"

"Paige laughed like Cruella de Vil, and I'm not even kidding." Layla leans forward, all serious.

"It wasn't that bad." I roll my eyes.

"Oh, trust me. It was bad. I was sitting right next to her, and quick as a flash I slapped my hand over her mouth, but I wasn't fast enough." She shakes her head mournfully.

"I couldn't help it. I was still a little mad about the whole thing where he beat me out because of a stupid sinus infection."

"So her laugh echoed across the entire gym," Layla says slowly. "And it kept echoing and echoing until poor little Anthony Lakerson sat down on the stage and wept."

"No way," Tyler says.

"He didn't weep," I say.

"Oh, he cried." Layla nods. "He cried hard. He cried so hard his mom had to push her way down the bleachers and take him home."

"I felt really bad," I say. "I told him I was sorry later. It just kind of . . . popped out."

"The apology?" Tyler asks.

"The laugh."

He grins.

"Anyway." Layla gets back to her gummy bears. "Later Anthony told everyone he'd been cutting onions all week for his mom's big Christmas feast and that's why he started bawling in the middle of the stage and he thought maybe the onion fumes had gone into his ears and made him hear words differently. Like *roboost* instead of *robust*."

"And that's the Spelling Bee Horrificalness," I say.

"And now we know it's all Mr. Hillerman's fault." Layla looks at me.

"Teachers have a great responsibility in this life." Tyler nods.

"For good or for evil," Layla says soberly.

"Well, I'll have to remember I'm in the presence of a spelling snob then." Tyler smirks at me.

"I gave that up."

"Sort of like how I gave up meat." Layla chews a gummy bear.

"Except I gave mine up years ago, and Layla has now gone two hours," I say, grinning at my best friend.

"So, you're engaged," Tyler says.

"Yep. Hoping to follow in the tradition of my parents, set so grandly before me," Layla says dramatically. "You can come to their surprise anniversary party if you'd like to. Though, to warn you, there is a good possibility there will not be any animal products on the menu."

"When is this party?" Tyler asks.

"February 22. And we're going to spend the night in the park beforehand. Me and Paige." She pats my knee again.

I guess that means Peter has backed out. Like I knew he was going to.

"Yeah." I try to muster up some enthusiasm.

Tyler looks at me and then back at Layla. "Wait, just the two of you?"

"Yep! It's going to be great. We'll bring sleeping bags . . . we'll roast marshmallows. We'll sing 'Kumbaya.' It'll be epic."

"Uh-huh." Tyler looks back at me. "Have you thought about maybe asking a few more people to join you in this epicness?"

"Definitely not a word, Tyler." Layla shakes her head.

"Sure it is. *J-O-I-N*. Join. You know, when more people come spend the night at the park so you don't get murdered the night before your parents' anniversary party." He gives her a stern look. "Somehow I doubt that would be the best way to pay homage to their grand example for you."

I start laughing. Any guy who can dish it back to Layla is okay in my book.

Layla pauses and thinks about that. "I guess that would be good, huh."

Tyler nods. "Staying alive? I think so."

"No, having more people to sing 'Kumbaya.' Two people just don't really make a great campfire sing-along and no offense, Paige, but our voices don't mesh very well."

I shrug. No offense taken there. She speaks the truth.

Chapter 9

Sunday morning, my alarm goes off at seven.

Now, I love being a Christian. I love Jesus. I love reading my Bible, and I love that I can go to God anytime in prayer.

I don't love that church happens so early on one of the few mornings I have off from work. And I especially don't love the weeks when I'm teaching the two-year-olds' Sunday school class, because I have to be there thirty minutes before I normally would.

If there are any unperks of being a Christian, I consider less sleep one of them.

I finally talk myself into getting out of bed by seven fifteen, stumble to the shower, and turn the nozzle all the way to hot. Good showers only happen if the water is so hot that my feet are purple when I get out.

I stare into the mirror while I wait for the water to heat up. My eyes have big dark circles under them, and I swear I see a new wrinkle forming on the side of my right eye. I am twenty-two years old. This is not supposed to happen for many more years.

Maybe it's the very late night last night. Tyler and Layla both ended up staying until well past midnight. We ended up half watching, half talking through the rest of *Clueless* and then *Just Like Heaven*.

I take a quick shower, blow-dry my hair, and pull on a pair of jeans and a black long-sleeved Henley-style shirt. Rule number one in teaching the two-year-olds is that nice church clothes are a definite no. Particularly if your nice church clothes include a super-cute jersey skirt that has a fold-over waistband instead of an actual waistband that can't be pulled down.

Yeah. I learned that lesson the hard way.

I plug in my curling iron and look at my hair. It isn't as long as Layla's and it certainly isn't her pretty, chocolaty brown. My mother liked to tell me my hair was "golden brown," but that made it sound a lot prettier than it actually is.

Should I ever have the money someday for highlights, I'll make it blonde again like it was when I was a little kid.

My dad always tells me that you can marry more money in five minutes than you can make in a lifetime. Which is why my mental list of what I am looking for in a future husband includes the words *rich doctor*.

They're right below *frequent shaver*. An occasional five o'clock shadow is cute, but I really prefer a clean-shaven face.

Probably has something to do with being raised in Texas, where it consistently reaches ninety degrees and 100 percent humidity. The less you have to wear, the better, and that includes facial hair.

Which is also why *doesn't think a swimsuit is nice summer attire* is on my list. And that one is self-explanatory.

I get to church at eight thirty after making a stop at Starbucks. I am well on my way to becoming one of the esteemed gold-card members with how often I go there. I sip my macchiato, then look at the cup, frowning.

If I give up macchiatos, will I have enough to get highlights every month?

I take another sip and shake my head. Isn't worth it. I'll stay dishwater blonde or brown or whatever color my hair is. You can never underestimate the power of a personality, compliments of the wonder drug caffeine.

My coteacher, Rhonda Matthews, shows up at about eight forty-five. "Paige, I am *so* sorry." She hurries through the half door looking pretty harried. "Mandy woke up with a cold, Reid's alarm didn't go off, and Ben decided that he would only come to church with me if he got to pick out his outfit." She hustles her two-year-old son, Ben, into the room. Ben looks . . . colorful.

"Nice boots, Ben," I say. It's hard work to pull off red cowboy boots with green athletic pants about two inches too short for you.

"What do you say to Miss Paige, Benjamin?" Rhonda demands, hanging her purse and jacket on the hooks by the door. This is the thing about us Texan women. It may be seventy degrees out, but dang it, we are going to wear those cute jackets when it is supposed to be wintertime.

Ben pulls three fingers out of his mouth, slobber covering them. "Tanks, Mwiss Paid."

"Sure," I say. One of these days, I will figure out how to get that stain-master stuff sprayed on the jeans I wear on

Sunday school teaching days. And maybe some form of germ repellent.

Rhonda watches Ben wander off toward the toys and shakes her head. "I really need to go through his closet this week and pack away all the pants that size. Kids just grow up too fast, you know?"

"Mmm." I nod, like I do know. In my opinion, though, these kids are never going to grow up and stop putting everything in their mouths. You'd think parents would want their kids to finally reach that stage. I watch Ben gnaw on a plastic dinosaur he just picked up out of the toy bin, then finally look away.

If I ever invent germ repellent, I can seriously become a zillionaire. Sunday school teachers everywhere would thank me.

By the time it's nine fifteen, we have twenty-three kids and insanity. Two teachers are about eight teachers too few when it comes to controlling twenty-three children who know only three words very well: *Mine! No!* and *Hey!*

Somehow, we create some semblance of order and get everyone to sit in what might pass as a circle. "All right, guys, we're going to sing a few songs and then listen to a Bible story, okay?" I say in my best version of that lady from *Lamb Chop*.

"I *hate* to sing!" one boy screeches as he stands and runs for the toys.

"Yeah! Me too!" Ben yells.

"Tough," Rhonda says, pulling out her mom voice. "Now you *will* sit down in the circle and you *will* sing songs. You get it?" She takes both boys firmly by the hands and leads them back into the circle. "And, Wesley, I know your mother. And I am not above tattling on you."

Wesley, properly chastised, slinks into a seated position and eyes me with about as much sweetness as a dill pickle.

"Um. 'Jesus loves me! This I know,'" I start. Because really, there is no good way to start singing about the Savior's unending, unbelievable love when you are just told you can't play with the toys and your mother's friend is going to tell on you.

The kids join me one by one, and by the time we've sung it four times over, everyone is singing and a few of the braver kids are attempting to do the hand motions with me.

We sing "Jesus Loves the Little Children," "This Little Light of Mine," "I've Got the Joy, Joy, Joy, Joy," and then a new girl politely asks if we can please sing the theme from *The Little Mermaid*.

"It's really very easy to learn," she tells the other kids. "Everyone listen. 'Look at this stuff, isn't it neat?'"

"Gabriella," I interrupt. "How old are you again?"

"I'm four," she says, holding up three fingers.

"Yeah, honey, you're in the wrong class."

"But you're a very good singer," Rhonda tells her.

"Yes. Very good." I look up at Rhonda. "Is Tiffany still out there?"

Tiffany is the eighth grader who sits out by the check-in desk to make sure all the parents grab one of the panda, koala, or giraffe cards, depending on how old their child is, so they can check them back out. It is apparently a security system, but seeing as how Tiffany left her post fifteen minutes into class and someone can easily just grab a panda card and come take a child, I don't see that it does too much. I just try to remember which parent goes with each kid.

Rhonda sticks her head out the half door. "Nope," she says.

"Okay then. Gabriella, you're going to be our helper today. Does that sound good to you?"

She nods happily, like I've just told her she is going to go to Disney World.

I really should switch to the four-year-old class. But then I look over at Kayla, the most adorable little girl in the entire world, and change my mind.

"Okay. Story time," I say, and Rhonda takes over.

Rhonda is a master storyteller. I think every mom becomes one when she leaves the hospital. It's definitely a motherly thing.

Today's story is about David, the little shepherd boy who was anointed to become king.

Joshua raises his hand.

"Yes, Josh?" Rhonda asks.

"Why did they pour syrup on his head?"

"Not syrup," Rhonda says. "Oil. It is something they did back then to show honor. But," she says quickly, "it is *not* something we do today. So y'all leave your mama's pantry alone. Yes, ma'am?"

"Yes, ma'am," Ben says.

All the other kids nod solemnly.

Like I said, Rhonda is very motherly.

When she finishes telling the story, all the kids come and sit down at the tables to make their craft of gluing cotton balls onto a cardstock cutout of a sheep. I've written the memory verse for this week on the back of the sheep.

Then we let the kids play outside on the playground until their parents come to pick them up.

Rhonda gathers her purse, jacket, and son and then gives me a head wave. "Bye, Paige. I'll see you in two weeks for this madness again."

I laugh. "Bye, Rhonda." I pick up my Bible, purse, and jacket and walk down the hall to the singles' class.

I am almost there when I think about what Tyler said about singles' classes and how he much preferred the main service. Seeing as how Pastor Dan is still on sabbatical and I'll probably hear some talk about how Xbox is not just a biblical thing but a good thing for every Christian, I turn and head back down the crowded hallway to the auditorium.

The auditorium is packed with people coming in and people trying to leave and people standing in the way of everyone who is doing the previous two things.

Apparently, there is just something about aisles that begs people to stand in the middle of them and talk, completely blocking the way.

I find an empty row toward the back on the right side and set all my stuff down on one of the seats. Since most of the people I know go to either the first service or the singles' class, I hardly recognize anyone around me.

I sit down and smile to myself. I can sit here and worship Jesus however I want to without worrying about what my friends around me think. I can quietly take notes without being passed a note that has *Hey, we should go get donuts for Sunday school* scrawled on it.

I start getting excited.

Then I start getting worried that I am excited I am going to be alone.

The music begins and the lights dim into almost complete darkness. A young couple squeezes past me into my row, followed by an elderly woman and what looks like her teenage granddaughter.

I have saved myself two chairs. One on the aisle, one right inside just so I know I'll be sitting by myself.

Our music pastor, Victor, and his wife, Carrie, start harmonizing the beginning of a worship song. We all stand, as is customary.

I close my eyes and just listen for a few minutes as everyone around me starts to sing. The young couple two seats down don't have very good voices but sing out anyway. I also hear the elderly lady's gentle warble and the teen girl's soprano.

I start singing and suddenly the only voice I can hear, the only voice that really matters, is my sad, usually off-key voice. But it isn't an issue. Not right now. Not when it is just me and God.

I raise my hands without caring what the people around me think, sing the words, and feel peace for the first time in a few weeks.

Pastor Louis climbs onto the stage as the notes of the final song hang in the air. "Thanks so much, Victor and Carrie," he says while the auditorium claps politely and sits down.

I sit down and pull my Bible over. Pastor Louis talks for the next forty-five minutes on God's goodness and how it does not give us license to sin, but it gives us an example to follow. "We like to say that God is good all the time. And yes, He is good all the time. But have you ever asked yourself why?"

I blink. I have never asked myself that question.

"Look at Deuteronomy chapter 7. If you're like me, you skip over these important books and head straight to the

New Testament." A few people in the room chuckle. Pastor Louis turns the pages in his Bible and reads, "'For you are a holy people to the LORD your God; the LORD your God has chosen you to be a people for His own possession out of all the peoples who are on the face of the earth.' And a little farther down, he says, 'Know therefore that the LORD your God, He is God, the faithful God, who keeps His covenant and His lovingkindness to a thousandth generation with those who love Him and keep His commandments.'"

Pastor Louis looks up from his Bible. "You see? God is not good to us because we deserve it. God is not good to us because we are so needy and sad. And God is not good to us because of anything we've done or will do. No, God is good to us because He is good! His goodness is a part of Himself. And He is good to us because He chose us."

He looks around the room. "If you've ever felt like you're not good enough, like you're not strong enough, like you don't do enough, stop. Rest. Realize that God is good. And He has chosen you."

He starts flipping in his Bible again. "What has He chosen you for?" He points at the Bible. "Ephesians chapter 1: 'He chose us in Him before the foundation of the world, that we would be holy and blameless before Him.'"

He says a few more things, but I don't pay as close attention because I am busy writing down references and underlining *holy and blameless* in my Bible. Holy and blameless.

I know I'm not living holy or blameless. I mean, goodness, I haven't even had a chance to read my Bible in a week. I bite the inside of my cheek and make a note on my bulletin:

Set alarm for 30 min earlier tomorrow.

If I am so tired at the end of the day that I can't focus on my Bible reading, then maybe the alternative is to get up earlier and read in the mornings.

Pastor Louis finishes his sermon, the band plays two more songs, and then everyone is dismissed. The church erupts into a volcanic mass of chatter, laughter, children squealing, and the general sounds of people standing, stretching, and gathering their belongings.

"Hi there!" a cheerful woman behind me says.

I turn to see a plump, dark-haired woman about thirty-five standing there.

"Hi," I say.

"I'm Cindy." She shoves her hand toward me. "Are you new here? What's your name?"

"I'm Paige. And no, not new here. New to this service, though."

"Well, it's nice to meet you, Paige! God bless you!"

I haven't sneezed so I'm not sure what her exclamation is for, but I nod and give her a smile before pulling my jacket on and heading toward the door. "Bye." I wave to her, trying to be friendly.

I mash and cram my way through the crowded hallway all the way to the end of it where the youth room is. Apparently, we have a leaders' meeting today. What is with all these leaders' meetings lately anyway?

I've barely had a chance to look through the material since Tyler and Layla ended up staying over so late last night. I skimmed through it while I brushed my teeth last night and this morning. It looks like we're going to begin a new series on the basics of Christianity.

"Hola." Rick says "hello" in a bad Spanish accent as I walk in.

"No marshmallow gun?" I greet him.

"What? Come now, Paige. I am a responsible, peace-loving father." He rolls his eyes. "Sheesh."

I nod to the Mountain Dew in his hands. "Bad night?"

"Paige, I love my daughter, but I swear she's nocturnal. We had the raccoon of babies. We went home yesterday about four in the afternoon. She slept the entire day, all through dinner. Nat nursed her at ten, we laid her down, we all slept until midnight, and then we were all awake until . . ." He looks at his watch. "Well, it's almost eleven forty-five."

"Sorry, Rick."

"Just pray for me. I drove here and I have to drive home." He rubs his bleary eyes and nods to Julie and Trevor stacking the chairs so the janitor can clean the youth room this week. "Thanks, guys."

"Sure thing, Rick," Trevor says.

Rick looks at me. "So, what do you usually do first service again?"

"I teach the toddlers every other week. On the off weeks, I go to the main service."

Rick nods. "How would you like to start coming in here and helping out with the youth ministry on the off weeks?"

I set my stuff down on one of the chairs Julie and Trevor left for us. "What would I be doing?"

"Nothing, really. Just being here for the girls before and after, so if they have any questions or need anything, you're there. Pretty much what you do on Wednesday nights but without the teaching."

No extra teaching sounds okay. Then I can just continue going to the second service. As much as I like hearing the current lessons on how Gandalf is apparently an allegory to Christ, I'm not getting too much out of the singles' class.

Lord of the Rings just isn't my style. If I'm going to read a book, I want it to take place in the real world.

I shrug. "I can maybe do that."

"Great!" Rick looks genuinely thrilled.

Sam and Trisha walk in, and Tyler comes in last again. "Morning everyone," he says, smiling at me. He drops into the chair next to mine. "How was Sunday school?"

"I went to the service this morning."

He grins. "Really? I didn't even see you there. Bummer. We'll have to sit together next time."

"Yeah." I try to inflect some enthusiasm into my voice but honestly, I loved this morning. It was just me and God. I miss that.

"All right, guys, I won't make this long," Rick says. "I know you've probably all got plans, and I need to go sleep. But I did want to go over the new curriculum with you and make sure everyone's on the same page."

"What page is that?" Sam asks.

"Right now? Oh, page 1, I guess." Rick grabs his binder off the pulpit. "I actually wrote this over the last few months. I want it to be something where the kids are learning the same thing on Sundays and Wednesdays so it really sticks, you know? So, today we talked about sin and you guys will all do a short lesson on it, look up a few passages, and then I've got about ten or fifteen discussion questions on it." He taps his binder. "Any questions?"

Everyone shakes their heads and Rick nods. "Great. It's pretty straightforward. Plus, I'm excited about having all the small groups going through the same thing. All right. Have a good Sunday."

"Sleep well," I tell him.

"Thank you. Hopefully that will wait until after I get home." He yawns.

I head out to my car after waving good-bye to everyone. Layla texted me during the meeting.

Want to go look at dresses today?

I write her back as I walk across the parking lot. Sure. Leaving church now. Want me to come to your place and pick you up?

My phone buzzes as I climb into the car. Sounds great. See you soon!

I drive to Layla's apartment. I feel germy. Children have been all over me this morning. One little girl fell on the playground and spent the next ten minutes crying alligator tears and leaking snot all over my shoulder.

I don't feel very bridesmaid-y.

I get to her apartment, walk through Murder Alley and up her stairs, and knock on the door. "Come on in!" she yells from inside.

I walk in and she is standing in the kitchen, wearing a green apron and oven mitts. She has her hair in a haphazard bun on the top of her head. Peter is sitting on the couch watching football.

"Hey, Peter," I say, walking past him into the kitchen.

"Hi."

And there you have it, folks. The longest conversation I will have with Peter this week.

"What are you doing?" I ask Layla.

She grins at me and turns back to peering into her oven. "I'm cooking!"

I look around her kitchen. About nineteen dishes are stacked in the sink, flour dusts one of her counters, and there is a slimy bag of potato peelings on the counter. "You read the *Pioneer Woman* blog again today, didn't you?"

"Possibly. But don't those potatoes look amazing?"

I look in the oven too. She has some kind of potato casserole bubbling in the oven. It smells good, anyway.

"Did you guys not go to church today?" I ask her.

"We went to first service. There's a playoff game on today."

Priorities and all that.

"Oh," I say.

"Yeah. And I decided to get culinary while he's watching the game. Apparently, these potatoes are like the best potatoes ever known to man and perfect for football game days."

I'm not a huge potato fan, but I blame that on my way-distant Irish heritage. A family can only stomach so many potatoes before someone in the lineage can't stand them.

"How was Sunday school?" Layla closes the oven door and sets the timer for another five minutes. "What allegory did you study today? *Diary of a Wimpy Kid?*"

I grin. "I went to service instead."

"No way. You skipped out on singles' class?" she gasps. "People are going to think you up and married, you know."

"Maybe. It was really nice."

"Up and marrying?"

"Service."

"Right. It was a good sermon today."

"Rick asked me to start coming to the youth group on my off weeks from the toddler class," I tell her.

"Oh yeah? What did you say?"

I shrug again. "I said sure."

"You have a hard time telling him no."

I lean against the counter. "I do not."

"Do too. When was the last time you said, 'No, Rick. I can't do that'?" She leans against the opposite counter, crossing her flour-covered arms over her chest.

I think about it. "One time he asked me to chaperone a broomball game."

"And *I* said no for you because you were so sick you couldn't even text." Layla sticks her finger in the air. "Doesn't count."

"I don't know, Layla. I don't mind helping out."

"Mm-hmm." She opens the oven again and pulls the casserole out.

"What's in that?" Something about the way it's starting to congeal just seconds out of the oven doesn't look right to me.

"Potatoes, chives, cheese, milk, flour, and gelatin."

"Gelatin? Like Jell-O?"

"Like baking gelatin." Layla tosses me an empty box from the counter.

I look at the front of it. *Preserving Gelatin. 4 packages.*

"How much of this did you use?"

"All of the packages. It's what the Pioneer Woman said to do."

"Where's her blog?" I ask.

Layla points to the kitchen table, where her laptop is

set up. I click the touchpad, and the screen lights up to the blog.

"See?" Layla says, coming over behind me. She points to the screen. "Layer the potatoes, chives, and cheese in a nine-by-thirteen baking dish. Then pour the milk and flour mixture over it."

"Where does it mention gelatin?"

She frowns at the screen. "It did say it right after that. I scrolled down to see what direction was next, and it said to sprinkle four packages of preserving gelatin over the pan."

I scroll down. And get to her next recipe.

Whole Berry Breakfast Casserole.

It calls for four packages of gelatin.

I look back at the potato casserole, and the whole thing seems to be almost breathing. It looks alive.

Which is not how potato casserole should look.

"Oops," Layla says sadly.

"It smells good," I tell her, trying to be nice. It does smell good even if it looks strange. Potato casserole should not wiggle like that.

I am suddenly pretty certain I'm not going to be hungry the rest of the day.

Layla sighs, pulls off her oven mitts, and brushes the flour off her arms into the sink. "People like me shouldn't be allowed to cook."

"Oh come now, Layla. You made those brownies that one time, remember? Those were good."

"They were from a box. I've seen monkeys on YouTube who can make those brownies."

I snap my fingers. "And you made those green beans with garlic and brought them to the church potluck."

"From the frozen section. They were even in a steamable bag so all I did was throw them in the microwave." She sighs and washes her hands. "At least Peter can cook."

This is news to me. "He can?" I ask quietly. "What?"

"Lots of stuff. Pancakes. He made this meatball soup a few weeks ago at his apartment that was his mom's recipe growing up."

I had no idea.

"I'm going to get ready to go. I want to look like a bride and not like that girl with the crazy hair from whatever that Pixar movie is when I'm trying on wedding dresses." She disappears into her bedroom and closes the door.

This is awkward. Just Peter and me. I can't decide what will be more awkward. To join him in front of a football game I couldn't care less about? Or to stand around in the kitchen with a pan of potato Jell-O?

Eventually, the potato Jell-O starts scaring me, so I go into the living room and sit on the glider chair.

Peter looks over at me. "Smells good in there."

I blink, feeling what I imagine the first people to experience a movie with sound felt like.

They are speaking aloud!

"Well, it didn't turn out too well, so I wouldn't get your hopes too high."

He shrugs. "Okay."

A few minutes of complete silence go by, save for the low drone of the announcers on the TV.

"So," I say, "Layla said you can cook?"

"Hmm?"

"She said you can cook? Pancakes? Soup?"

"Oh," Peter says, looking at the TV. "My mom had left a

container of the soup in my freezer. I just stuck it in the pot and stirred it."

God bless their future children. I immediately start praying that one set of their parents will move into town so they at least have a chance of a good solid meal once a week.

Layla opens the door, looking cute in a gray sweater dress, black leggings, and boots. She pulls a red scarf around her neck and grabs her jacket.

My dashboard showed it was seventy-one degrees when I was driving over here after church. She is going to roast, but I don't say anything.

It is January, after all.

"Ready?" she asks me cheerfully.

I stand and nod. "Yep."

"Bye, sweetie." She leans over to kiss Peter. I look away. It is awkward watching friends kiss.

"Bye. Have fun." Peter offers her a smile before turning back to the TV.

Layla opens the door; I grab my purse and follow her out.

"I vote we go to Panda for lunch first," Layla suggests.

"Didn't we just have Panda?"

"You can never have too much Panda Express, Paige. Never. And anyway, I'm buying. My grandpa just sent me a big check as a wedding present."

"You don't want to save that money for something other than fast-food Chinese?" I ask her, unlocking my car.

She slides into the passenger seat, and we both buckle our seat belts while I turn the ignition.

She shrugs at me. "Like what?"

"I don't know. A down payment on a house? Or at least an apartment without Murder Alley?"

She waves her hand. "Potato, po-tah-to. What you call Murder Alley, I call a peaceful stroll. And anyway, Peter wants us to move into his apartment after the wedding." She makes a face, and I feel my nose wrinkling as well.

Peter, with all his charming personality and engaging wit, is not the best housekeeper. And yes, I am being sarcastic.

"That places freaks me out. I just know something lives there with him." Layla shudders.

I gag. Now I really am not hungry.

"Or we can just go look at dresses," Layla says after a second.

"Good idea." I back out of my parking place. "Where am I driving to?"

"Marcello's. We'll start there."

Marcello's is a big national wedding dress chain, which usually means they can offer better prices but the dresses are not as unique as the smaller boutiques. However, the biggest reason to go to Marcello's is their legendary customer service. Supposedly, from the moment you walk in, people wait on you hand and foot. You want coffee? You get it. You want a caramel macchiato? You get it.

One of our friends who used to be in the singles' class told us that she'd mentioned offhand something about being hungry for shrimp while she was there with her mother-in-law, and one of the ladies who worked there came out a second later with a full shrimp dinner for her.

I kind of want to go and just see if all the buzz is right.

It's about a thirty-minute drive from Layla's apartment, so Layla starts messing with the radio, tuning it to a country station. "I think I want to walk down the aisle to Keith Urban," she says dreamily.

"Sadly, I'm pretty sure he's already taken. And for that matter, so are you. And anyway, I'm pretty sure he's too short for you."

Layla laughs. "No, you dork. I meant I want to walk down the aisle to one of Keith Urban's *songs*."

"Like what? The song where the girl is like a bird? The song where the girl is like a song?"

She purses her lips. "True. He doesn't really have very good wedding songs, does he?"

"Not so much." Not in my opinion anyway. But I am way more traditional than Layla. I think brides should walk down the aisle to that "Here Comes the Bride" song.

I pull into Marcello's and we both just sit in the car for a few minutes, staring up at the huge, beautiful building in front of us.

"Wow," Layla whispers.

"Yeah." I nod.

Huge, beautiful white dresses hang in the windows on mannequins who are poised to marry other faceless mannequins in black tuxedos.

"I bet they get some Mr. Potato Head parts at their wedding." I elbow Layla.

She looks over at me. "Whose wedding?"

"The mannequins. Because they're faceless. So they'll need Mr. Potato Head's . . ." I sigh. "Never mind."

"You have the weirdest sense of humor sometimes," Layla says, climbing out of the car.

This, coming from Layla Prestwick.

We walk through the doors and a tiny woman looks up from a reception desk. "Welcome to Marcello's." She smiles at both of us. "Who is the bride?"

"I am." Layla raises a hand like she's back in kindergarten.

"Wonderful! Congratulations. Let me see which of our consultants is free. Would you care to have a seat?" She points to a comfy-looking couch underneath a white archway covered in vines and twinkle lights. "Can I get either of you anything to drink?"

Time to test the waters. "Actually, do you guys happen to have caramel macchiatos?"

She nods. "Small, medium, or large?"

This is reason enough to get married right here. I look over at Layla, who shrugs.

"Two larges, I guess."

"I'll have those right out. While you're waiting, miss, please look through our catalog and see if anything catches your eye." She hands Layla a book three inches thick. "If it does, fold the corner down and the consultant will pull the dress for you to try on."

"Okay." Layla starts to look overwhelmed.

"Dresses are in the front; veils and accessories are in the back." She disappears behind a wall of white dresses.

I look at Layla. Her eyes are big. "Paige," she whispers. "There's like three million dresses in here."

"Good thing you aren't getting married until October."

"We may have to move it even further out. Holy cow." She opens the catalog and makes a face. "Nope. Ick. Oh wow. Not my style. Ew . . ." On and on she goes for the first thirty pages.

The woman comes back holding two huge white mugs with *Marcello's—It's your day!* written on them in blue.

A little corny, if you ask me. Which no one has.

"And Liza will be your consultant today. She'll be right out."

"Thank you," Layla says. She looks back at the catalog, cradling her hot mug. "That one isn't bad."

I taste my steaming macchiato. It is amazing. It tastes like they have a Starbucks on site, which for all I know, they easily could have.

A very tall, large-boned woman comes around the wall of wedding dresses a few minutes later. "Hello there," she says, her voice very deep. "My name is Liza. I'll be assisting you today. I see Greta already got you coffee. Can I get you anything else?"

"Not right now," Layla says.

"Wonderful. What are your names?"

"I'm Layla. This is Paige."

"Hi," I say. "Great macchiato."

"Yes, Pedro is our barista. He's very talented."

Pedro. Why can't Layla be marrying the Spanish version of Peter, who can obviously make killer macchiatos?

"Please follow me, ladies."

Liza leads us around the wall of dresses, down a red, dimly lit hallway, and into a good-sized, well-lit room with mirrors on every wall. "This will be your fitting room. Please make yourselves comfortable. Now, Layla, what did you have in mind?"

Layla starts spouting off all kinds of words like *lace*, *white*, and *strapless* while I look around the room. There is a white sofa. A coffee table. A few wedding magazines. And a brochure.

Welcome to Marcello's!

There is a list of all the different types of food trays they have available. I look up at the woman, suddenly starving. As soon as Layla finishes listing every quality she can think of for her dream dress, I break in. "Can we actually get one of these cheese plates? And the chocolate and fruit plate?"

Liza smiles at me. "Of course, of course. And, Layla, I'll be right back with a selection of potential dresses for you as well."

"Thanks!" we both say at the same time.

Liza leaves and we both just look at each other. Layla suddenly jumps off the couch. *"I am getting married!"* she squeals, jumping up and down.

I laugh.

Ten minutes later, Liza is back with two trays of food and a rolling hanging bar with ten different dresses wrapped in thick, plastic garment bags.

"All right. Here are the trays." Liza sets the cheese and chocolate in front of me on the coffee table.

"Thank you."

"And here are the dresses." Liza turns to Layla. "I guessed you are around a size 4 or so?"

Layla nods.

"Here's a camisole and a tiered underskirt that I'd like you to put on. I'll be right back." Liza steps out of the room to give Layla a little bit of privacy. I lean back on the couch, munching on a slice of Gruyère cheese. I love this particular type of cheese. On months where for whatever reason I suddenly end up with more cash than usual, I always buy cheese and chocolate. Even saying the word *Gruyère* makes me feel fancy.

"I can't believe I'm doing this. I can't believe I'm doing this," Layla says over and over while she changes out of her sweater dress and into the camisole that looks more like a corset.

"Me neither. Do you need help?"

She blows her breath out and tries hooking the hooks in the back, staring at herself in the mirror. "Augh. Yes, please."

I finish my cheese, stand, and go around behind her. "Okay. You'll have to suck it in."

"I am sucking it in!"

"Mmm. Try blowing it out then."

She exhales deeply and I cinch the hooks together. It is like an armpit to belly button bra.

Looks ever so comfortable.

I get all the hooks hooked and pat her shoulder blade. "There you go. You can breathe again."

"Ha. That's what you think," she gasps. "I suddenly have a lot more respect for my great-grandmother. Oh my goodness. I can't sit down in something like this!"

"Well, you certainly won't slouch." I smush back into the couch while she wrestles the underskirt on. She levels me with a glare, and I immediately sit straight up. "Sorry."

"Hmph."

"On the plus side, your figure looks very nice right now."

She finishes pulling on the skirt and turns to look at herself in the mirror. "Wow, you're right!" She pats her abdomen. "This just eliminated like six of the last brownies I ate!"

Liza knocks on the door and then sticks her head in. "All set?"

"I think so. Is it supposed to be this tight?" Layla asks.

Liza goes over behind Layla and tugs on the camisole. "Oh yes. If not tighter. This is what's going to keep the dress from sliding around on your wedding day."

"Tighter?" Layla says weakly.

Liza gives Layla a polite smile. "Yes. Okay. We'll start with the first dress."

Liza shoves the yards and yards and yards of white fluffy lace over Layla's head, cinches up the back, and directs her to stand in front of the mirrors.

Layla giggles. And twirls. And preens in the mirror. "Oh my goodness! Peter is going to lose his socks." Layla giggles again.

I smile, but then I think about Peter and the reaction he will most likely have, if it is anything like his normal reaction to things. One time, Layla set a kitchen rag on fire while she was trying to cook oatmeal on her gas range, and Peter and I were over at her apartment. She jumped around the kitchen screaming for someone to call 911, grabbed the edge of the rag while continuing to scream, threw it in the sink with the screaming still going strong, and ran water over it.

By that point, I was up, running to the kitchen, calming Layla down, and helping her scrub the char off the cook top.

And Peter? Peter waited until the smoke alarm turned back off before he said, "Is breakfast almost ready, Layla?"

I stare at my best friend in the most beautiful dress she's ever worn, looking absolutely radiant, and suddenly get very, very sad.

She whirls to me then, a huge smile on her face. "What do you think? Is it the one?"

The dress? Sure. The groom? I am not so sure. The marriage itself?

All I can think is, I am losing my best friend to the Tin Man, and I bite back tears along with the Gruyère.

Chapter
10

Monday and Tuesday are a blur. I wake up, get dressed, go to work, work all day on banquet preparations, go home, work on the lesson for youth group and a few things for taxes coming up at work, go to bed, and do the whole thing over again.

Wednesday morning, I'm sitting at my desk when Mark walks in the door, whistling. "Good morning, Paige. It looks like the Teller family's birth mother delivered last night." He smiles at me. "Big, healthy boy."

I grin. I love the Tellers. They first came to us about eight months ago, and every time, without fail, when Mrs. Teller comes into the agency, she brings everyone in the office Starbucks.

Including me. She is a favorite. Plus, she is young and really cute and her husband is about the most disturbingly affectionate man ever. If they are in the same room, he is either holding her hand, caressing her shoulder, or wrapping his arms around her waist.

So, while I love her, I alternate between really liking and feeling really awkward around him.

"What did they name him?" I ask.

Mark pulls his phone out of his pocket and scrolls to his notebook app. Mark can't remember anything. He even has to program his phone to tell him when it's his daughter's birthday.

I find that just sad.

"Samuel Michael," Mark says. "Nine pounds, nine ounces."

"Oh my gosh," I gasp, thinking of their poor, tiny birth mother.

Mark nods. "But Rachel is doing well too. Candace is at the hospital with them today, so she won't be coming in."

"Okay." This isn't uncommon in a field that involves pregnant women. I pull up Candace's schedule on my computer and start calling the clients she has meetings with today to let them know she'll have to reschedule.

Peggy has a meeting with a potential birth mother at a coffeehouse, so it ends up just being Mark and me for most of the morning. Which is nice, because I actually get some work done. My goal every year is to get taxes filed and done by the beginning of March so I'm not stressing out that whole month.

I try not to think too deeply about the fact that filing taxes for an adoption agency six weeks before deadline has become one of my primary goals in life. It tends to depress me.

I remember back when I was about seventeen or eighteen and had plans to change the world. I was going to be the best family counselor in the state, I was going to change children's and families' lives for the better, and I remember being so totally on fire for Christ that I dragged six of the people who worked with me at Tratoria's Pizza to church. Four of them have become Christians, and the last time I looked on Facebook, three of them are married, one with a baby on the way.

I look at my computer and the receipts stacked in front of me and just sigh. Sometimes, I like being an adult. I like being able to set the thermostat in my apartment at the temperature I want, I like having single possession of my remote control, unless Layla is over, and I like being able to go to Starbucks at nine at night and order a regular macchiato without my mom hinting that maybe I should be drinking decaf by then.

I don't like all the work that comes with being an adult. Or the tiredness. Or just the lack of passion.

I click around on my computer and look out the front window. It's time for a change. I just don't know where to even begin.

* * * * *

I hang up the phone at noon and cross another thing off my list for the banquet. So far, we have three speakers—a local TV personality who has adopted his three kids, a March of Dimes representative, and a girl about my age who was adopted when she was an infant and is now a beauty pageant queen.

We don't mess around with adoption fund-raising. Mark has been doing this banquet since he first opened the agency, and every year it just gets bigger. We had to rent one of the ballrooms at the Marriott for this year's.

I pull out my lunch cooler and open a cheese stick. Cheese and a packaged salad aren't necessarily the most filling lunch, but it is more nutritious than yesterday's lunch of Oreos and fruit snacks. Even though, according to the package, the fruit snacks contain real fruit.

Right.

Layla texts me at twelve thirty, right as I am putting my lunch away and clicking off the blogs about party planning.

JUST HEARD ONE OF THE BANDS WE ARE THINKING ABOUT IS TOTALLY BOOKED UNTIL MAY. ☹ ☹ ☹

I write her back. WE'LL FIND SOMEONE ELSE. DON'T WORRY ABOUT IT.

I've already booked one of the bands for the banquet. They are a swing band, so I figured it would be fun dance music. And Mark actually liked the demo I gave him, which is something of a miracle. Mark is all about the music and the dancing at these banquets.

Much to all of our chagrin.

*　*　*　*　*

Youth group goes well. The girls really learn from the lesson on sin, and honestly, I do too. Rick has an interesting way of looking at things. He doesn't make a lot of sense in person, but for whatever reason, he can write well.

After the class is over, I gather all the extra pencils the girls used, and everyone has already headed back to the youth room for snacks. I grab my jacket, Bible, and leader's guide and follow a group of sophomore guys down the hall.

Nichole approaches me as I walk in. "Hey, so I think I can meet again tomorrow." She had to cancel last

Thursday because her mom had already scheduled a dentist appointment for her.

I nod. "I'll pick you up at five thirty." I'll be skipping my workout again this week, but who am I kidding? I haven't had the time to work out in about a month.

A few of the other girls come over and we end up talking about a new movie that has just come out that a few of them have seen. "Oh, Paige, it is *sooo* cute," Tasha gushes. "It's the best movie I've ever seen!"

I know Tasha well. "You always think that," I tell her, grinning.

"I do not!"

"I present Exhibit A," I say. *"Cheaper by the Dozen 2."*

"Oh yeah! That's a great movie!"

Obviously this girl needs some serious movie therapy. And quite possibly some kind of a brain scan.

"I really need to organize a movie night for you," I say offhandedly.

"Oh, Paige, would you?" one girl says.

"Can I come too?" another one jumps in.

Suddenly all six girls are jumping up and down about the movie night at my place.

"I'm so excited!" Brittany, one of the girls, says. "When are we having it?"

"Um," I say, trying to defuse their enthusiasm. I can barely find time to eat. How in the world am I going to pull off a movie night?

"Friday?" Tasha suggests.

"Friday works for me!" Brittany says.

"I mean, I guess . . . that might wor—" I barely get the word *work* out of my mouth when all of the girls explode, and somehow they multiply.

"Movie night at Paige's on Friday!" Tasha yells.

"Sweet," Tyler says, coming over. "How about *Gladiator*?"

"Ick," Brittany says. "And no boys allowed. This is a girls' movie night."

Tyler backs away to the snack table, hands up surrender-style. "My bad, my bad." He grins at me.

"Okay, guys, listen." I try to corral the madness. And how are there suddenly twelve girls excited about this?

"I'll bring popcorn," Tasha says.

"And my mom will *totally* make cookies," Paris Kleinman says.

That part sounds good. Mrs. Kleinman makes the most amazing sugar cookies I've ever tasted. Paris will probably bring them and they'll be shaped like those clapperboard things that directors use. Or a movie camera. Or, considering the talent Mrs. Kleinman has, a rendering of a poster of whatever movie we decide to watch. She has basically a full-time job making cookies for everyone at the church.

"Well," I say, feeling myself weakening.

What do I really have planned for Friday night anyway?

"We can all get there about six and pitch in for pizza!" Tasha suggests.

"Yeah!" seven of the girls shout.

I leave church with my entire Friday night planned without my help.

* * * * *

Candace walks in Thursday, weaves her fingers together under her chin, and says, "Okay, Paige. You can't hate me forever."

"What?" I smile up at her from my desk. "I've never hated you."

"Right. Hold on to that feeling."

"Why?"

She shakes her head and disappears into her office. Five minutes later, my e-mail notification dings.

So sorry, Paige. I need these by Monday. ☹ ☹

Three home-study audios are attached to the e-mail.

Normally, one home study takes me about six hours to transcribe. Six uninterrupted hours, which never happens. The home studies end up being about thirty single-spaced pages and have to be perfect because they are legal documents.

I bite my bottom lip. Taxes and banquet preparation officially take a backseat, and it looks like I will be working late tonight. Especially because I can't work late tomorrow, since it's my job to pick up the pizza before heading back to my apartment to watch *Tangled*.

And I really, really don't want to come in over the weekend.

Particularly since my weekend is going to include more listening to bands for the anniversary party. Layla found one she was almost sure of last night on the band's website. I've never heard of them. Plus, she says she might want to go back to Marcello's and look at more dresses.

Which means there is potential for more of the amazing cheese and chocolate platters at Marcello's. Not a chance I am willing to give up, even if it means I have to work my tail off all day and night tonight and try on thirty bridesmaid dresses like I know Layla will want me to do.

It was really good cheese and chocolate. The only thing I hope is that the bridesmaids don't have to wear that awful corset.

I pull up a blank document on my computer, slip on my headphones, get my foot pedal ready, and start transcribing. The bummer about transcribing at the office during business hours is that every single time the phone rings, I have to stop and answer it, totally disrupting my flow.

But I manage to crank through one home study by the time I get my late lunch of peanut butter and jelly on stale bread and a Ziploc bag of dried mangos I found hidden in the back of my pantry.

It's a lunch of champions for those who haven't gone grocery shopping in over a week again.

Peggy comes in from her lunch appointment and sets an envelope with my name written on it on the desk in front of me. I am attempting to eat a mango while typing. It is not going well.

"From the Tellers," she says, tapping the envelope. "And you are not as talented as you think you are."

"Thanks. And thanks." I pause Candace's recording right in the middle of her description of the clients' living room. I don't really want to know why the state cares so much about whether or not the couple has plug covers installed already. Usually, it's at least six months if not a year from the time of a home study before a client gets matched with a birth mother. And really, how quickly do babies start sticking things in outlets anyway?

I rip open the envelope. It's a bright yellow card with *Thank You!* written across the front in happy, flowery letters.

If Mrs. Teller were a card, this would be it.

I open it, and a Starbucks card and a picture fall out. I grin.

Paige,
Thank you for your unending sweetness to us during a time of emotional stress! We will never forget your kindness or your smiles when we would come in for what was often a very hard meeting. Thank you! May God bless you!

Love,
Gabe, Cassie, and Samuel Teller

She's drawn a big smiley face below Samuel's name. The picture is of the three of them at the hospital, I assume. Samuel has a little striped hat on his head and Mrs. Teller has obviously been crying. Actually, both Mr. and Mrs. Teller look like they have been crying. I squint at the picture. And so does Samuel. Though I doubt that his crying is from happiness like I am sure his parents' tears are.

I smile and tuck the note in my desk along with a few others I've gotten from clients. It makes my chest get all warm when I see a couple I really love finally get their dream baby.

I pocket the Starbucks card and get back to work. Candace owes me a macchiato for dropping three of these on me at once.

By five o'clock, I am about ten minutes away from finishing the second one. I click over to the third. It's a four-hour tape. I squeeze my eyes shut. I do not want to stay here until nine. Plus, I promised to take Nichole out at five thirty. I've been putting off calling her to cancel because I was hoping I'd finish sooner than I thought.

Plus, what kind of person cancels on a girl who has already gone through so much?

Candace tries to sneak by my desk to leave.

"Hey!" I shout.

"Sorry. I'm so sorry. I thought I'd already given you the first two, I honestly did. And then all of their lawyers called me last night and said they needed them this week, and I realized I'd never given them to you to transcribe. I'm so sorry," Candace says, a hundred miles a minute.

"Venti. Caramel. Macchiato," I say very slowly.

"Yes, ma'am. I'll have it on your desk at nine tomorrow morning."

"Macchiato," I say again as she opens the door.

"Right. Got it," Candace says. But I know exactly what I'll read on my phone at eight forty-five tomorrow morning. WAIT, DO YOU WANT A CARAMEL LATTE OR A CARAMEL FRAPPUCINO?

Candace isn't a Starbucks regular, so she tends to get mixed up once she gets inside and starts listening to other people's orders. One time, she made a Starbucks run for Peggy and me and came back with a tall, decaf, iced skinny mocha with an extra shot for me.

I asked her to bring me a grande caramel macchiato and an apple fritter.

And besides that, I do not understand the concept of ordering an extra shot of decaf. Why? To what end?

I look at the clock. It is now five fifteen. I have finally finished transcribing the second home study, and if I don't get any red lights and maybe speed a tiny bit, I can get to Nichole's house by five thirty.

It just means I'll have to work on the third home study during the day tomorrow and bring home banquet stuff to work on over the weekend.

Joy.

I grab my purse, sling on my jacket, and run for my car. I drive as fast as I dare, since I'm not really in the financial place to afford to pay for a speeding ticket. My dad always flirts with ten miles an hour over the speed limit. No matter where he drives.

But he also makes twice my salary.

I get to Nichole's apartment at five thirty-seven. Not quite the timing I was hoping for. I hurry out of my car, run up the walk, and tap on the door.

"I am so sorry," I say when she opens the door.

She shrugs. "No big deal. Mom's here, so let me tell her I'm leaving." She opens the door a little wider. "Come on in. I'll get my jacket too."

I step into her apartment. She and her mom have just moved here, so there are still boxes stacked against walls and piles of things in different places.

There is a long shelf against the wall by the door that has a bunch of jars on it. I step closer to look at them. They're filled with rocks, dirt, and little tiny bushes that look like they've been planted by gnomes.

"My mom builds terrariums," Nichole says, coming back into the room with her jacket.

"Oh," I say, because really, what else can you say to that? Terrariums and an extra shot of decaf are about on the same level of usefulness in my mind. But then again, so are goldfish, and there are plenty of happy goldfish owners out there.

I assume they are happy anyway. I've never asked them.

"So," I say, climbing back in my car. Nichole buckles her seat belt on the passenger side. "Where would you like to go?"

We end up going back to Starbucks, and I use some of what the Tellers gave me to buy our drinks. Nichole talks for the next hour about her dad and how she and her mom are doing.

"I just don't understand why he left." She gets quiet and sips her vanilla bean Frappucino, tears shining in her eyes.

And my heart just breaks. "I don't either."

"Do you think this is God's plan for my life?" she asks quietly several minutes later.

I dig in my purse and come out with my Bible, which is still in there from Wednesday night youth group. I read a verse in Isaiah a few months ago that I remember all of a sudden. I flip through until I find the purple highlighted section. "The LORD will guide you always; he will satisfy your needs," I read out loud to her.

She takes another sip of her Frappucino. "I don't feel satisfied."

I look at her and force a smile. I don't either.

Chapter
11

I manage to finish the last home study transcription during the day on Friday. And Candace even manages to get my Starbucks order right. "I wrote it down," she says, proudly setting the venti caramel macchiato on my desk. "And I'm sorry again."

I take a sip and nod. "You're forgiven."

I reconsider my words as I stuff tax preparation forms and last-minute banquet calls that need to be made into a file folder and clip it with binder clips so I don't lose anything. Tomorrow is looking like a fun Saturday.

And I don't even know what to think about tonight. Last I heard from Brittany, who texted me at four thirty, eighteen girls are now coming over to my apartment tonight. Eighteen. I have no idea where they're going to park, much less sit. I have a used couch I bought at a garage sale four years ago, an overstuffed chair, and four tiny kitchen chairs. And that's it for furniture.

Another thing, how much pizza do eighteen teenage girls eat? I drive to a local pizza parlor pondering the question.

A slice a person? Two? I can usually eat two, but I'm not growing anymore, and I'm also not as concerned about my figure as I was in high school.

Back in my "I'll just take one slice" days.

I pity past me.

But then again, I'm not in high school where people are constantly judging you by your appearance anymore either. Now, I am in an office with two women who are always on Atkins and always telling me how lucky I am to be naturally thin.

There are outside factors to this not caring as much.

I end up getting three pizzas and drive home with my car smelling strongly of pepperoni and grease. The signs of a good pizza.

I climb the stairs to my apartment and balance the pizzas on one arm while I unlock the door and go inside. I tried to straighten up a little bit before I left this morning just in case I ended up running late getting back home. There wasn't too much to straighten up.

I haven't been home enough to make a mess.

I turn the oven on low, shove the pizzas in to stay warm, and go change before the girls start showing up. As much as I like leggings, boots, and sweater dresses, movie-watching attire while lounging on a couch eating pizza they are not.

My doorbell rings at exactly six o'clock. I've changed into my faded and nearly-ripped-in-the-back-pocket jeans, socks, and my old college sweatshirt. Three girls are standing on my porch. "Hi, Paige!" They all grin excitedly at me as they come inside. I think two are seniors and one is a sophomore.

By six thirty, the sound in my apartment is reaching decibels it has never reached. Girls are everywhere — giggling, eating, drinking Cokes that one of the girls brought, and oohing over the cookies Mrs. Kleinman made.

That are, in fact, decorated just like the paper lanterns in *Tangled*. It just makes me laugh when Paris walks in the door with the cookies. "Your mom is the best." I take the huge box of cookies from her. "And holy cow. How many of us does she think there are going to be?"

Paris shrugs. "She says if I have extras to just leave them with you as a thank-you for having us over."

I am suddenly much more concerned about my figure.

I finally get all the girls to sit down with their pizza around six forty-five. I push the DVD in and turn the volume up. I turn around and try not to shake my head.

There isn't even breathing room, the girls are all packed in so tight. Nine girls have squished together on the couch, two of them are sharing the chair, and all four of the kitchen chairs have been dragged to the living room. The rest of the girls ended up on the floor.

The movie starts and you can immediately tell who's seen it before. Some girls sing along to the songs, others whisper the lines with the characters, which honestly is one of my biggest pet peeves. Particularly if I am watching a movie I've never seen before.

But the other girls don't seem to mind.

I set the cookies in front of everyone about halfway through the movie. "Everyone has to take at least two cookies," I say over the movie.

"No problem." Brittany grabs three. "These are Mrs. Kleinman's cookies, huh? They are *amazing*."

Paris's shoulders straighten proudly, and I smile to myself. It's a good thing to be proud of your mom.

I miss my mom. Most of the time I stay so busy I don't notice, but every so often, a girl just needs her mom.

Particularly if you've got a great mom like mine.

The movie ends forty-five minutes later and none of the girls moves. "That is *sooo* good!" Tasha squeals from the couch. "That is the best movie ever!"

I laugh. "Today, anyway."

She grins at me.

And then the chattering starts again. And it doesn't cease until the very last girl leaves at eleven thirty. And then there is silence.

Just me, half a pizza, and forty-two cookies left.

My floor is covered in cookie crumbs, my kitchen counter has pizza sauce and paper plates all over it, and someone spilled a Coke on the tile in the entryway and only used a dry paper towel to soak it up, so now the whole area is sticky.

I look at everything that needs to be done, at the bursting file folder of work stuff, and then at my bed.

And the bed wins out. Right after a shower to get rid of the greasy feeling I have all over my face.

I climb beneath the covers and look at my Bible sitting on the bedside table behind me. I am so tired that my eyes are burning.

"Tomorrow," I promise myself as I turn out the light. Maybe I'll even get in a nice hike with my Bible like I used to do.

Then I close my tired eyes and am out before I have another thought.

* * * * *

I wake up blissfully at eight forty-five on Saturday.

The latest I've slept in weeks.

I roll over and look at the clock before rolling to my back and staring at the ceiling.

My to-do list for the day reels through my brain.

Shower, get dressed.

Breakfast.

Banquet calls.

Tax prep.

Clean bathroom and kitchen.

Band previewing with Layla at one.

Call Mom.

Clean up Coke spill in entryway.

It isn't my favorite way to wake up. Particularly on a Saturday. I like to wake up slowly, make coffee, and then spend a quiet breakfast reading.

I get out of the shower a few minutes later, pull on a pair of jeans and a gray sweater, and blow-dry my hair. I come out to the kitchen to make coffee just as my phone rings.

It's my mom. "Hi, honey."

"Hi, Mom." I grin. One, because I'm excited to talk to my mom, and two, because I can cross two things off the list now.

"Just calling because we're getting ready to go to the store and I wanted to see what you want when you get here soon," she says.

I frown and walk over to my planner, checking the date. "I'm not coming for about six weeks, Mom."

"I know. But I want to have everything ready."

I grin. Mom misses me too.

"I'm good with whatever, Mom."

"I'm thinking we can go to Carroways for dinner one night."

"Perfect." My favorite local restaurant. They have the best onion rings in the whole state of Texas.

"And I'll make a brisket, of course. And Dad's going to make his rolls."

My dad doesn't cook. He once ruined an entire batch of pancake batter because he misread tablespoon instead of teaspoon of salt. But for whatever reason, Dad can make the lightest, fluffiest, buttery-est, yeastiest rolls ever. It's a miracle of nature. Mom always tells me she thinks God gave Dad that gift because, otherwise, she wouldn't have taken a second look at him way back in their dating days.

"Daddy is a nerd, honey," she'd say then.

And then Dad would sigh, remind her that his nerdiness was why they were now able to afford a nice house, and then he'd go make another batch of the rolls, just so Mom didn't get any ideas about leaving him for someone who didn't still wear knee socks.

Yep. That's my dad.

I suddenly have a strong craving for brisket and rolls, and the oatmeal I am making never looked worse. "That sounds so good right now."

"And I'll make you sweet potatoes."

My mother is about the most southern cook I've ever met. I've heard this rumor that sweet potatoes can actually be healthy for you, but considering I've never seen them any way but fried or covered in butter, brown sugar, and marshmallows, I have a hard time believing it.

The oatmeal really doesn't look good now.

"When do you think you'll get here?" Mom asks.

"I have to work that Thursday, so I'll probably just leave as soon as I get off work." If I have my duffel bag in the car when I go to work that morning, I can leave straight from the office. "So, maybe around eight?"

"So, not in time for dinner but maybe in time for dessert?"

"That's in time for dinner, Mom. We can just have a late night."

She laughs. "Sweetie, Daddy's doctor told him he has to start eating lighter meals earlier at night, so we've been eating grilled chicken on salads at five o'clock for the past month."

I have a hard time imagining my father going along with that diet plan. "And he's really doing it?"

"He sure is," Mom says proudly. "We eat every night at five, and then we each get a small snack around seven. I've been making us that fat-free popcorn and adding a little of that no-salt seasoning to it."

Really can't picture Dad willingly eating like that. My father is the king of beef and carbs. His favorite meal is steak with a huge loaded baked potato and about six of his rolls.

"Wow," I say.

"We're getting healthy. I've even got him up walking with me every morning at six before he goes to work."

I try picturing that one and suddenly realize that my parents are getting older. Eating at five, walking at six in the morning. Old people do that. If my mother tells me she's started wearing khakis as lounge pants, I'll have to look into retirement communities for them.

"Wow," I say again, trying to calculate how old my parents are. I don't remember them being this old before.

"Yes. But don't worry, sweetie. I'll make all of your favorite meals while you're here. It's good to allow yourself to splurge every once in a while."

"Uh-huh." I look at my congealing oatmeal. Maybe her comment is God's sign to me that I should go get an apple fritter from Starbucks and just not worry about my eating-out budget today.

I wince, thinking of my eating-out budget. Sometimes I miss being a little kid who doesn't get the concept that money isn't endless. At some point, you can run out. It is a jarring lesson to realize. I learned it three weeks after I moved into this apartment and suddenly noticed I had exactly $212 in the bank.

And nothing else.

There were lots of prayers said before that first paycheck finally arrived.

"So what do you have planned for today?" Mom asks.

I push the oatmeal aside and grab a paper towel and some of my floor cleaner spray. "I've got to do some cleaning and some work on the agency taxes before I meet Layla to preview bands for her parents' party."

"You've been very busy lately."

I scrub the Coke spill, throw the paper towel away, and see my half-finished wreath as I put the floor cleaner away. "Yeah," I say sadly. "Very busy."

"Sometimes life is like that. But sometimes it's our own fault. Can you cut anything out? I remember how you always needed your downtime."

I think about it. I can't cut out Layla's parents'

anniversary. Or work-related busyness. And I would probably be the worst Christian on the planet to cut out the youth group or Sunday school stuff. And after all that, there isn't too much left. I've already skipped working out for the last two weeks. And I barely have time for laundry and grocery shopping.

"Not really," I say.

"Well. Just think about it. And I'll let you go, honey. Dad looks like he's ready to go to the store."

"He goes with you now?" I am legitimately shocked. I think I can remember two times in the entirety of my childhood when Dad went to the grocery store with Mom. And I am pretty sure both of those times were when we were completely out of something and it was Mom's birthday and Dad felt bad that she had to go by herself on her birthday.

"Sure," Mom says all nonchalant like it's no big deal. "He goes with me every week now."

That's the final straw. My parents are officially old.

"Wow," I say again because really, what else can I say?

"Have a good morning, sweetie. Love you."

"Love you too, Mom." I hang up my cell phone and pocket it. Coke spill is done, breakfast is done. I only had one bite of oatmeal, but it will have to hold me over until lunch because there is no way I am eating more of it.

Oatmeal is cheap for a reason.

I grab the cleaning supplies and spend the next thirty minutes scrubbing my toilet, shower, sink, and kitchen. Then I vacuum all of the cookie crumbs out of my carpet. Then I look at the plate of cookies sitting on the kitchen counter.

A cookie has milk and eggs in it, right? Those are basically breakfast ingredients.

I eat a cookie and then glance at the clock. It is ten, and maybe if I hurry I can get a good head start on the work stuff before it's time to meet Layla.

My phone buzzes in my pocket and I pull it out. Tyler.

"Hello?" I answer because I always feel a little weird saying, "Hi, Person's Name!" when I don't know them very well.

"Hey, Paige. It's Tyler," he says, warmly.

"Hi, Tyler. How are you?"

"I'm good. Listen, I know you're crazy busy all the time, but I was wondering if maybe you'd be interested in meeting me for lunch."

"Lunch," I repeat, looking at the clock, at the list of people I need to call, and then at the huge tax folder on my kitchen table.

"Right. It's this meal you have midway between breakfast and dinner, though to be honest, I usually end up eating breakfast and lunch all close together and then I'm starving for dinner."

"Today? Like now?"

"Well, like two hours or so. I've figured out that shock and surprise is the best way to get you to say yes to hanging out with me."

I laugh. I like Tyler, I do. He is very laid-back. Sometimes that can be a good quality to have in a friend.

"I don't know. I have a ton of stuff to do for work."

"Like what?"

"Taxes," I say.

"Eh. Those aren't due until April, right?"

He has a point. "Yes." I draw out the word. "But they will take me a while. And the earlier I file them, the earlier I can stop worrying about them, especially since I've got Layla's party in about three weeks. And I have like fifteen people I have to call for this banquet the agency is putting on the weekend after the party."

"You take a lot of responsibility for things that aren't your problem," Tyler states. And before I have time to think about that and get mad, he says, "Now. Lunch. Let's say I'll pick you up at eleven thirty, and we'll go get hamburgers at Greg's."

My mouth waters at the thought. Greg's has the best hamburgers in the city. Thick, juicy, piled high with all the extras.

"Well, I'm also meeting Layla at one to listen to some bands for her parents' anniversary party."

"Surely it doesn't take you an hour and a half to eat one of Greg's hamburgers," Tyler says. "I mean, it only takes me about three minutes. And that's if I'm remembering to actually chew."

I half laugh, but I keep staring at the tax file. "Tyler—" I prepare to tell him I don't think it will work for today.

"Done," he says. "I'll see you at eleven thirty. That gives you about an hour and a half to work on those taxes. And I'll drop you off at Layla's anniversary band thing." He hangs up. Probably so I don't have the chance to tell him all the reasons why that is not a good idea.

Reason number one—Layla will flip out if she sees Tyler drop me off at the lounge where one of the bands is playing. She'll probably tell Liza, or whoever our consultant is next time we look at dresses, that I need to see a selection of dresses as well.

Reason number two—I had a cookie for breakfast.

Following that up with a hamburger for lunch does not sound like the healthiest day to me, particularly after listening to my parents' new lifestyle changes.

Reason number three—Tyler is very sweet and charming, but at the end of the day, I have a job, and even though he thinks I take too much responsibility for things in my life, if I don't, who will?

True to his word, Tyler knocks on my door at exactly eleven thirty.

I look up from my laptop. I have been able to call all of the people on my list and input most of our numbers into the online tax-filing system. But not all of them.

"This is bad timing," I tell him, opening the door.

"It's nice to see you too!" Tyler says brightly, coming into my apartment. "You look great as well."

I gaze at him and sigh with a smile. "Thank you. It's good to see you, and you look nice." He does look nice. Dark-rinsed, straight-cut jeans and a white polo shirt. I am very jealous of the tan he already has.

It is still winter, for goodness' sake.

His hair is shiny and curly, like he swiped at it with a towel when he got out of the shower and then forgot about it. I like it like that. It fits his carefree attitude.

"I'm like halfway through inputting the numbers," I tell him, going over to my laptop and tapping on the unfinished stack of receipts, paychecks, and bills. "And I haven't even started trying to calculate all the rest."

"Don't y'all have an accountant?"

"You're looking at her."

"I thought your degree was in counseling."

I nod. "It is."

"So you take a job at an adoption agency to do accounting stuff instead?"

I bite my lip. "No." I'd taken the job because Mark had said they really needed a secretary, and if I could fill in there, then as soon as they hired another secretary, I could become a counselor and work with the birth mothers there.

That was a year ago.

I sigh. "It's complicated."

"Hmm." He doesn't look like he believes me. "Let's go. I'm hungry and we've only got a little bit before you have to meet Layla."

"And that's another thing."

"Layla?"

"If you drop me off at the lounge, Layla will freak out."

"Don't worry," Tyler says. "I enforce the use of seat belts in my car. She has nothing to worry about."

"You obviously don't know Layla. She is about the worst, most unsafe driver in this city. She doesn't care about seat belts."

He shrugs. "Well, then I don't see the problem. You'll be fed, on time, and arrive there alive." He shrugs again.

"It's not the safety thing or the punctual thing." I try to figure out the best way to tell him my concerns without being weird about it. On the one hand, I don't want him to drop me off at the lounge because Layla will throw a fiesta. On the other hand, I can't tell him the reason why, because it will sound like either I like him or I think he should like me.

This all sounds very immature. I thought I'd left all this behind in Austin when I moved here for college.

"What is it then?" Tyler asks.

I sigh. "Never mind."

"Okay. Let's go."

I am out of excuses. I look at him for a long minute and finally go to get my purse. "Fine."

"Thanks for suffering through my presence." He grins, opening my front door.

"No, I mean, it's not that at all, Tyler," I say quickly, face flushing.

"Sure," he says, but he's still grinning. "I'm hurt, Paige. Deeply hurt."

"You look deeply hurt." I lock my door behind us and follow him down the stairs.

"I hide my emotions well. It's what my third-grade teacher wrote on my report card."

Somehow I have trouble believing that of Tyler Jennings.

We get to Greg's, and Tyler has to park in the parking lot for the shoe store next door. "Busy," he says offhandedly.

I've never been here when it isn't busy.

The line, thankfully though, isn't too long. Tyler doesn't even look at the menu suspended above the counter. "Know what you want?" he asks me.

"Sure. And I can get mine." I reach in my purse for my wallet.

Tyler waves a hand. "Right. I ask you to lunch and you pay. That's real gentlemanly. I'd have to call my mother afterward and apologize for not following the upbringing she labored to give me."

I laugh.

A cashier waves us over, and Tyler lets me go in front of him. "I want just the regular cheeseburger," I tell the cashier.

"Anything to drink?"

"Water, please."

"Sheesh, Paige, just get a drink."

I level a look at Tyler. "Fine. A Coke."

"And for you, sir?"

"The double cheeseburger with fries and a Coke, please."
He hands the cashier his credit card.

The cashier gives us two cups and a receipt. I fill my cup
with Coke and follow Tyler over to a little booth by the
windows. The restaurant is packed and very loud. We sit
down and Tyler grins at me. "Now, is this so painful?"

"I don't mean that your company is painful, Tyler."

"I should hope not. I try to be polite. I heard once that
politeness is the tenth fruit of the Spirit."

I grin.

One of the servers brings our burgers over, and Tyler
folds his hands in front of him on the table. "Let me pray real
quick. Jesus, thank You for this time with Paige, help her to
have fun listening intently with Layla, and bless this food.
Amen."

"Amen," I echo.

"So, Paige," he says, after swallowing his first bite. I am
still chewing mine.

"Mmm?" I say, trying not to spew a mouthful of delicious
cheeseburger all over the table.

"This insane schedule you keep up. How do you do it?"

I swallow, frowning. "What do you mean?"

"I mean, how do you do it? Do you live on espresso? How
do you even remember everything you're supposed to do?"

I reach into my purse and pull out my planner. The
denim cover is starting to tear. Which is fine by me, because
I'd seen one in Target a while back I thought was adorable.

"I make sure I write everything down," I tell him.

He reaches across the table and takes my planner from me. Which isn't necessarily something I want him to do. I write *everything* down. Birthdays, dentist appointments, deadlines, when I need to get the oil changed in my car, and when I last started my period.

Reading that planner is like reading the diary I don't have time to keep.

"One o'clock, Layla at Paparazzi Lounge," Tyler reads out loud. "Six o'clock, bring dinner to the Hannigers."

"Crap." I close my eyes.

"That doesn't sound too tasty."

"No, I forgot." I sigh. I haven't looked all the way down on the square for today, apparently. "It's the family of one of the girls in my small group. Her mom just had major surgery and she's a single parent, and Rick passed around a sign-up sheet to take them dinner." I try to figure out what groceries I have. Enough to make a casserole?

There is no way. Not unless the Hannigers want a mustard, Swiss, and oatmeal casserole.

"You're taking them dinner on Thursday too?"

"There were a lot of open slots on the sign-up sheet. I don't want them to not have any food. Didn't you see it at youth group?"

Tyler nods. "I'm taking them a pizza next week. Look, Paige." He closes my planner and sets it on the table. He stops, pursing his lips and looking at me.

"What?"

He lets his breath out and shakes his head. "Nothing."

"No, really, what?"

He shakes his head again. "Eat your cheeseburger. It can wait for a later date."

I am in the middle of a bite when he says the word *date*. I try not to make a big deal about it, but I look up at him anyway. He is calmly eating a fry, watching a short little toddler help his daddy refill his Coke from the machine.

Does he think this is a date? Or did he mean "date" as on a calendar?

I chew quietly. Do *I* think this is a date? I think through what has happened today. He suggested coming, he drove me here, he paid.

All three things that, by themselves, wouldn't necessarily mean date, but when added up collectively . . .

Oh boy.

I am on a date. And I didn't even know it until just a minute ago.

"So, I am reading through the new youth Bible study that Rick wants us to go through and I—"

"Tyler," I interrupt as soon as I finish swallowing.

He looks at me. "What's up, Paige?"

"We're on a date."

He grins. "I like you."

"This is not good."

"You have no problem saying what you think."

"I don't have time for a relationship."

"I especially like your honesty."

"I mean, I barely have time to maintain proper dental hygiene."

He starts laughing then. "Paige, chill." He holds his hands up and leans back in his seat. "Just take a deep breath for a second."

I clamp my mouth shut and inhale through my nose like they tell me to do in those Pilates videos I watch every so often. I like Tyler, I really do. He is fun, he is very cute, and he is a huge hit with Rick and the freshman guys, so I figure he has to be a decent guy. But the thought of adding something else—particularly something that takes so much time—to my calendar makes my eyeballs shake.

"Paige," Tyler says, leaning forward and reaching for my hands. He grins at me, his blue eyes crinkling, hands warm. "Look. I'd be lying if I said I don't think you are beautiful or that I'm not interested in dating you. But I knew from the first three minutes after I'd met you that dating you probably wasn't going to happen unless I suddenly became pregnant and had to go meet with you for weekly counseling sessions."

I try to force myself to not blush. Even if there is no chance of dating Tyler, it's always nice to hear someone of the opposite sex tell you that you're beautiful. Particularly while he's holding your hands.

He rubs his thumbs over the backs of my hands, then lets them go. He leans back again. "And let's face it, the odds of my becoming pregnant are pretty slim. I mean, there's my whole belief in abstinence to consider."

I shake my head. "You're so weird."

"And yet, I still managed to get you to have lunch with me." He licks his finger and draws a line in the air. "That is one for me. Two, actually, because I believe I had dinner with you nearly two weeks ago as well."

I open my mouth and then close it again. We did have dinner almost two weeks ago.

"Paige, I know that you're crazy busy. And honestly, I think you need to learn how to say no to a few of those things. But how about in the meantime we just get to know each other as friends?"

I smile at him. "Sounds like a plan."

"Good. Friends it is then."

We finish our burgers and talk about the new Bible study Rick wrote for the youth group. And then Tyler parks in front of Paparazzi Lounge at 12:50.

"Early," he announces as he shifts into Park. "Am I good? Are you impressed?"

"Yes and yes," I say. "Thank you. And thanks for lunch."

"My pleasure."

I grab my purse and start to open the door.

"In a rush?" he says.

"Well, I mean, we're here."

"Is Layla's car here yet?"

I look around. I don't see it, which honestly makes me feel better. Though I am going to have to tell her that Tyler dropped me off, since she will have to give me a ride home, and I don't think she'll just accept no reason for why I haven't driven here myself.

"No," I tell him.

"See? That was easy to say, huh?"

"What?"

"*No.* It's not a hard word to say."

"Does this have to do with my schedule?" I ask him.

He grins. "Pretty and smart. I really do like you, Paige."

"There's something you need to know about Layla," I close his car door and shift to face him. "She's crazy."

"I guessed this."

"No, I mean, really. She's nuts. And now that she's getting married, she's become even more nuts."

"You still seem to like her," Tyler says.

"Most of the time I do. But if she sees that you gave me a

ride here and then figures out that we had lunch before this, she'll call your mother to see how many people you'll be inviting to our wedding so we can go ahead and book a reception space." I let my breath out after my long run-on sentence. I am becoming like Layla. It is not necessarily a good thing. "I just didn't want to say anything before because it sounds really weird."

Tyler listens to me, nodding. "Got it. We don't know each other. I've never seen you before. What is your name?"

"You don't have to go to that extreme. I'm just saying. Layla has a knack for being overly dramat—"

Right then, I see Layla's Jetta pull into the space right beside us. Layla glances over at us, sunglasses on her face, looks away, and then whips her head back. Her lips form the words. *Oh. My. Gosh.*

She rips her sunglasses off her face and jumps out of her car, obviously giddy. I sigh and look at Tyler. "Sorry. I'm so sorry."

"Hi, Paige! Hi, Tyler!" She is so loud I can hear her perfectly inside Tyler's car with all the doors and windows closed.

I open the door. "Hello, Layla."

"So, are you guys going out now? Oh, I'm *so* excited!"

Tyler grins at me and then looks at Layla. "Y'all have fun listening to the bands."

Layla starts squealing about how excited she is and heads to the door, chattering happily about how long she's waited for this day, the day that I would show up to hear a band play in my boyfriend's car.

I sigh and start to climb out of the car. Tyler reaches over and grabs my hand. "Oh, and Paige?" he says, grinning at me.

I look at him.

"I really prefer a black suit for a wedding. A tux is just so stiff, you know?"

I level him with a smoldering look, he starts laughing, and I climb out of the car. "This is all your fault, Jennings." I close the door.

He waves three fingers at me while holding the steering wheel and backs out of the parking lot. Layla is holding open the door to Paparazzi's, still talking. "And oh, Paige, wouldn't it be so wonderful if we can find little houses in the same neighborhood? We can be all, 'I'm out of sugar!' and the other one can run over with the cup of sugar." She sighs happily.

I stare at Layla — at the expression of pure joy on her face, at the tightly dressed hostess inside the door — and just sigh.

"It would be nice to have someone to borrow sugar from," I say. Maybe my oatmeal would taste a little better then.

Chapter 12

Sunday morning I pull on a gray jersey skirt, red ballet flats, and a bright red sweater. It is my official "well, I guess what we call winter is over" outfit, and it comes out every February.

It is now February.

Basically, I can look forward to seventy-degree weather and more party planning. Layla cannot make up her mind on a band to save her life. And the agency banquet just had its first vendor cancellation in six years of banquets.

"I'm so sorry," Tina said on the phone last night from Flowers R Us. "We didn't realize we'd double booked for your party and a wedding. And honestly, we're just not staffed to handle it. I'm refunding your money. I apologize."

Which leaves me with a few weeks to find another florist to make eighty-four table centerpieces that look both fun and classy.

I grab my Bible and my purse, lock the door behind me, and hurry down the stairs. I traded my time to make coffee for sleeping in, so I have to get coffee at the church.

Which is always a coin toss on whether or not it will be good. One lady who serves at church in the mornings can make the perfect pot of coffee and leave you feeling like all is right with the world. And the other lady can make you swear off coffee for the rest of your earthly life.

I drive to church, end up actually finding a parking spot in the very last row of the parking lot by the youth room, and hurry inside. Rick asked me to start coming to the youth Sunday school on the days I'm not teaching the two-year-olds, so here I am.

"Paige!" two girls say excitedly when I walk into the youth room. The place is dead save for four girls and one guy, who looks like he hasn't slept in thirty-six hours.

"Hey, guys," I say, walking over. I set my Bible and purse on a chair and turn back to the group of kids. "How are you guys?"

One of the girls is Allison Hanniger, the girl in my small group whose mom just had surgery. I ended up stopping and getting them one of the to-go boxes you can order from a local barbecue place. It had shredded beef, creamed corn, rolls, potato salad, and brownies in it.

I figured I couldn't go wrong with that.

And went ahead and blew my eating-out budget until July.

"Paige, thank you so much for dinner last night," Allison says, smiling at me. Allison is a very cute girl. If she already looks like that as a fourteen-year-old, her mom will have some issues with boys flocking to her house when she gets a little older.

"Sure."

"It was wonderful. And Mom is already feeling a lot better. Creamed corn is her favorite thing to eat."

"Wow, that's great!" I say. Mrs. Hanniger is one of those church moms who I want to be more like. She is constantly doing something for someone. When I got to their house last night, it about killed her to sit there and watch me leave dinner on the table instead of making me sit down and eat with them.

"You're *sure* you can't stay?" she asked me for the eighth time. "There is more here than we'll eat in a week."

"Then enjoy the leftovers," I said, giving Allison a hug and waving to her little brother, Michael.

I never knew Allison's dad. He was killed in a car accident when Allison was five. She barely remembers her father. Mrs. Hanniger always told me that if it hadn't been for Grace Church, she wouldn't have made it through that time. "So of course, I'm going to give back now," she always says while doing something around the church.

I go back down the church hall for my coffee. It is still a little early, so there isn't the mad rush for the caffeine like when I usually show up to the coffee table.

I carefully peek into the kitchen to see who is running the coffeepot today.

"Well, good morning, Paige!"

It is Melba Waters. I force a smile. Caffeine and I will not be friends this morning, apparently. I look longingly at the shiny, stainless-steel pot. We won't even be neighbors. Melba Waters destroys coffee.

"Hi, Mrs. Waters."

"Go ahead and get some, sweetie. It's all ready now." She pats my hand.

"Oh, that's okay. I think I'll just get some tea today." I pray that the Lipton tea bag I am holding, which has probably been there since 1995, will still contain enough caffeine to ward off my incoming headache.

Melba shrugs. "Suit yourself, dear."

I walk sadly back down to the youth room with my tea. *Tea.* In my opinion, the only reason to drink tea is if you're sitting opposite Mr. Darcy looking at Pemberley's beautiful lake. I look around. No lake, no Mr. Darcy. Only the beige-painted hallway and sixteen-year-old Justin, who is about to go into the youth room.

"Hey, Paige," he says, his voice cracking slightly when he says my name. He clears his throat. "Hey," he says again, an octave deeper.

I love Justin.

"How's it going, Justin?"

"Fine. How are you?"

"I'm drinking tea."

He steps three steps back from me. "Look, I can't get sick. School just started back up, and if you saw the Mount Everest that is my homework, you'd offer to get me a sherpa."

"Chill. I'm not sick. And I won't get you a sherpa. They're going extinct. Too many fleece jackets are being made right now." I dunk the tea bag up and down in the water. Maybe if I get it really, really strong, it will taste like coffee.

I take a sip and try not to gag.

"Are you okay, Paige?"

"Justin. There is a reason the early American settlers threw all that tea in the ocean." I make a face.

"Taxes?"

"Taste."

"My mom makes me drink green tea the second I tell her I'm not feeling good," Justin says. "One day I fell in gym and busted up my knee and Mom made me drink green tea until the swelling went down." He sighs and looks a little sick even remembering. "Two weeks I drank that stuff."

"I'm sorry."

"What's wrong?" Rick asks, poking his head out of the youth room.

"Justin had to drink green tea for two weeks, and I'm going to need Starbucks," I say, still gagging.

"Okay. Well, in the meantime, come on in here. I have to teach you how to run the words."

"What words?" I ask. "Please don't tell me you use a teleprompter." I walk into the youth room and follow Rick over to a computer.

"It's for the music, weirdo. So it's pretty user friendly."

"Is it a computer?" I put my hands behind my back like my dad used to tell me to do anytime we were in an electronics store.

Rick looks at me. "Com-pu-ter," he says slowly, touching the top of the screen. "It's a wonderful invention, really. Has changed the way we live and move and breathe."

"Rick."

"Look, it's basically just a slide show. Everything is all set up and in there. All you do is click the arrow to switch to the next slide. See?" He pushes a button and the first verse of "Come Thou Fount of Every Blessing" pops up on the computer screen and on the wall at the front of the room.

"Wow," I say. "I didn't even know y'all did music on Sundays."

"You really don't pay attention during leaders' meetings, do you?" Rick asks.

"You've talked about it?"

"I spent most of the last one complaining about how hard it is to find bass players in this youth group." Rick sighs.

"You have a bass player?" I wave my hand at the front of the room. "There's a whole band?"

"What did you think the drums were for?"

I shrug. The whole youth room looks like someone's garage. There is exposed ductwork in the ceiling, the whole place is painted gray, and there are cement floors. Not to mention the odor that always seems to hang around in here, though I think that's due to too many thirteen-year-old boys, who haven't quite gotten the hang of daily deodorant, mixing with eighteen-year-old guys, who haven't quite gotten the idea behind a *hint* of cologne as opposed to bathing in it.

"Anyway." Rick points to the computer. "Good?"

"I thought I was just supposed to sit in here and be an adult presence for the girls."

Rick grins. "Well, life changes sometimes. Which is a good segue into my lesson." He claps his hands and whistles loudly. "Round it up, guys!"

Fifty-some-odd kids fall into their seats. Six of them walk up to the front and pick up guitars I hadn't noticed there and one sits down behind the drums. Bethany sits behind the keyboard. Rick stands beside me and operates the soundboard.

"Wow," I whisper.

"I know. I feel powerful here," he whispers back.

"Hi there," Ben, one of the senior guys, says into the microphone. "Good morning."

Everyone mumbles something that may have been "good morning" back to him while Rick pushes six or seven little knobs and buttons around. He looks very professional.

"Everyone stand up, please." Ben starts strumming and I immediately panic. Whatever he is strumming is definitely not "Come Thou Fount." Then the drums start and I get even more panicked.

"This isn't the right song!" I hiss to Rick.

He frowns at me. "Put the words up, Paige."

I click the button right as Ben starts singing. "Come thou fount of every blessing," he sings and the rest of the kids sing with him.

Wow. This song has taken a makeover in here. I didn't even know you were allowed to play drums to hymns.

Ben leads the kids in four songs, and I am so focused on making sure I'm clicking the button at the right time that I don't even notice the extra thirty or so kids who trickle into the room during the music. Our youth group is exploding.

Rick thanks the band, grabs his Bible, and walks up there as the band goes to their seats. "All right, guys, turn to James."

I walk back to my chair and listen for the next thirty minutes as Rick teaches on serving. "You guys are single. You guys have very few real responsibilities. You guys have the ability to be totally focused on Christ. So how are you spending that singleness? Doing things for yourself? Or serving Jesus with the time you have right now?"

I write a note in the margin of my Bible. *Am I serving Jesus with the time I have now?*

I am single too. I have very few responsibilities. Other than showing up for my job every weekday morning and paying my rent on the fifteenth of every month, I don't have much else to be responsible for.

So why am I so busy?

Tyler's voice from yesterday's lunch comes back into my brain. *"I think you need to learn how to say no."*

I know how to say no.

"Paige, will you pray for us?" Rick asks me suddenly.

I jump and then nod. "Sure."

"By the way, everyone, if you haven't met Paige, she leads the freshmen girls on Wednesday nights and is one of the best people I know, so get to know her," Rick says.

"Let's pray," I say, feeling a blush creep up my cheeks. "Jesus, thank You for this time, thank You for this day, help us use it to serve and honor You. Amen."

"Amen," Rick echoes. "Don't forget to stack your chairs on your way out!"

Chaos erupts and for the next ten minutes all I hear are loud voices and metal clanging against metal. A few girls come over and chatter about how much fun they had at the movie night last week.

"We should totally do that every week!" Brittany says.

"Dude, you shouldn't just invite yourself over." Tasha elbows Brittany in the ribs.

Now even the girls are saying *dude*? This greatly concerns me. I don't know what it is about that word, but it just grates somewhere back in my left temporal lobe.

"I don't know about every week," I say slowly when all the girls get quiet and look at me, and I suddenly realize they are waiting for my thoughts on it.

"Every other week then," Brittany says. "And we can all just keep pitching in for pizza, and I bet if Paris's mom can't make cookies, our moms would make some snacks for us to bring."

And with that, my apartment gets booked every other Friday night until graduation in May. I think about the question Rick asked during the lesson and bite my lip. Maybe this is the way God wants me to serve Him with my time.

"Your apartment is so cool," Tasha says to me. "I can't wait until I get to move out and get my own apartment."

I remember when I used to think that. Back before I realized that having an apartment means having to pay for rent and utilities.

I wave good-bye to the girls and walk back down the hallway for church, squeezing through the crowded hallways filled with chattering, happy people. I find the same row I sat in last week all by myself and sit down, smiling. Alone. I might be weird, but I love worshipping God when it is just me and my thoughts.

"Paige!"

I look up as Layla comes into the row. "What are you doing here?" I ask as she pulls me up to give me a hug.

"Dude, we totally just skipped the singles' class!" she squeals.

"Not you too," I moan. Seriously, there are so many other wonderful choices to express the word *friend*.

"Yep! Rebels, we are. Is this where you're sitting? We'll sit by you. Oh, this is nice! I haven't been to big church in, goodness, I don't even know how long."

"Too long if you're still calling it big church." I wave at Peter. "Hi, Peter."

"Hey."

"Well." Layla dumps all her stuff in front of the seat next to me. "We're here now."

Yes, they are. Peter squeezes past me and sits on the other

side of Layla. I try not to sigh as the worship band takes the stage. So much for being all by myself.

"Why don't we all stand?" Victor, the music pastor, says into the microphone. Everyone in the room stands and he starts strumming his guitar.

"Hey, guys."

Tyler is suddenly standing right beside me. He looks down the row at the extra empty seats. "Can I sit with you?" he whispers as everyone starts singing.

"Before the throne," the congregation sings.

"Oh!" Layla squeals, turning to see Tyler standing there. "Peter! Move down so Tyler can sit by Paige." She half nudges, half pushes Peter down a seat and then grabs my arm and yanks me over so Tyler can get the aisle seat I previously had.

"Thanks." He grins at me.

"Sure."

Now I am not only not alone, I am surrounded. Layla's sweet soprano is on my right. Tyler's surprisingly good voice is on my left.

I can't sing loudly now. And I also don't feel comfortable closing my eyes and raising my hands like last week.

We sing three songs, and then Pastor Louis climbs onto the stage. "Thank you, guys, that is great music. Let's pray, shall we?"

He prays and preaches for the next thirty minutes. Tyler takes notes from the sermon on his bulletin, and Layla keeps giving me sidelong grins through the whole thing.

It is very hard to pay attention.

The service ends, and I pick up my Bible and jacket. Now I am slightly depressed, and I have a headache from the lack of caffeine this morning.

"So," Layla says, drawing the word out. "What are you two up to for lunch?"

I cannot eat out. Especially when I really won't have the spare funds to eat out until the summer. And I still have to be saving for a bridesmaid dress, the inevitable shower I'll throw for Layla, and a wedding gift. I am already planning on a quiet afternoon at home, finally finishing that wreath and probably eating peanut butter and crackers.

"Well," I start, about to tell them my grand plan of hot gluing muslin fabric rosettes to a grapevine wreath.

"Because I am thinking we should all go to that little sandwich shop down the street. Last time I was there, I had the best peach iced tea I've ever had in my life."

Too much tea in this day.

"I had tea today already," I say. "And I really shouldn't eat out."

Layla shrugs. "It's on me. And why did you have tea?"

"Mrs. Daugherty wasn't doing the coffee this morning," I say sadly.

"Oh." Layla nods. "I'm sorry. You should have texted me. I would have brought you coffee. And anyway, there's a Starbucks right beside the sandwich shop. Just go in there and grab a macchiato before you come get lunch."

"I'm not sure businesses appreciate when customers do that," I say.

"You really think you'll have some left by the time you get back to the sandwich shop?" she asks, shocked.

I think about it and my head aches even thinking that much. "True." I need caffeine or an Excedrin, but one of the two.

"See? So it's settled." Layla grins brightly. "Yay! We'll see you two there! We have to go find Rick and ask him a quick question about the ceremony."

"You're having Rick do the wedding?" I ask, a little shocked. Layla likes Rick, but she's always said he is too crazy to ever perform her wedding.

"You just never know what he's going to say next," she told me right after they first got engaged. "That's a big no in my book for a preacher to do at the ceremony. I want to know *exactly* what he's going to say."

Layla nods to me now. "Of course, Paige. We're closest to him of all the pastors."

"Right, but earlier you said that —"

"Well, I just decided that even if he's unpredictable, at least he knows us. Plus, his premarital sessions have got to be more entertaining than some of our other pastors'," she says to me under her breath.

I smile. "Yes. There is that."

"So. Peach iced tea?" she asks again.

Peter shrugs. "I'm pretty much up for anything." Which might have been the longest sentence I've ever heard him say.

Tyler shrugs as well. "Why not? I like sandwiches. I like iced tea."

"*Peach* iced tea," Layla corrects him. "Peach. There's a huge difference between regular iced tea and the goodness that is peach iced tea."

"Four hundred calories and some high fructose corn syrup?" Tyler asks.

"Taste," Layla says.

"Oh. Right." Tyler picks up his Bible. "I'll stick with just the regular stuff."

"Your loss," she says. "Okay. We'll see you there. You guys should go on ahead and get us a table." Layla takes Peter's arm. They leave the sanctuary, walking back down the hall to the youth room.

I follow Tyler out into the bright sunshine. It is probably sixty-five degrees outside. Welcome to spring, apparently.

"Where's your car?" Tyler asks me. I point over to the lot by the youth room and he nods. "Why don't you just ride with me? I'm right there, and the sandwich place is just a couple of minutes away."

And here comes Accidental Date Number Two. And exactly what Layla is likely hoping for, seeing as how the sandwich shop is only a few blocks away and she easily could have fit all four of us in her Jetta. We could have waited while they talked to Rick. I've been to the sandwich shop once with Rick and Natalie, and it isn't crowded at all.

"Look, Tyler." I hold up my hands and squint at him in the bright sunlight.

"I know, I know. Consider it free gas." He leads me to his car.

"You know what?"

"You don't have time to date, you wish I'd just leave you alone, Layla's already got your engagement ring from me all picked out, whatever." He unlocks his truck and opens the passenger door. "Hop in."

I bite my lip. "I wasn't going to say that."

"Really," he says, but it isn't a question. He leans one arm against the open passenger door, ducks his head closer to mine, and gives me a disbelieving look. "What were you going to say?"

I cross my arms over my chest and think about it. Which is hard to do with him standing so close. "Well, she really is going to overreact," I say finally. "I mean, she went on and on about the ride you gave me to the lounge for like seriously forty-five minutes, and I couldn't even hear the band's first three songs and—"

"Get in the car, Paige."

"Fine."

He closes the door after I get settled onto the seat and comes around the front to his side. "So." He turns the key in the ignition. "Sandwiches."

"Something between two slices of bread? They're really a neat invention. I'm surprised you've never heard of them."

"I lead a sheltered life." He grins at me. "No, I was going to ask, what kind of sandwiches are we talking? Like Subway sandwiches or like guy sandwiches?"

"Jared's a guy, and he seems to like Subway."

"No, not guy with a little *g*. Big *G* Guy. As in Guy Fieri. Food Network? My mom loves him." Tyler sighs at the windshield. "Honestly, I have big envy problems when it comes to his job."

"Because he makes sandwiches?" I haven't watched too many of his shows. I am not the biggest fan of cooking shows. When I sit down to watch TV, I want it to be HGTV so I can dream about decorating my future house.

"Great-looking sandwiches," Tyler says. "Huge. And with stuff like roasted chicken and homemade mayonnaise."

Another thing I am not a fan of: mayonnaise. Even the name grosses me out. I make a face.

"What?" Tyler looks over at me.

"I don't like mayonnaise."

"Why not?"

"It's gross."

Tyler looks at me like he is still waiting, and I frown. Do I really need another reason?

"It tastes like fake food. Like American cheese."

"Hey," Tyler says, a warning ring in his voice. He holds up a hand. "American cheese is not fake."

"It is too fake. It's not cheese at all. It makes me feel sad for all the poor Americans who live over in Switzerland and have to defend their native country's namesake cheese."

Tyler laughs. "Well, I guess you have a point."

"Oh, stop here," I say quickly as he drives past the Starbucks. "I really need some caffeine."

"I thought the sandwich shop had legendary iced tea."

"Real caffeine. None of this watered-down, weak stuff."

He grins and pulls into the Starbucks parking lot.

"I'll be right back." I grab my purse. "Do you want anything?"

"I'll take the watered-down, weak stuff." He shakes his head.

I run inside, order, pay, and wait while they make my caramel macchiato. If I am going to continue to drink these things, I am really going to have to find the time to work out again. Maybe I can start getting up earlier and working out before going to work, since my evenings are quickly getting filled up with other activities.

Getting up earlier. There is an unwelcome thought.

"Venti caramel macchiato!" the barista yells.

"Thanks." I take my drink and go back out to Tyler's truck. The sandwich shop is right across a planter median thing filled with some sort of holly bushes. "You know," I say, opening his truck door. "We can just walk."

"Eh, then we're taking up space at the wrong restaurant." He looks at my drink. "I've got a five-gallon bucket you can take with you next time. Save Starbucks a cup."

"Hardy har har." I roll my eyes and sip my drink. Tyler drives the thirty seconds to the sandwich place and parks in front. Layla and Peter aren't there yet, which isn't surprising seeing as how they went to go talk to Rick.

Rick can be a bit long-winded.

Tyler makes no move to get out of the truck, so I sit there as well, drinking my coffee so I don't have to take the cup in with me to lunch. Slowly, my headache starts to ease.

"So," Tyler says. "Tell me about Peter."

"Peter who?"

"Peter, your best friend's fiancé Peter." Tyler gives me a weird look.

"What? There are lots of Peters. Peter Pan. Peter Rabbit. And we just heard a whole sermon taught from First Peter."

"Well, I meant Peter . . . you know, I don't even know his last name."

"Schofield."

"Peter Schofield. Peter and Layla Schofield."

I nod as he practices their names. "You have very nice diction."

"You know, your sarcasm level goes up the more caffeine you consume." He grins at me.

"No, it's just when I get tired. I'm sorry."

He shrugs. "I thought it was kind of funny, actually. So, Peter."

"What do you want to know about him?"

"I don't know. I'm about to have lunch with him. Is there anything I should know?"

"Like will he attack you with one of the plastic forks and steal your sandwich?"

"Like what is he *like*?" Tyler annunciates.

"Peter . . ." My voice trails off while I try to think of the nicest way to describe him. "Peter is . . ." I pause again, taking a drink of coffee.

Tyler is watching me. "I'm getting the feeling you're not really a fan of his."

"Let's just say I won't be wearing a shirt with his face on it anytime soon," I say quietly. I feel bad publicly declaring that I don't like my best friend's soon-to-be husband.

"That's tough."

I wave a hand. "It's not like I think he's a bad guy or anything. We just, uh, don't have a lot in common, I guess." Like spoken sentences and expressions and the ability to be considered more than just a mammal.

"Stuff in common is good. Is he a sports guy?"

I think about it. He does spend a lot of time watching games on TV. "I guess so."

"Like football? Baseball? Snowboarding?"

"Mmm. Sure." I finish off the macchiato.

"You know, I think I'll just ask him what he's interested in," Tyler says after another minute.

"Probably for the best." I nod.

Layla's Jetta heads into the parking lot. Peter is driving.

"I thought you were going to save a table," Layla says when we climb out of the truck.

"I had to finish my coffee," I tell her. "And we are the only two cars here."

She looks around. It is true.

"Are they open today?" She walks over to their door to peer at the sign. "They're open."

"They're just not very good," I say.

"Then why are we here?" Tyler slings his keys around his finger.

Layla sighs. "Peach iced tea, Tyler. I thought we'd gone over this."

"You'd sacrifice a decent sandwich for peach iced tea?" Tyler asks Layla, then turns to Peter. "Do you like the sandwiches here?"

Peter shrugs.

I would take that as a no, but I actually have no idea if Peter likes the sandwiches or not. I've only heard Peter's opinion of something once, and it was when he was dissing *Beauty and the Beast*, which I happen to love. So, it was not an opinion I agreed with.

"Guys, this isn't just peach-flavored tea; this is peach iced tea. With that thick, syrupy stuff they pour into it. It's worth a bad sandwich. I swear it to you on my dead rabbit Waldo's grave," Layla says.

"You had a rabbit named Waldo?" Tyler asks.

"She even knitted a red-and-white striped sweater for it. Don't get her started," I say in a hushed voice.

Not hushed enough, because Layla glares at me. "He was cold," she says icily.

"He had fur," I say.

"He did not . . . have very much."

"All right, I'm hungry. Let's just eat here." Tyler opens the door to the shop and the smell of freshly baked bread wafts out in a warm breeze. "Smells good." Tyler shrugs.

I follow Layla in and frown. "Is this the right sandwich shop?"

She is frowning as well. "It looks different." She sniffs. "Smells different too."

"I know. It smells good," I say.

"Oh no. What if they got good bread and got rid of the peach tea?"

A guy comes out from a back room then, holding a dish towel. "Oh, I'm sorry," he says, obviously flustered. "That bell thing I have for the door never works. Welcome to the Sandwich Shop."

Layla elbows me. "Was that the name of it before?"

"I don't know. We always just called it the sandwich shop," I whisper back.

"I've heard you have legendary peach iced tea," Tyler says nicely to the man.

"Oh, we've only been in business for a week," the guy says and Layla sighs. "You're thinking of the place that used to be here, and yes, they did have wonderful iced tea."

"Well, this is awful," Layla says.

"Not that you're in business," I tell the man quickly. "She just really liked their peach tea."

"I understand," the poor man says. "We have flavored teas as well, but not peach, I'm afraid. Mango is the closest I have to it."

Layla sighs again. "Oh."

"Your bread smells great." Tyler looks at the menu suspended above the counter for a minute. "I'll take your turkey club."

"White, wheat, or rye?"

"Wheat, please."

The man nods, snapping latex gloves over his hands. "Can I get anyone else anything?"

Layla mutters something under her breath.

"What?" I ask her.

"A ham sandwich on white," she gripes.

The man looks at me. "And for you, Miss?"

I try to make up for Layla's rudeness. "A turkey, please. Wheat bread, please. Mustard only, please. Thank you, please." I may have gone a little overboard.

"No lettuce or tomatoes or anything?"

"Oh. Yes, please. All of that, please. Just no mayonnaise, please." I really just need to stop, so I clamp my lips shut as Tyler gives me a strange look.

"And for you, sir?" the man asks Peter.

"The club on wheat."

"You got it."

Layla pays and we all pick out bags of chips and get our drinks. Layla sits at a table overlooking the parking lot, still complaining about the tea.

"I mean, seriously. Mango is nowhere close to peach. Other than being fruit, they have nothing in common," she whispers.

"They're both orange," I say.

"And they have similar textures," Tyler says.

"And they both—"

Layla holds up a hand, stopping me midsentence. "I'm content with my Dr Pepper."

"Really?" I ask.

"Not yet. But I will be."

I grin. The man brings our sandwiches out, and they look really good.

"So, Peter, what do you do?" Tyler asks after he finishes blessing the food.

Peter looks up at him, and I am suddenly curious as well. What does Peter do? I have no idea. Layla has just always talked about him pushing papers around all day.

"I'm an estate planner."

I take a bite of my sandwich, still curious about what Peter does. Is that code for an architect of big houses?

"Like wills?" Tyler asks.

"Right. I do the nonlegal stuff."

"People come to him to help them prepare for their deaths," Layla says.

No wonder Peter is so quiet and depressing. My job is stressful, but at least at the end of the day, I help with a happy part of people's lives.

"Wow," Tyler says. "That's a very needed field. My grandfather didn't do anything to prepare for after he died, and you wouldn't believe all the stuff my grandmother had to deal with."

Peter nods. It is apparently the end of the conversation, because the whole table falls quiet.

"So, Rick's doing the wedding?" I ask Layla.

"Yep. Confirmed it today. We start premarital counseling in August. I'm a little scared."

Of marriage? I want to ask, but obviously I can't with Peter and Tyler sitting there. So I say, "Of premarital counseling?"

"Yeah. I mean, Rick is very strange. Even you have to agree with that."

"I do," I say.

"That's the other thing," Layla says. "'I do'? I mean, I'm

all for traditions, but I really think we should write our own vows." She sighs at Peter. "Don't you think that would be romantic?"

"Mmm," Peter hums around a bite of sandwich.

"Then we can write whatever we want to in the vows. None of the stuff that just seems like it's there for filler, you know?"

"Like what?" I ask.

"I don't know. Just the legalese-y sounding stuff. 'I, Layla' and all that stuff. I never walk around saying things like, 'I, Layla, think this sandwich is good.'"

I grin. Tyler laughs.

"I mean, I know there's good stuff in traditional vows. And I don't want to throw the china out with the dishwater," she says.

"What?" I ask.

"The floaties out with the pool water?" She frowns.

"The baby out with the bathwater?" Tyler suggests.

"That's the one!" Layla points at Tyler. "I don't want to throw the baby out with the bathwater."

I laugh. "Oh, Layla."

"What? Who even comes up with those clichés? And seriously, if you have such a dirty baby that after washing him, you can't even see him in the bath, that's a bigger parenting problem, I'd say."

* * * * *

Tyler drops me back at my car at one. "See? That wasn't so bad." Tyler grins at me as he brakes beside my car in the empty parking lot.

"Only because Layla was so distracted that the place didn't have her peach tea."

"Layla is funny."

"Yes, she is." I look over at him, debating whether or not I should ask the question.

He smiles at me. "What?"

"Do you think Peter is a good match for Layla?"

"Do you?"

"I asked you first."

He leans back in his seat, shifting his truck into Park. "Well, I've only spent today with them together. I really don't know them that well."

"First impressions."

Tyler squints into the bright sun coming through the windshield and doesn't say anything for a few minutes. "He's quiet," Tyler says, finally. "But Layla is very chatty. So maybe that's a good thing."

I nod. "Maybe." I pick up my purse from the floorboard and smile. "Well, thanks again for the ride, Tyler."

"Sure thing. Anytime."

I open the car door and climb out.

"Paige?" Tyler smiles at me. "I hope you're able to take the afternoon and do something that you want to do."

"Thanks." First things first, I am going to finish that wreath.

"Maybe next weekend we can go on a picnic or something," he says. "The weather is really nice right now."

Something is happening next weekend, but at the moment, I can't remember what it is. "I'll have to check my planner."

"I figured." He grins at me. "That's why I gave you advanced notice this time."

I pull the planner out of my purse and turn to February. "Oh yeah. I can't do next weekend. Rick is going to be out of town all weekend with the junior highers on their retreat, and I told Natalie I'd go stay with her and help take care of the baby."

"Maybe the weekend after that." Tyler nods.

I check those dates. "Friday night, I have a bunch of high school girls coming over for a movie night again, Layla wants me to go party shopping with her on Saturday, and then Sunday I told my boss I'd help him clean the office."

Tyler narrows his eyes at me. "The next weekend."

"That's when Layla's party is."

"Weekend after that."

"We have a big adoption fund-raiser banquet thing on Saturday night, so I'll be spending the day getting everything set up for that."

"And Sunday?"

I check. I don't have anything written down yet for that Sunday. But with the anniversary party out of the way, I imagine Layla will want to start on the wedding planning.

"Probably helping Layla."

Tyler shakes his head. "You are crazy."

"I'm just busy."

"You cannot say no, can you?"

"What would you have me say no to?" I wave a hand at my planner. "My pastor? My boss? My best friend?" I take a deep breath. "I'm sorry," I say quickly, quietly. "I didn't mean to yell."

He watches me for a minute and then nods. "Go home,

Paige. Change into comfy clothes, put in one of your favorite movies, and just *chill*. Can you do that for me?"

The overstuffed tax folder is still sitting in my apartment, but I nod just to please Tyler.

"Thank you," he says. "And thanks for coming to lunch with me."

"Sure. Sorry again."

"Stop apologizing, Paige. It's all good." He smiles at me and waves. "See you on Wednesday night for youth group."

"Okay." I close the truck door, and he waits until I climb into my car and then lets me leave first. I am tired. More than just physically.

Chapter 13

I drive home, walk up the stairs to my apartment, unlock the door, and head inside. I go straight over to my closet, pull out a pair of sweatpants, and am just getting ready to change when my doorbell rings.

I look at my phone. No missed calls, no missed texts. Surely it is just a solicitor. I set the sweatpants down and walk over to the door, looking through the peephole.

It's Lucy, one of the high school girls. I open the door, confused to see her. She isn't looking at me. She is looking back down the steps.

"Lucy?"

She turns and her face is splotchy and she has tears in her eyes. "I didn't know where else to go," she says quietly. "Can I come in?"

I open the door wider, my heart sinking to my knees, my brain automatically going to the worst possible things that could have happened to her. I don't know Lucy very well. She is one of the quieter girls, but she was here for movie night. I am pretty sure she is a senior in high school.

She comes inside and I point to the couch. "You can sit there." I go into the kitchen and all I can find to drink is water, so I pour her a glass, dampen a paper towel, grab the tissue box, and carry all of it back over to the couch. She is sniffling, tears welling up in her eyes.

"Here." I hand her the wet paper towel. She mashes it against her eyes. I set the water and tissues on the coffee table and then sit down beside her. I am so bad at this. Do I touch her? Give her space? Give her a hug? Give her time by herself? Ask her what happened? Sit there in silence?

I decide to just keep my hands together in my lap and sit quietly. She dabs her face with the paper towel, blows her nose, and drinks most of the water before she finally starts talking.

"I just had a huge fight with my dad," she says, tears flowing again.

"Are you okay? I mean, he didn't . . ." I can't even say the words. I don't know very much about Lucy, but I know her parents are divorced and her mom isn't really in the picture.

"No, no," she says quickly, shaking her head, swiping at her eyes with the paper towel. She sniffs and shrugs. "I have this amazing opportunity to be a camp leader this year at a Christian camp that specializes in helping special-needs kids."

"Your dad doesn't want you to go," I say when she cries again.

She shakes her head and talks through her tears. "He says I'll be blowing all my chances at a scholarship and that will put me back a year and then I'll be the one who doesn't have enough motivation to stick it out in school and medical schools won't accept me because of that."

I listen quietly. I'm not sure what she wants me to say. I'm not even sure I know what I'm supposed to say. I'm sorry? Disobey your dad and go to the camp? Obey your dad and go to college?

She sniffles. "I just don't know what to do. I don't want to go against my dad, but this is the only time in my life that I'll be able to do something like the camp. But if he's right, I don't want to sacrifice my ability to go to medical school, because I really feel like God's calling me to be a doctor." She blows her breath out and stares out my window.

I watch her for a second, rubbing my face. Lucy is one of those girls who can do whatever she wants to. She's beautiful, with long, thick blonde hair, and she's brilliant. I rub my cheek, watching her tear-stained face for a minute.

On the one hand, I wish I was eighteen and had the whole world open to me again. I hadn't made any major life decisions, but I had everything figured out. I was going to become a counselor and work with the kids who hurt the most and change lives for the better. Which just makes me a little depressed thinking about my life and how it has turned out in these last five years.

On the other hand, I am thankful I'm not in the middle of feeling pressured to figure out my whole life.

I squeeze my eyes closed for a minute. *God. Words, please!*

"Lucy," I start slowly.

She looks at me, still dabbing her face with the paper towel.

"When do you have to let the camp know whether or not you can come?"

"By the end of the month." She sniffles.

I nod. "Well . . ." I am seeing my afternoon of finishing

that wreath slipping through my fingers. But what kind of awful person would I be not to help a hurting girl in need? I pat her arm. "Let's go make some chocolate-chip cookies." I stand. "Sometimes the world makes more sense after cookies."

Lucy doesn't leave until almost eight o'clock. We talk through the pros and cons of each choice, why her dad is so stuck on her going to college, and what she wants to do. And then we talk about it all again and again. I never tell her what I think she should do, and I never offer advice. I just listen. And mix up cookies and then bake a frozen pizza for us to eat for dinner.

She turns to hug me right before she walks out the door. "Thank you, Paige." She hugs me tight, holding a plastic container of cookies in one hand. "You're the best."

"Let me know what you decide to do," I say.

"I will."

After she leaves, I close and lock the door behind her and then look around my apartment. I have taxes to work on, a florist to find, pans to wash, and a cookie-making mess to clean up. I had been considering getting up a little earlier tomorrow morning to work out before I go to work.

It seems like an even better idea now after spending the afternoon eating cookie dough, but a horrible idea considering how late I will probably be up cleaning.

I stack all the dishes in the sink, run some hot soapy water over them, and then just let them soak. I rub a sponge over the counter and wipe up all the sugar remnants and then sit down at the computer to do some floral research.

I've already called around ten florists for the banquet.

They like to start planning the next year's banquet as soon as one is over. It's a lot of work.

The band is another story.

Mark is one of the best bosses I've ever had just because, most of the time, he lets me do my own thing. I do my work, he does his, he gives me more work to do, and I do it without him looking over my shoulder the whole time. It drives me absolutely nuts when people are constantly looking over my shoulder.

Well, the music selection for the banquet turns Mark into the exact opposite of a best boss. He wants to know every little thing I do with the music. What bands I am thinking about, what the band looks like, acts like, sounds like, and what they charge. Whereas everything else for the banquet, he just gives me a budget and a green light.

I am so thankful we finally booked the swing band. Four weeks before the banquet is cutting it way too close.

I Google florists in Dallas and four million results pop up. And I'm not even exaggerating. Apparently, the floral industry here isn't suffering for competition.

I scroll down the page, cross-checking the listings with the florists I've already called. A place called At First Sight catches my attention, and I click over to their webpage.

They have some pretty designs on their site. And a few of the pictures are of large weddings and other events, so they obviously can do something on a larger scale. I write down their contact info on my yellow legal pad. I'll call them in the morning.

I look at the tax stuff and just shake my head. It is already ten thirty. My goal of getting taxes done by March is looking progressively more and more like a failure.

Chapter 14

I get to work a few minutes before eight the next morning. Without having worked out.

In a little over a month.

I am feeling it too. It is not my favorite feeling.

At First Sight florist opens at eight fifteen, so as soon as the four changes into a five on the digital clock on my desk, I dial.

"Good morning and thanks for calling At First Sight florists," a friendly lady answers the phone.

"Hi, I've got a bit of a catastrophe, and I hope you can help." I might as well be honest.

"Well, honey, I've been in this business for thirty-two years, and it's been my experience that flowers can usually help in a catastrophe."

"It's not really that kind of catastrophe." I explain about the banquet and how the florist I already booked had canceled. "And so, I need eighty-four table centerpieces by the last weekend of February."

"Mm-hmm, mm-hmm," she says through the whole

thing, like she is writing it down. "Okay," she says with a sigh when I finish. "Eighty-four, huh? Do you know what you'd like them to look like?"

"I'd like red roses." This is my first year to be officially in charge of the banquet completely, and I want it to be spectacular. Last year, I was working here when they had it, but I was new, so I didn't plan hardly any of it.

"All right. Big arrangements? Small? And what kind of price range are we looking at here?"

I tell her our budget and she responds with another, "Mm-hmm."

"And somewhere in the middle as far as the size," I tell her.

She is quiet for a minute. "Okay, sweetie. Here's what I'm going to do. I'll get together three different designs for you, and if you can come here around two o'clock this afternoon, I'll have them ready and be ready for you to sign the contract. Does that sound like a good plan?"

"Does that mean you'll do it?"

"If you like the designs, then sure. Consider me your florist."

"Thank you!" I gush as Peggy and Candace walk in. "Thank you, thank you!"

"No worries, dear. We'll get this figured out. I'll see you at two."

I hang up, grinning. My day is already looking good. "Good morning," I say cheerfully to Peggy and Candace.

"Happy today, hmm?" Peggy asks. "Date tonight?"

"No, she's happier than just a date," Candace says before I can answer. She looks at me, studying my face. "Did you just win that thousand-dollar Starbucks gift card competition?"

"There's a competition for a thousand-dollar Starbucks gift card?" I gasp.

"That obviously isn't it." Peggy picks up her message slips from her box.

"I think I found a florist for the banquet."

"I thought you found one months ago," Candace says.

"They called me Friday and canceled."

"Well, that is mean," Candace says.

"I agree." Then I frown. "What did you mean when you said I was happier than just a date?"

"I can't explain it." Candace turns to Peggy. "You've seen Paige before she goes on a date." Candace shrugs. They both start to walk toward their offices.

"Wait." I hold up my hands. "What's wrong with me before I go on a date?"

"Oh, nothing, dear," Candace says.

"No, really. I should probably know this."

She sighs. "You get . . . tense?" She looks at Peggy.

"Apprehensive." Peggy nods.

"No I don't," I protest.

"Honey." Candace rolls her eyes. "I am trained in the field of recognizing when someone is tense or not. Trust me. You tense up. Big time. I'm surprised you've never gotten cramps. In your neck. Or your back."

She is back to fragments. Candace is serious.

I lean back in my chair, frowning. "Really?"

"Sorry, Paige," Peggy says, smiling motherly at me. "It's true."

"Remember that kid with the bleached shirt?" Candace asks Peggy.

"Major tenseness." Peggy nods.

"Okay." I hold up my hands again. "Michael was weird. And I did not know this before I went out with him. Of course I was going to be tense for a blind date." Natalie set me up with him, and I still haven't forgiven her for that one.

I don't like giving blind dates my home address, so he'd shown up at my work to pick me up wearing a T-shirt with a bleached design of a Mario Brother on it—that he had created himself.

"It's Luigi," he said proudly, puffing out his chest.

I had very good reasons to be tense that night.

"Or that guy you went out with a few times a little while ago . . . what was his name?" Candace asks, frowning at Peggy.

"Anthony," Peggy supplies.

Anthony Myerson. It's been a long time since I'd thought about him. He made Michael the Mario Brothers fan look normal. I'm not sure what I ever saw in him, but I went out with him two or three times.

"Come to think of it, you have very interesting taste in men." Candace sits on the edge of my desk, angling her body so she can see me. "Why do you think that's the case?"

Great. Now I am going to get a counseling session on my dating life. My day isn't looking as bright all of a sudden.

"I d-don't . . . know," I stutter.

"She has a wonderful father, so it's not father issues," Peggy says.

"I know." Candace is looking at me with a studying frown. "You are a great puzzle to me, Paige Alder. And a good study for us." She stares at me a minute longer. "I think I'll do it."

"Do what?" I ask, suddenly very scared.

"I'm going to find out what's wrong with you." She nods and hops off the desk.

What am I supposed to say to that? Gee, thanks? Don't worry about it? I'd prefer to stay a puzzle?

"Okay," I say slowly.

"Paige," Peggy says, her tone placating. "There's nothing wrong with you. You are God's creation, and you are beautiful and intelligent."

"Y'all aren't going to charge me by the hour, are you?"

"I want you to see the wonderful person you are in God's eyes," Peggy says.

"And I want you to start dating a guy who actually deserves someone as amazing as you are and not some loser who thinks that chocolate will kill you," Candace adds.

Peggy laughs. "Oh yeah!" She grins. "What was his name again?"

"Will Rakers," I supply, rubbing my head. Maybe my real issue isn't my horrible taste in men as much as my habit of having them meet me at work.

"Now he was funny."

"That's because it wasn't your M&Ms he flushed down the toilet." Peggy rolls her eyes at Candace.

She laughs.

"The point I'm trying to make, Paige, is that you should sit down and write out a list of qualities you want in a future husband," Candace says.

"I have a list of qualities. I've never written it down, but I know them."

"Tell me three of them." She crosses her arms over her chest.

"I'll even name five," I tell her haughtily, checking the

list off on my fingers. "Rich doctor, frequent shaver, high-class chef, doesn't wear skinny jeans, and appreciates HGTV," I finish.

Peggy and Candace just exchange a look.

"What?" I protest.

"None of those things is a quality," Peggy says.

"Not even one," Candace adds. "No qualities. At all."

"Doesn't wear skinny jeans?" I say. "That is a definite quality."

"Paige," Peggy says.

I sigh.

"Look, honey, you have the . . ." Peggy squints at the ceiling, obviously looking for a nice word to use. "Tendency. You have the tendency to say yes to everything."

This sounds vaguely like what Tyler told me on our last nondate.

"I do not," I say.

"Ahem, I'll give you examples." Peggy starts ticking them off on her fingers. "Michael, Anthony, and Will. There's three."

"Waterskiing with Layla's family," Candace adds.

I wince. I hate water. And I hate skiing. And yet, somehow I found myself strapped to the heaviest skis in the world, grasping onto a handle tied to a rope that was attached to a boat. I had to have my arm set back in the socket and wore a brace for three weeks afterward.

And none of my cute summer outfits looked cute with an Ace bandage brace.

"What's-his-face from your Sunday school class who needed help moving," Peggy says.

I'd shown up to Gavin's all set to help and found him and three guys playing Xbox in an apartment that hadn't even started being boxed up. So I spent the rest of the day boxing up his closet while he and his friends tried to kill each other in whatever the horribly violent game was.

I can concede that one.

"That friend of yours who, thank the good Lord, finally moved back home to Michigan or wherever she was from, who kept asking you to go to dinner and forgetting her wallet," Candace says.

Aubrey Benterly. Once she finally moved, I had to eat rice cakes for every meal for four months just to get money back into my savings. She called me up at least three times a week with some crisis she needed to talk about. "Let's just meet at Olive Garden," she'd say in tears.

"And then the winner of them all, Luke Prestwick," Candace says.

I sigh.

Luke Prestwick. I cried over him for two months.

A few months after getting this job, I'd confessed the whole Luke saga to Candace and Peggy. And then I decided that maybe his moving to California was a blessing in disguise.

Maybe.

I try not to think about him.

"Look, Paige," Peggy says in a more gentle voice. "I'm not against you helping people. In fact, it's one of the qualities I love best about you."

"And it totally comes across in your work here," Candace says. "That's why you've got a drawerful of thank-you cards and pictures from all of our clients." She pulls open my top drawer as Exhibit A. I have stacks and stacks of cards, letters, and pictures in there.

"What did you do last week?" Peggy asks.

I frown. "What do you mean?"

"I mean, I've seen your planner. Get it out. I want to see what you did last week."

I pull my planner out of my purse, open it to last week, and set it on my desk. Peggy and Candace read quietly for a minute.

Candace shakes her head. "Good gracious, girl. When do you even have time to eat?"

"Or shower?" Peggy asks.

"Or sit and watch a movie?" Candace says.

I sigh again. "I don't know what you guys expect me to do." I close my planner and shove it back in my purse. "Nothing in there is bad. It's church stuff or best-friend stuff or work stuff. I can't cut out any of it."

"I'm just suggesting that maybe you look into the mirror and practice saying the word *no*," Peggy says gently.

"And I'm seconding that suggestion." Candace nods. "It's a lesson I had to learn, and it's one I've always been thankful for." She looks at me for a long minute and then pats the top of my hand. "A need does not constitute a call, sweetie."

Peggy smiles softly at me. "We'll let you do your work. Just think about it."

I nod. Candace walks around my desk and gives me one of those awkward hugs when one person is seated. "I love you, honey. It's the only reason I'm giving you a hard time."

I nod again. They both walk down to their offices, flipping through their voice-mail slips. I look at my computer, pulling up the banquet spreadsheet I created, and bite my lip.

Do I really have that big of a problem saying no?

I shake my head. They are overreacting. I can say no. I mean, I've said no to Tyler asking me out like eight times by this point. Which maybe is a bigger issue I have. Apparently, I can't say no to needy, weird guys, but a normal, sweet Christian guy I have no problem turning down.

Maybe I do need help.

* * * * *

At First Sight is about fifteen minutes from the office, but since it's a work-related visit, Mark agreed that he and Peggy would cover the phone. I love work-related errands. They are like a field trip.

The day is absolutely beautiful. Sunshine, blue skies, probably seventy-five degrees, and low humidity, which is something of a miracle in Dallas.

The florist is in a little strip mall right next door to a tailor. I park in front and walk in.

Some days, I wish I'd gone into floral design. The place smells amazing.

"Hey there." An older lady who looks a lot like the actress Kathy Bates smiles at me from behind a long worktable and rubs her hands on a towel. "Can I help you?"

"I'm Paige Alder. I called you this morning from Lawman Adoption Agency."

She nods. "I am expecting you. I'm Sandra. Come on in to the back room. Can I get you anything? Water? Coke? I think I've even got a pitcher of sweet tea in there." She waves for me to follow her.

"No thanks." See? I can say no.

"It's my famous sweet tea." She leads me into a small

white room with a wicker coffee table and two wicker chairs. She nods to one of the chairs.

"Okay then," I say. "Sweet tea sounds good."

Sandra leaves and I nod to myself. Sweet tea does sound good. So it's fine.

"Here you go." She comes back in with a tall glass a minute later. "And I'll be right back with your arrangements. I just finished the last one a few minutes ago."

"Thank you."

"Don't thank me until you've seen them." She grins. She comes back holding two different arrangements. "Let me grab the last," she says and then is back a minute later.

She sets them all on the table in front of me, and I feel myself relaxing. They are absolutely stunning. The smaller one is too small for what I am thinking, but I will have a hard time deciding between the larger and the middle-sized one.

"And all of these are within my budget?" I ask her.

"Yes, they are." She pushes a pair of bifocals up on her face. "Now, you said you need eighty-four of these?"

"Right."

"Totally doable." She nods. "You just let me know which one you like or if you want any changes made to them." She sits back in the other wicker chair and smiles at me. "Is this a fancy event?"

"Yeah. It's as close to black tie as you can get," I tell her. She nods.

I study the flowers, thinking. "Okay, another question. If I get the medium-sized ones and we make it this size but with fewer flowers, can I get two extra-large arrangements for the stage?"

She purses her lips, thinking. "Red roses as well?"

"Yes."

"Mmm. We can probably do that. I might have to add some filler greenery in there, but that will bring the price down a little bit so it's a comfortable fit for your budget."

I like this lady. I sip her sweet tea and can see why she is famous for it. "Are you guys open on Saturday?"

"Until noon."

"My friend is planning an anniversary party for her parents. I might have her come by." It would be much easier on us both if someone else was making the centerpieces for Layla's party. Particularly if she really wants us to sleep in the park the night before.

I am still praying she'll change her mind on that one.

I leave the florist feeling a little more relieved about the banquet. Sandra says she'll get to the Marriott at two o'clock on the last Saturday in February. Which gives us four hours to get the arrangements on the tables and stage before the banquet actually starts.

Surely that is enough time.

I get back to work and check the florist off my list of things to do. Mark comes over to my desk around four.

"Paige, did you already confirm with the speakers?"

I nod and flip through my file on the banquet. "Yes, sir. All of them should be there at five, and I've already arranged with the Marriott to have three wireless microphones for them, as well as one on the podium as a backup."

Mark looks impressed. "Very thorough." He smiles at me proudly. "And when is the band getting there?"

"I think they're coming at three to rehearse. I told them they'd go on at six fifteen." The way the banquet is set up, Mark will open the evening, say grace, and then we'll serve dinner. The Marriott is giving us a great discount on their catering service, so we are using them. When dinner starts to wrap up, the band will take a break, we'll hear from Owen Roberts, the TV guy; Alexa Thomas, the lady from March of Dimes; and Camilla Carson, the beauty pageant girl. Then the band will play again, and they'll have an open dance floor until the night ends around ten with the silent auction winners.

It will be a big night.

"And the auction items?" Mark asks.

Again, I flip around in my file folder. Mark spent the past year going to different businesses and asking for donations for our auction. All of the proceeds go straight to helping lower-income families adopt. Add the auction money to the ticket sales and we usually exceed $20,000 to $30,000 in one night.

The biggest item he got to auction off is a seventy-two-inch flat-screen TV. Which just seems ridiculously huge for a TV. And it makes me feel sad for the poor news anchors on television these days. I would be horribly self-conscious if I knew my face was seventy-two inches and in high definition in someone's house.

I tell him which businesses are bringing the auction items and which ones we need to pick up from the day before. He nods and then smiles at me again. "You're a great secretary," he says and goes back to his office.

I think he means it as a compliment. But as he leaves, I just sit there and stare at the banquet file.

I will most likely never be a counselor at Lawman Adoption Agency.

I *am* a good secretary. Too good for my own good.

Chapter 15

There is a text waiting from Tyler when I finally call it a day at five thirty.

JUST WANTED TO APOLOGIZE FOR WHAT I SAID YESTER-DAY AFTER LUNCH — I CAN BE TOO BLUNT SOMETIMES. HOPE YOU ARE HAVING A GREAT DAY, PAIGE.

I write him back.

NO BIG DEAL. YOU ARE MOST LIKELY RIGHT. THANKS FOR BEING HONEST WITH ME. I'LL SEE YOU WEDNESDAY NIGHT.

I drive home. I am planning on going home and changing before heading back to the grocery store. I decided to dress up today, and my heels are killing my feet.

I climb my apartment stairs and find a white envelope taped to the door.

I am half creeped out. First, because that means someone has been on my porch and stuck a note to my door without me being there. Second, because it doesn't have a name or anything on it.

I pull it off slowly and open it. It is a card.

Paige, thought you could use this.

Inside is a Chili's gift card. And it isn't signed. I turn the card over to check. Even the handwriting is indistinguishable. All caps.

Great. Now, how am I supposed to write a thank-you note? I smile though and walk inside. Looks like ribs are in my future tonight.

I call Layla.

"Hey, Paige," she answers, sounding busy.

"Did you leave me a Chili's gift card?"

"Did I what?" Her voice gets muffled. "Peter, no, I don't like that there. Hang on a second, Paige."

She starts talking to Peter, and I decide to change my clothes. I kick off my heels, find a pair of ratty jeans, and grab a TCU T-shirt.

"Sorry, Paige. Peter went with me to the grocery store, and he hasn't quite gotten my pantry system down."

"You have a pantry system?" Layla's pantry looks like a canned-good donation stash. Nothing is grouped together that I can tell.

"Sure I do. I organize by expiration date."

Only Layla would do that.

"Now, what do you want?" she asks me. "We can't go to Chili's tonight. Mom and Dad want to take us out to dinner. Though, they'd probably love for you to join us, so you should just come along."

"No, no, I'm fine." I can indeed say the word *no*. Twice today, as a matter of fact. It isn't my fault that Sandra seduced me into saying *yes* to her sweet tea. I am looking forward to telling Peggy and Candace tomorrow about my victories.

"Anyway, I don't think we're going to Chili's. Mom said something about Panera. But if you're craving Chili's, I can probably convince them to go there."

Suddenly, I am craving macaroni and cheese. "No, Layla, really. I don't want to invite myself to your dinner tonight. Someone left a Chili's gift card on my door, and I'm just calling to say thank you, if it was you."

"Oh, well, it wasn't me. Though I probably owe you more than a Chili's gift card for all the work you've done for Mom and Dad's party. Speaking of which, I finally bought all the stuff to make the invitations."

I frown. "Wait, what?" Last I'd heard, she was going to just send e-vites. And that was after her other brilliant idea of having them made by some lady she'd found at an online craft fair.

"Yep. I got cream-colored paper, some burlap and muslin, and some blue lacy accents that match Mom and Dad's wedding colors." She sounds proud of herself.

I rub my forehead. "How many people are you inviting again?"

"So far, I've got a hundred and twenty. But those are individuals, so probably around . . ." She blows her breath out. "Oh I don't know, maybe seventy invitations?"

Seventy invitations. All handmade.

I sit down at my kitchen table.

"The party is in two weeks, Layla," I say quietly.

"Right. I figure we can crank them out this weekend and have them all ready to be mailed on Monday. That's still plenty of notice for a party. And I've already been talking to all our out-of-town relatives and Mom and Dad's best friends for like the last four months."

"I can't help this weekend, though, Layla. Remember? Rick is going out of town, and Natalie asked me to come stay with her and the baby."

"Oh." Layla gets quiet for a minute. "I bet Natalie wouldn't mind if we worked on invitations at her house. I'll text her and see if that's okay. And we're meeting Mom and Dad at Panera in like fifteen minutes, so I've got to go. Are you going to come?"

"No, thanks though," I say quietly.

"All right. See you later." She hangs up, and I rub my forehead.

Sometimes Layla has no idea how much work goes into things.

* * * * *

The week alternates between crawling and flying by. I spend every day working on the banquet stuff at work and Layla's party stuff at night.

The one bright spot is when I tell Rick and Tyler about the gift card on my porch. Rick just says, "That's cool," and leaves.

"Well, hopefully you like fajitas then," Tyler says nonchalantly, following Rick.

I did not mention that the gift card is to Chili's.

Since he left, I didn't follow him. But it does make something deep in the pit of my stomach get a little bit warmer.

Friday after work, I drive straight to Natalie's house and

get there about five fifteen. I'd brought my duffel bag with me so I could head right over there. Rick left at seven this morning for the retreat, so Natalie has been home by herself for a while.

I don't totally understand why she needs my help. Claire is only four weeks old. How much trouble can she be already?

Natalie opens the door looking like a truck ran over her, backed up, and ran over her again. Her hair is greasy and pulled back in a ponytail. She is wearing sweatpants and a pink ratty T-shirt that says *Anybody Want A Peanut?* and has a picture of Fezzik on it.

"Thank God!" She grabs me in a hug.

I hug her back with one arm since I am holding my duffel bag with the other. She lets go and rubs her eyes. "She hasn't slept at *all* in the last thirty-six hours," she moans. "She sort of napped for about ten minutes today after nursing, but the second I set her down in her bassinet, she woke back up."

"She's quiet now," I say, walking inside.

I haven't been over to their house since Claire was born. Natalie usually kept a house that looked like it belonged in a Pottery Barn catalog.

Today, pillows are strewn everywhere, there is a huge pile of laundry on the couch, and random blankets, pacifiers, and diapers are all over the floor.

Claire is propped into a corner of the couch, looking at me, sucking on a pacifier.

"See what I mean?" Natalie yawns. "She just *stares* at me like that."

"Hey, precious," I croon, sitting down on the couch next to her. She doesn't even blink but just stares straight at me, pacifier moving up and down in her mouth.

It is a little disconcerting.

"I have read every single article online about getting your baby to sleep." Natalie sits down on the pile of laundry. "And nothing works. I've tried the swing, I've tried the bouncer, I've tried the Moby wrap, I've tried singing, and I've given her three baths with that lavender-y baby soap." She shakes her head slowly. "And still she stares. Or cries."

"Maybe Fezzik's head is scaring her." I nod to Andre the Giant's head on her shirt. He does have kind of a creepy expression.

"No way. My daughter cannot be scared of *The Princess Bride*. No way."

I look back at Claire, and she is still staring at me. "Maybe she's hungry?"

"I've been nursing her for an hour every three hours," Natalie says, exhaustion straining across her face. "She can't be hungry. And I've changed her diaper eighteen times today."

"She's had *eighteen* dirty diapers?" Rick is going to need to get a second job just to pay for diapers.

"No, she's had two. But I just thought maybe she wasn't comfortable, so I kept changing her, hoping she'd go to sleep."

I grin. "Well, when was the last time you fed her?"

"Twenty minutes ago."

"Okay. Go take a shower and a couple-hour nap. I've got Claire. And we'll have dinner waiting when you wake up."

I am pretty sure I've never seen Natalie so happy. "Really? Really, Paige?"

"Good night, Nat."

She jumps off the couch and runs for her bedroom.

I look at Claire. I've never spent very much time with such a small baby, but it can't be that hard, can it?

It can.

After twenty minutes, I can see why Natalie's hair hasn't been washed in so long. First off, it takes two hands to hold Claire, and the second I set her down to do something, she flips out with these horrible squawky sounds that verge somewhere between a cry and what I imagine a dinosaur hatching sounded like.

I finally just reconcile myself to holding her the rest of Natalie's nap and calling in a pizza or something instead of making dinner. I pick her up carefully, still a little afraid that I might drop her and she will shatter into a million pieces on the floor. Her head lolls around so much. It scares me.

My phone starts ringing an hour after I get there. It is Layla.

"Hey!" she says cheerfully. I can hear music in the background. "Just calling to let you know I'm on my way with the invitations!"

I try to think positively. Maybe she already finished the invites, and she is coming by to show the finished product to me.

"I'm at Natalie's, remember?" I cradle the phone between my cheek and my shoulder while I hold Claire in the rocking chair. She is looking at me with wide, dark eyes, her pacifier bobbing up and down.

"Right. I called Nat last week and she said that was fine to bring the invitations over to work on. Actually, I even suggested we watch a movie or something while we work on them, and she said that would be great."

"Well, she hasn't slept in three days," I tell Layla. "She's taking a nap right now. And Claire cries anytime you set her down."

"So I'll work on the invitations and keep you company while you hold Claire. Be there in ten."

She hangs up, probably so I can't continue to debate with her.

I look down at Claire, rocking slowly back and forth in the chair. I never did much babysitting. Young babies waver between grossing me out and making me nervous. You can never predict what an infant is going to do.

Claire is still staring at me. I remember my mom telling me once that the only way she could get me to sleep in the beginning was by swaddling me up so tight she could stand me up against the wall.

It can't hurt to try.

I lay a blanket out on the floor, wrap Claire up as tightly as I dare, and settle back into the chair with the baby burrito.

"So," I say quietly, rubbing a finger over her soft baby cheeks. "What do you think of the world so far?"

She seems to relax a little when I stroke her cheek, so I keep lightly brushing my finger over and around her cheeks, her forehead, her tiny chin, and her little Dippin' Dot of a nose. She keeps melting farther and farther into my arm, and a few minutes later, her eyelids start to flutter.

Which of course is when Layla knocks on the door. I squint at the front door, see we never locked it after I got here, and ever-so-slowly fish my cell phone out of my pocket and text Layla, all while keeping the same rhythm rocking.

As soon as I finish texting, I keep stroking my finger over her face. Layla creeps through the door, finger over her mouth, holding two paper grocery sacks.

Claire's eyes are half closed now. Her pacifier isn't bobbing up and down nearly as much.

I nod to the huge baby swing in the corner. Layla reads my mind and goes over and turns the swing on and then closes the drapes since the sun is shining directly on the swing.

Claire's eyes shut all the way.

I hold my breath, ease to my feet, still half rocking Claire in my arms, sway over to the swing, and ever-so-slowly set her into it.

And, miracle of all miracles, she stays asleep.

I breathe for the first time in ten minutes, and Layla nods at Claire.

"You're an old pro," she whispers to me.

"She hasn't slept in thirty-six hours," I whisper back. "It's inevitable she'd fall asleep eventually."

We tiptoe to the kitchen and Layla opens her bags. "Well, I brought all the invitation stuff. And I actually got the chance to make one this week after I got off work. What do you think?"

She holds it up. Layla is not crafty at all. She is forever saying that if people out there are willing to take the time and energy to make crafts, she would take the time and energy to work and make money to pay them for their crafts.

"Wow," I say because I'm not sure what else to say to her invitation. I pictured something totally different when she mentioned burlap and lace. The invite is half a sheet of cream-colored paper with scraps of burlap and lace haphazardly glued on it around the wording.

"Yep. It's terrible, huh?"

"Well," I say, not wanting to be mean.

"You can't lie to your best friend. It's awful. It's proof I should never be allowed to handle a glue stick."

"Well," I say again. "I mean, I think I just had something different in mind."

"I should hope so."

I pick a scrap of burlap from the bag and twist it in my fingers until it looks like a mini rosette. "What if we do more of this style? With lace accents."

Layla shakes her head. "See? How did you do that? I spent eight hours working on that invitation, and you made something gorgeous in fifteen seconds."

"You seriously spent eight hours working on this?"

"Some of us have to be good at shopping." Layla sighs with the burden of her responsibility.

I laugh.

"Anyway, I figured Natalie could use some groceries, so I brought a few things for her too." Layla pulls a frozen lasagna, a few bags of frozen vegetables, some Marie Callendar's frozen meals, two loaves of French bread, and two packages of Oreos from the other bag.

"Wow," I say, this time in admiration. "Natalie will love you."

"That's my goal. I want a beautiful wedding with a killer ceremony. The best way to get to the heart of the pastor is through his wife."

I grin.

Natalie comes walking out of her bedroom at seven thirty, just as I am paying the pizza delivery guy for our extra-large pepperoni pizza. We managed to get thirty invitations put together, and they are scattered all over Natalie's dining room table, glue drying.

"She is *sleeping*?" Natalie whispers, staring open-mouthed at her daughter who is still snoozing away in the swing.

"I swaddled her up. I hope that's okay. She hasn't budged since I laid her down."

Natalie just keeps staring. "You. Are. A. Miracle. Worker. And you can never leave."

"Did you get some sleep?" I ask her, trying to distract her from that thought, because the idea of living with Rick and Natalie is not necessarily a welcome one.

"*Glorious* sleep." She squints at the clock hanging on her wall. "If she's sleeping, I'm going to eat dinner before I wake her up to eat."

"You have to wake babies up to eat?" Layla asks.

"You do when you're first nursing. I'm bursting here."

Layla holds up her hands. "Too much information, Nat."

Natalie opens the pizza box and inhales. "Wow, you guys did not have to get pizza," she says, pulling two slices onto a plate. "This is so not on my list of what I was going to eat after Claire was born."

I grin.

Natalie squeezes her eyes closed. "Lord, thank You for these girls, for their generosity, for their sweet hearts, and for my precious daughter. And may this pizza be free of all calories. Amen."

Layla nods and gets two slices for herself. "Amen and amen."

"So what are these?" Natalie stands with her paper plate and looks at the mess of invitations covering her kitchen table.

"My parents' party. Rick says y'all are coming," Layla says.

"Did he now?" Natalie rolls her eyes and takes a bite of

pizza. "He has no idea what kind of work it is to be a mother and be nursing eight hours a day every single day."

"I for one would be a little weirded out, though, if I walked in and Rick was nursing," I say.

"I'd be *way* more than a little weirded out," Layla declares.

Natalie shrugs. "I don't know. It would be nice to be able to split the nightly duties."

New parents should just avoid thinking.

Chapter 16

I get home Monday night, dragging my duffel bag into my apartment and yawning. I am exhausted. I went straight to work from Natalie's this morning, and I didn't get a complete night's sleep any of the three nights I was there.

I can't imagine being Natalie. At least I know I am going to sleep tonight.

I look at the clock on my phone. It is six. The odds are good that I will be in bed by eight.

Kicking my duffel bag in the general direction of my bedroom, I slump down on the couch and close my eyes. Next week starts the general panic that will be my life for the next two weekends. I should soak up every second I can and just lie on the couch with my eyes closed.

My phone buzzes in my back pocket. I roll over to my side, dig it out, and answer it without checking the caller ID.

"Hello?"

"Paige?"

Tyler. "Hi," I say, shifting back to a sitting position and rubbing my eyes.

"Did I wake you up?"

"Mmm. No."

"You weren't at church."

No, we weren't. Claire finally decided to go to sleep at six in the morning. I spent the whole night taking shifts with Natalie.

"Mm-mmm," I mumble.

"Are you sick? Dying? Take your pulse for me."

"Tyler, I'm fine. I spent the weekend at Natalie's, remember? I didn't get any sleep."

He is quiet for a minute. "Did you just get home?"

"Yeah."

"Well, I'll let you go relax then."

I nod and then realize he never mentioned why he was calling. "Did you need something?" I ask him right before I hang up.

"What?"

"I mean, were you just calling to ask me to take my temperature?"

"Pulse, Paige," he says, and I can hear the grin in his voice. "I'm calling to see if you want to go get dessert at that Italian place by church, but we can definitely do it another night."

My mouth starts watering. But it still isn't enough to keep my eyes open. Sometimes you have to choose sleep over eating.

Even if the eating does involve a delicious hot-baked apple dough thing topped with cinnamon ice cream and the company of a cute, very sweet guy.

I blink. Apparently I *am* tired.

"Another night sounds good." I try to let him down gently.

"How about I come there and we watch a movie or something instead?"

"Um, tonight?"

"Yeah!"

Obviously he hasn't been able to tell how tired I am from my voice. I rub my forehead, thinking about Tyler.

I like the way his hair curls.

"Well," I say, thinking about it. I can maybe stay awake through a movie.

Maybe.

"Paige," Tyler says, half gently, half reprimanding. "No."

"No what?"

"No. You can tell me no."

"I have." Many times over.

"Not often enough. Come on. You can't hurt my feelings. I promise. You need to learn how to do this. Just because there's an opportunity to do something does not mean you have to be the one to do it."

Candace's words from last week swim through my sleep-muddled brain. *"A need does not constitute a call."*

Apparently they think similarly.

"So. Do it."

"Do what?" I ask him.

"Tell me no."

"No."

"There, see? It wasn't that hard."

I smile. "Bye, Tyler."

"Good night, Paige."

I hang up, walk into the kitchen, and pull out a cheese stick. And look at it. How often has this been my dinner over the past month?

I shake my head as I walk to my bedroom. I change into my pajamas, pull back the covers, and see my Bible sitting on my bedside table.

I forgot to pack it and bring it to Natalie's.

I wouldn't have had the time to read there anyway.

I pick it up, but the words all run together. I am too tired to read. I can't even remember the last time I read anything.

But I am serving. Surely that counts for something.

Then I fall asleep.

* * * * *

Tuesday, we have our official staff meeting to discuss the budget. I push the button on the answering machine at ten o'clock so the machine will play my "we're here, just not available" message, grab my file folder with all the banquet information, and walk into Mark's office.

Mark's office is where we always have staff meetings because his is really the only office large enough to have them, other than the waiting room where I work, but that isn't too conducive to meetings.

Candace and Peggy are already in there, sitting on the chairs in front of his desk. Mark nods to the other chair he brought in for me.

"All right," he says. "Let's start this. Paige, I'm going to need a rundown of the hour-by-hour schedule, as well as all of the vendors."

We spend the next hour going over the banquet. It is eighteen days away, and this is the time of year when Mark goes into stressed-out mode. I've heard horror stories about what he is usually like.

He doesn't seem that bad to me.

Probably because I've done all the work on the banquet.

"Wow," he says finally, leaning back in his chair. "You definitely covered all the bases. And the infield. And the outfield."

"Thanks." I tuck all the papers back into the folder. I am glad he likes my work, but something sinks in my stomach. Yet again, I am making myself the perfect secretary.

Why hire a replacement when you don't need one?

My dream of being a counselor is looking further and further away.

* * * * *

Between Friday night's movie night when the girls talked me into watching *Bewitched* and the weekend spent helping Layla iron out the last-minute details for her parents' party that is one week away, I stayed so busy that I barely had time to think.

"I think I'm going to tell them I've made reservations at that really nice restaurant downtown. What's the name of it?" Layla asks, making a pot of coffee on Sunday night. I sit at her kitchen table, staring at the mess of papers, brochures, and plans all over the table.

"Gustavo's?"

"Right. And I'm going to rent a limo to take them to the restaurant, but really it's going to take them to the park where we'll all be."

I nod. "Sounds like a good, expensive plan," I say as she puts the sugar bowl on the table.

"Just the way Dad likes it." She grins.

Layla pours me a cup of coffee and then sits down catty-corner to me with her own cup. "And the weather even looks good."

I nod, scooping a couple of teaspoons of sugar into my cup. I checked the weather as well.

"Do you have a sleeping bag?" Layla asks me, sipping her coffee.

I sigh. She is still bent on spending the night in the park. I told her that surely if we were there by five in the morning, we'd be fine.

"I just want to be safe," she told me on the phone yesterday. "It would ruin everything if the park was already taken."

"I just want *us* to be safe," I tell her now.

"Well, me too. I mean, if we get kidnapped, that would definitely put a damper on the party." Layla grins. "Don't worry about it. I already talked to Peter and he's going to join us."

Now this is awkward. My best friend, her fiancé, and I are all spending the night in a dark, empty park together.

I give her a look. She smiles cheekily. "And don't worry, you get to sleep in between Peter and me."

"Oh joy."

"You can tell me if he snores then."

"Is that a deal breaker?"

She thinks about it. "Not if it's one of those snores that can be solved with one of those weird bandages on his nose."

"What?"

"Sleep Right? Breathe Bright?" Then she grins. "First star I see tonight?"

"You are so strange."

"Oh!" she says quickly and pulls out one of the papers from the stack under the sugar bowl. "That reminds me. I remembered that Aunt MaryAnn and Aunt MaryLou aren't speaking to each other. We'll have to move one of them to a different table."

"MaryAnn and MaryLou," I echo.

"My dad's mom has a thing for Marys." Layla shrugs. "I think Dad's just happy his name isn't Mary Andrew like in *Kate and Leopold*."

I grin.

We switch the aunts around, and then Layla sits back, sipping her coffee and nodding at the table seating chart. "Perfect."

"When are the tables getting there?" She rented the tables and chairs from a place in town.

"Noon, I think. Which gives us about five hours before people start showing up to decorate. The band is getting there at four thirtyish. And the invitations told everyone to get there by five thirty at the latest."

"And your parents come at six," I say.

"Right."

We both sit quietly, staring at the mess on the table for a few minutes, sipping our coffee.

"I can't believe it's almost here," Layla says. "All this work. And it's almost over."

"Your mom and dad are going to be so happy." I smile at her. "This really is about the sweetest thing ever."

"Well, I mean, they did everything for me. I figure this is the least I can do for them." She gets up to refill her coffee mug. "Now," she says as she comes back over with the coffeepot to top mine off, "let's talk about you."

"What about me?"

"I don't know. We've been so busy with this party planning and you've been so nuts with the banquet stuff and church stuff that I feel like we haven't talked about anything but business in forever. What's going on?" She puts the coffeepot back and sits down again.

I rub my finger on the coffee cup, thinking.

And then think some more.

Once you take out the party, the banquet, and the church-related stuff, I have very little left to talk about.

I work. But that is mostly last-minute details for the banquet lately.

Layla is still talking. "Like, I mean, what have you been reading lately? Oh and I saw this skirt at T. J. Maxx the other day that I totally want to show you because you could definitely make one just like it and it would be adorable."

When was the last time I sewed, much less read my Bible or even a different book? I rub a hand through my hair, still thinking. I love to sew. I love to read. I love to work out, and goodness knows, by the way my jeans are currently fitting, I haven't even had time for that lately.

Layla is just looking at me, and I blink. "Sorry, what?"

"I said, what are you reading in your Bible right now?"

"Oh. Well, I haven't really had a lot of time lately." I fidget, feeling the twinge of guilt that I hate. I hurry on. "But I've been serving. A lot. I figure that has to count for something, right?"

Layla swallows her coffee and shrugs. "I really appreciate all you're doing for me with this party, but if we weren't ever talking in the middle of it, I'd really miss you." She shrugs again. "I know that I've asked you to do a ton and I really do need to stop doing that, but, friend—you also need to feel free to tell me no. I'll live, you know."

I smile shortly at her.

"I mean, if you're sacrificing things like your devotional time for this . . ." She pauses and then shakes her head. "It's totally not worth that, Paige."

I don't say anything. Just keep rubbing my coffee mug with my thumb.

Thinking.

What if service for God isn't the same thing as time with Him?

My stomach gets tight at that thought.

I guess Layla can tell how uncomfortable I am, because she switches to yet another uncomfortable topic.

"And then there's the matter of Tyler."

I try to hold back the sigh.

"Spare me the dramatic sound effects, Paige. He obviously likes you. And for goodness' sake, I hope you like him. He's smart, he's sweet, he seems to have a good thing going with God." She ticks the points off on her fingers. "If you tell me that he has asked you out and you've said no, I'll cry right here into my coffee."

It looks like there are going to be some things I do not discuss with my best friend. Salty coffee is just no good unless there's a dose of caramel in there too, and this is just the plain stuff.

"Paige," Layla says, her voice softening. She reaches over and grabs my hand, making me look her in the eyes. "Look, I've been waiting for a great guy to come along for you for pretty much forever. Especially since you seem to attract every weirdo in the state, including my brother."

I smile. That is a long, complicated story.

"Just give it a chance. That's all I'm saying." Then she nods. "Now. Go home. Don't think about the party or the banquet the rest of the night, okay? And actually, I don't even want your help until Friday night at the park."

"Layla," I protest.

"No, I'm serious."

"You have way too much to do."

"What?" She shrugs. "We've already done everything. The caterer is delivering, the florist is delivering, the chairs and table and dance floor are being delivered. The only thing I have to do is pick up the linens from Aunt MaryAnn and I'm done." She rolls her eyes. "Surely I can accomplish that."

She has a point.

I drive home and climb the stairs to my dark, quiet apartment. The silence has never really bothered me, but tonight, for whatever reason, it's so quiet that it almost feels loud.

I lock the door behind me and sit on the couch.

When did I get so busy?

I've always been one of those people who has a lot going on, but never like this. Last year, I worked forty-hour weeks, went on the occasional date on Friday nights, spent the weekends crafting, watching movies, hanging out with Layla, and then felt rested and ready for Monday.

Every week.

I used to be able to read my Bible for over an hour if I wanted to at night. I never fell asleep during a devotional.

Ever.

I sigh, close my eyes, and lean my head back.

"What should I do, Lord?"

I honestly can't see any way to cut anything out of my life—without letting someone down.

Again, Candace's words filter through my brain.

"A need does not constitute a call."

What does that even mean?

Chapter 17

I arrive to work on Monday feeling haggard.

Which is not a word I like using to describe myself. Particularly since I immediately think of those awful troll dolls that were popular when I was a kid. I look at my reflection in my rearview mirror and wince.

I should have used more hairspray today. Not to mention more blush. My face looks stark and white.

"Wow, Paige . . ." Candace looks up from my desk when I walk in. She makes a face at me. "Sleep much?"

"I'm fine."

She pulls a file from my drawer, stands from my chair, and walks over to me, frowning. "Don't take this the wrong way, sweetie, but when I was twenty-two years old, I looked a lot younger than you."

Well, it isn't the sweetest thing she's ever said to me.

Peggy comes in then, holding a cup of coffee, her bifocals perched on the end of her nose. "Can you grab that Myerson file too, Candace?" She looks over and sees me. "Are you feeling okay, Paige?"

"I'm fine."

"She's not fine," Candace says to Peggy.

Peggy looks at me over her glasses, and I suddenly have a flashback to when I was eight and got sent to the principal's office for writing notes during class.

"I'm *fine*," I insist.

Peggy just narrows her eyes at me. Then she exchanges a glance with Candace, who nods.

"Go home, Paige," Peggy says.

"I'm sorry, what?"

"Go home," Candace says this time. "You are not welcome here."

"Guys, listen, it's sweet of you to be concerned, but I'm—"

"You're not fine," Candace interrupts.

Peggy comes over and leans up against my desk. "Go home. Candace and I can take turns covering the phones today. Go read. Go watch a movie. Go take a bath. I don't care. Do whatever it is that you haven't had the time to do in the last six months."

"I can't take off work right before the banquet. Are you kidding? Mark would kill me."

Candace shrugs. "He won't kill you. Besides, you're working overtime all day next Saturday. Consider this part of your weekend."

I stare at them, but they just calmly return my gaze.

"Bye, Paige!" Candace says, perkily. "Have a great day! Thanks for stopping by."

Peggy grins. "See you tomorrow."

I gape at them but they immediately set to work ignoring me. Candace starts writing down all the voice-mail messages, and Peggy leans over to check the e-mails.

After five minutes of being ignored, I finally walk out.

Now what am I going to do?

I stare into the sunlight of the beautiful spring-like day and suddenly feel completely giddy. I have the whole day to do whatever I want.

The *whole day*.

I don't even know where to begin. I climb back in my car and just sit there, feeling this huge mix of relief, excitement, guilt, and exhaustion.

I decide to tackle the exhaustion first and drive straight to the closest drive-thru Starbucks and get myself an iced venti caramel macchiato, and since it's a special day, I get extra caramel drizzled on top.

Then I go home. I change out of my skirt into a pair of yoga pants and a short-sleeve shirt, find my favorite fuzzy slippers, and grab my Bible.

First things first.

I read a couple of psalms while sipping my macchiato and then flip over to the New Testament. I turn pages until I am in Luke.

The story of Jairus and his daughter catches my eye.

I've read the story before, but I start reading it again. Jairus's daughter was very sick, so Jairus did the one thing he could to help her — he ran to Jesus and begged Him to come heal his daughter.

Jesus agreed and started that way, but on His way there, He got sidetracked by a frail woman who had been bleeding for twelve years. In the meantime, one of Jairus's servants came and told Jairus that his daughter had died.

I read it, my heart hurting for Jairus. He did all he could. He went to Jesus. He asked for help. Jesus even said yes.

And still his daughter died.

If only Jesus had hurried.

I swallow my coffee. Come to think of it, I can't remember a time when Jesus did rush. Even when one of His best friends was dying, it still took Jesus a good three days to get to Lazarus.

Why did He wait? Why did He go so slowly sometimes?

I leave my Bible open on the couch and go get my glue gun and my half-finished wreath. I know Jesus cared. The Bible tells over and over about how God is love and how Jesus loved.

So why wait?

I plug my glue gun in and wait for the glue to melt. I have the muslin rosettes all ready to go. It is a huge grapevine wreath, and I love the idea of little clusters of rosettes glued all over it.

Why did You wait, Lord? Why didn't You hurry and heal the little girl? Or Lazarus?

Jairus even had to stand there and watch while the woman who had been sick for twelve years — the exact age of Jairus's daughter — got healed instead of his little girl.

I bite my lip and press a rosette into place.

Jesus, that must have broken Jairus's heart.

I finish gluing the rosettes on the wreath and stand back, admiring it. It turned out exactly how I envisioned it several months ago.

I pick up my Bible again.

Jesus was speaking to Jairus. "Do not be afraid any longer; only believe, and she will be made well."

I stare at those words for a long time.

Do not be afraid any longer.

Do not be afraid any longer.

Jesus didn't care. He didn't care about the things that didn't matter. He didn't care about the people pushing Him to do things on their timetable and not His. He didn't care about rushing around, trying to heal every person in the world.

He didn't care about pleasing people.

But He did care about Jairus. And He obviously cared about Jairus's daughter, since He then went to Jairus's house and raised her from the dead.

Maybe He cared so much that He waited to answer Jairus until the moment when every last hope was gone and all he could do was turn to Jesus.

Lord, I'm overwhelmed.

Gently, I hear His answer.

I need to cut some things out. I pull my planner out of my purse and look at the full weeks I have ahead.

And then I pick up the phone and dial. I start with Geraldine, the church secretary. "I'll only be able to teach the two-year-old class once a month now," I tell her. It is more important right now that I have time for Jesus to teach me.

I call Rick.

"Hey, what's up, Paige?"

"I want to help the youth group girls, Rick, but I can't help them if I have nothing left to give."

"I agree. Let's talk about you taking a full-time job here instead of working at the agency."

"Not right now," I tell him. "I need to work on me first. I can't come to Sunday school anymore. I need to be in church myself."

Rick gives a soft laugh. "Atta girl," he says after a minute.

"This is exactly what I've been wanting to hear from you for the past six months."

"Why did you keep asking me to do things then?"

"Because I really do want you to come work for the youth group. The girls adore you. You'd be a great asset to this ministry."

"Not right now," I say again.

"But maybe someday. Just pray about it, Paige. That's all I'm asking you to do. And it's about time you learn to say no."

I hang up with Rick and make myself a sandwich and sit down to watch HGTV until I fall asleep, somewhere around someone finding a new home with a great backyard.

I wake up at four.

And for the first time in months, I feel rested. I take a long, hot shower and then actually take my time blow-drying my hair and putting on makeup. I haven't played with makeup in months. I even experiment with some shimmery brown eyeshadow and decide it is actually kind of flattering on me.

I curl my hair into long, beachy curls and smile at myself in the mirror. This is the Paige I remember.

My sewing machine is sitting dusty and sad at the bottom of my closet, so I dig out the machine and the box of extra fabric I have and move it all to the kitchen table. Summer is coming, and a long time ago I bought some white eyelet fabric that will make a really cute skirt.

While I sew, I think. I pray. I listen for the first time in weeks.

"Do not be afraid any longer."

"A need does not constitute a call."

Sometimes it is okay to not please everyone.

At five thirty, I finish hemming my simple A-line skirt and pick up my cell phone.

"Hey, Paige," Tyler says easily after two rings. "How are you?"

"What are you doing for dinner?" I ask him, feeling a little nervous. I have never asked out a guy—ever.

Ever. Ever. Ever.

But considering he has asked me like twelve times, I figure this is maybe just an overdue response to one of those.

"Dinner, huh?" Tyler drawls, and I hear the smile in his voice.

"Dinner. At California Pizza Kitchen."

"Tonight?"

"Right now."

He laughs. "Well. Pizza sounds a lot better than the instant macaroni and cheese I was about to make."

"Is that a yes?" I fold the skirt up and try not to read too much into how excited I am.

"Yes ma'am. It's a definite yes. I'll even pick you up so you don't have the chance to change your mind."

I grin.

Tyler knocks on my door twenty minutes later, just as I am sliding my dangle earrings through my ears. I changed out of the yoga pants and into jeans, ballet flats, a white lacy cami, and a gray cardigan with three-quarter-length sleeves. I feel like I look cute in an unassuming kind of way.

Unassuming is always a good look to go for when you are the one asking the guy out. I think. Like I said, I don't have a lot of experience with it.

I open the door and Tyler grins at me. "Wow," he says, eyebrows going up. "You look great!"

"Thanks." I feel myself blushing.

"No seriously. You look . . ." He studies me for a minute, and the blush just gets deeper into the marrow of my cheekbones. "I don't know. Happy?" He nods to my hair. "I didn't realize your hair was so long."

Which is probably another way of saying, "Gosh, you've had your hair in a sloppy bun for most of the time I've known you."

"I had a good day," I tell him.

"Yeah? What did you do?"

I grin. "Nothing." And it is actually the honest-to-goodness truth.

We get to the restaurant, which is in an outdoor mall, park in the huge parking lot, walk inside, and discover that there is a thirty-minute wait. "On a Monday?" I ask the hostess, shocked.

She sighs at me, looking frazzled. "You're telling me. I have midterms in two weeks. I was planning on an easy shift and then studying the rest of the night."

"I'm sorry." I look at Tyler. "Want to go somewhere else?"

He shakes his head. "How far does this buzzer thing reach?" He points to the round black disc I hold.

She shrugs. "I don't know. Pretty far."

"We'll be outside then," he says.

We walk back outside. It is cooling off, but in Dallas, that means it's still seventy degrees and about 60 percent humidity. I look up at him. "Well. What do you want to do?"

He points to a bench. "We can just sit there, if you want."

I sit. The bench is facing the parking lot, and it's right between two planters filled with mini trees and flowers. There is music playing and it sounds like Michael Bublé, though I don't recognize the song.

Tyler sits down and smiles at me. "So. Nothing? You didn't do anything all day?"

"I got to work this morning and got sent home."

He squints at me. "You're not sick, right?" He scoots a couple of inches away.

"Relax. I just got a little overwhelmed, that's all."

He looks at me and a strange expression crosses his face, then he blinks it away and smiles. "Well. I won't say I told you so."

"Go ahead and say it."

"I told you so."

"You know, for not knowing me very long, you sure seem to be comfortable telling me exactly what you're thinking," I say, rolling my eyes.

He grins. "So, what do you plan on doing to prevent days like today from happening again?"

"Days like today? Absolutely nothing. Today was great!" I wave my hands as I talk. "I finally finished that wreath I've been trying to finish for the past six weeks. I watched HGTV. I did my makeup. Tyler, I took a *nap*." I grab his forearm. "For like two *hours*." I pull away, shaking my head. "I can't even remember the last time I sat down to watch TV, much less the last time I curled my hair."

"Your hair does look very nice." He grins at me.

"Thank you." I nod. "This is what I used to look like."

"Before what? The Munchkins invaded?"

"You're a dork."

"Speaking of saying exactly what you're thinking." He grins again.

I ignore him. "No, before life got all crazy. Up until today, I thought that God's plan was for me to spend my singleness serving Him with every spare minute of my time."

"And now you don't?" Tyler frowns.

"No, now I just have a different idea of what serving really means."

The buzzer goes off in my hands before Tyler can respond. We walk inside and hand it to the hostess, who then grabs a couple of menus and leads us to the far back corner of the restaurant. "Is this table okay?" She points to a booth in the corner.

"Great, thank you," Tyler tells her.

I sit down and take my menu from the hostess. I love California Pizza Kitchen and I'm not entirely sure why. It's loud, the baby two tables across from us is screaming while his frazzled mother scrambles around trying to get him to stop, there is what seems like a lady and her adult son debating some political policy next to us, and the whole place smells vaguely of pepperoni and yeast.

Even so. I always ask to come here every year on my birthday when Mom and Dad come into town.

I barely glance at the menu before closing it.

"Already know what you're getting?" Tyler asks.

"Yep." I get the same thing every single time I come. Pear and Gorgonzola Pizza, mango iced tea, and if I'm still hungry or feel like having pizza for lunch the next day, tiramisu for dessert.

It is delicious.

Tyler wrinkles his nose when I tell him what I'm ordering. "Pears on pizza?"

"What? People put dead, canned, salty fish on pizza. I ask you, which one is weirder?"

"Whatever. I'm getting the meat lovers." He folds his menu and sets it on the table in front of him. "So, what did you mean by you have a new idea of what serving God looks like?"

I sigh, trying to think of the right way to put what I am feeling into words. I see why the Bible mentions that the Holy Spirit prays for us when words just won't work. Words lack a lot.

The waitress comes by then, which gives me another couple of minutes to figure out how to phrase it. We order, she nods and takes our menus with her.

Tyler looks over at me, waiting.

"It's just . . ." I spread my hands out, thinking. "So, before yesterday, I would have said that I am serving God by everything I'm doing."

"Okay," Tyler says.

I tell him about reading the story of Jairus and his daughter. The waitress brings our drinks, and I play with my straw wrapper while I talk. "So, Jesus didn't even rush when it was something like that," I say.

Tyler nods. "I've actually noticed that before. Jesus knew He only had thirty-three years here, but He didn't hurry around. He taught, He spent time with His disciples, and He spent time with God."

"Right." I take a sip of my delicious mango tea and nod. "So, I've basically decided my priorities need to be worked on a little bit."

"Good." Tyler grins at me. "And I'm stoked to see that California Pizza Kitchen with me made the priority list." He reaches across the table and picks up my fingers, rubbing his thumb along my knuckles.

I feel myself blushing, and I hope the poor restaurant lighting is working in my favor. I like Tyler. I think he is funny, and he seems to have a good head on his shoulders.

But goodness knows I'm not ready for a real relationship right now.

I need to get my other serious relationship up and running normally again first.

Thankfully, the waitress shows up with our pizzas right then. Tyler ducks his head and squeezes his eyes shut when she leaves, still holding my hand.

"Lord, thank You for this time with Paige, thank You for this delicious dinner, and please just continue to guide Paige in the right way. Amen." He smiles at me and lets go of my hand.

"Amen," I echo, pulling a slice of pizza off the plate.

"So, are you excited for the next couple of weeks?" Tyler asks, after he swallows a bite of his pizza. "Isn't Layla's parents' thing this weekend?"

I nod. I need to call Layla when I leave here and make sure she doesn't need anything.

Then I catch myself. If Layla needs something, she will call me.

"Yeah." I chew a bite of delectableness and swallow. "She wants me to spend the night in the park with Peter and her on Friday to save the space for the party."

"Sounds good and awkward," Tyler says.

"See? Thank you. I knew I wasn't the only one who thought so."

"I've got an idea," he says a few seconds later. "How about Peter and I stay the night in the park and make sure no one takes it the next morning? You and Layla can join us for a picnic or something there that night and then just bring us breakfast in the morning."

"Really?" I try not to get too excited at the prospect of not having to spend the night in the park. Not only was I going to be sleeping between my best friend and her fiancé, the idea of staying the night someplace so badly lit and so close to bugs and all sorts of nature doesn't sound like a great night of sleep to me.

"As long as you bring coffee," Tyler says. Then he takes a deep breath, looking at a slice of pizza. "Lots and lots of coffee."

"Wow, Tyler, I don't know what to say."

"You'd better just go ahead and say yes. I've even got camping supplies. It'll be like a bonding thing with Peter."

"Yes, well, good luck with that," I say quietly and then immediately regret it. "Sorry."

Tyler grins. "Maybe he's just more of a quiet guy. I mean, come on, all I saw growing up was how the girls always fawned over the silent, stoic types." He rolls his eyes at me. "Needless to say, I wasn't either one."

I nod. Tyler is not very quiet, that is a fact.

"Well, it's the whole Mr. Darcy image that's killing you," I tell him. "No one does silent and stoic better than him."

"I'll take your word for it."

"You don't have to just take my word. I actually own the movie. You can watch it." I grin. "I even own both the five-hour version and the two-hour version."

"There is a *five-hour* version?" Tyler shakes his head.

"Seriously. Who has five hours to watch a movie?"

"I think we'll have more than five hours at the park on Friday. I'll bring my laptop and we can watch the whole thing."

"Or," Tyler says, overannunciating the word, "we can do something fun."

"What is more fun than five hours of Mr. Darcy?"

"Oh, let me think," Tyler says sarcastically.

"See? It's hard to even think of more fun ideas."

"That is not the problem. The problem is so many ideas are better that I'm having trouble narrowing them down."

I laugh.

He drops me off at my apartment two hours later. I am stuffed to the top of my scalp, and I even have a box with half my pizza left over. Tyler talked me into saving the rest of the pizza for tomorrow and splitting the tiramisu with him tonight.

It was a good decision.

"Thanks for dinner," I say for the twelfth time as we stand at the base of my stairs. "I really didn't mean for you to pay."

Somehow, he talked the waitress into giving him the check while I was in the restroom, even though I specifically told her when I ordered that dinner was on me.

Tyler grins at me, and I can kind of see how he managed to coerce the waitress into doing what he asked. He has a really nice smile. And the subtle look in his blue eyes is making my stomach feel squirrely.

I clear my throat and look away. "Well, thanks again." I try to sound nonchalant. I hope he is picking up my vibes about this not really being a date as much as just two friends hanging out.

"Sure thing," he says. "So, I'll see you on Wednesday night at youth group. Rick says we're meeting early again."

"Of course we are." I nod.

"And I'll get in touch with Peter about Friday, if you'll let Layla know."

I nod again. "Will do. Have a good night, Tyler."

"You too, Paige. Thanks for letting me join you for dinner."

Tyler waits until I've climbed the stairs and unlocked my door before he waves and walks back to his truck in the parking lot. I close and lock the door behind me.

I can't even remember the last time I had such a great day.

Chapter
18

The week passes by in a blur of phone calls from Layla with last-minute favors, last-minute work on the banquet, and quiet nights at home. Other than Wednesday night, I spend every night at my apartment, either working on things for Layla while movies play in the background or quietly eating my dinner while reading my Bible.

It is a relaxing but fast week.

I leave work on Friday and drive straight to a local barbecue place. Who am I kidding—I won't be able to eat out until Christmas, but at least I am going out on a good note. I buy a huge container of shredded beef doused in the infamous sauce, a package of rolls, coleslaw, baked potatoes, creamed corn, and two gallons of sweet tea.

We do picnics right here in Texas.

Layla is pulling up to the park just as I am.

"And the weather is even supposed to be gorgeous!" she squeals, getting out of her car without even a hello.

"Hello." I grin at her.

"Hi. So, I think this is a good idea," she says, coming

over to my car and tucking a stray strand of hair back into her bun. She looks adorable. She is wearing jeans, a flowing pastel-pink tank top, and a light blue cardigan. Her hair is in a low bun and she has a headband on.

If I dressed like that, I'd look like a commercial for Easter candy, but Layla is my friend who can pull off anything. It causes both admiration and envy.

But I'm getting over it. Sort of.

I hand Layla the barbecue and pick up the box with all the sides. "We'll have to come back for the tea."

"Good grief, Paige, how many of us are there going to be tonight?"

"Layla, boys eat a lot." A lot more than I ever imagined. I watched Tyler polish off his dinner, a slice of my pizza, a salad, and half the dessert at dinner the other night. Now I know why Natalie was always complaining about her grocery bills after she married Rick.

Layla just mumbles something under her breath.

I walk across the grass to the gazebo and set the box down. "So." I stand, hands on my hips. "What's the plan of action?"

"Well, the biggest thing is going to be letting people who come by know that we are reserving the gazebo, the big open space right there, and the area by the parking lot." Layla sets the barbecue beside the box and points out the area she is talking about.

"The band will be performing in here, and the dance floor will be right there." She points to the area right below the gazebo. "The tables for the food will be along that side of the dance floor, and then I've got tables coming for people to eat at."

I nod. "This is going to be beautiful, Layla."

"I hope so. I picked up a bunch of twinkle lights at the dollar store this week. Want to help me wrap the gazebo while we wait for the boys?"

We spend the next ten minutes working on some of the gazebo, though I spend more time swiping away cobwebs with a napkin than wrapping lights around the posts. Tyler shows up right at six wearing athletic shorts and a University of Texas T-shirt.

"I have a ladder I could have brought." He watches us stand on the benches that line the gazebo walls.

This particular gazebo always makes me want to burst out into "You are sixteen going on seventeen," from *The Sound of Music*.

But I refrain tonight. We want Tyler to stay, after all, and my voice isn't known for causing gasps of enraptured awe.

Layla shrugs. "Eh. We can stand on the benches for now. I've got my uncle bringing in some other lighting for the dance floor tomorrow, and I bet he'll have a ladder with him. We can finish putting up all these little twinkle lights everywhere then."

Peter pulls up and gets out of his car. He pockets his keys in his Nike shorts and walks over. Layla waves from on top of the bench. "Hi, honey!"

"Hey," Peter says, smiling shortly at her.

"Hi, Peter." Tyler reaches his hand out to shake Peter's. "How was your day?"

Peter shrugs and watches us work on the lights for a minute.

I will take that as, "Eh, it was okay."

I guess Tyler decides to do the same because he shrugs and turns back to us. "What can I do for you guys?"

"There's a big blanket in my trunk for us to use during dinner." I dig my keys out of my pocket and toss them to Tyler. "And a grocery sack with plates and cups and stuff. If you will grab those things, we can eat while it's still mildly warm."

Tyler nods and walks across the grass to my car. He comes back a few minutes later, and Layla announces that she is starving and it's time to eat.

Tyler says a quick prayer for us, and then we load up our plates and sit in a circle on the blanket on the grass. It really is a beautiful night. The sun is starting to fall and the humidity level is dropping. The guys will have a nice night here.

Thank goodness all my fears about rain have been wrong.

"So, I have prepared a spreadsheet." Layla wipes her mouth with a napkin and digs in her back pocket.

"Oh boy," I say, rolling my eyes. Layla is Queen of Last-Minute Organization. The second we are almost done with something is when she will spend eighty hours writing up an organizational chart.

It made studying with her in high school migraine inducing.

"Relax, Paige. It's just a list of everything that needs to be done tomorrow, and see? It even has a little box next to each item to write a little check mark in." She smiles proudly at her three-page list. "I am on top of things."

"Eating those motivational mints again?" I ask her.

"Spearmint." She nods.

"What time will you guys be back in the morning?" Tyler asks, finishing off his barbecue sandwich.

I look over at Layla, who shrugs. "I was thinking around

seven," she says. "We'll come and start getting stuff set up and y'all can go home and sleep or shower or whatever and then maybe around twoish you can come back and watch the park while Paige and I go shower and get ready."

"What time does the party start?" Peter asks.

"Five," Layla says.

Layla's parents are coming at six. It is all falling together. I look up at the darkening sky and then at my watch. It's seven thirty. That gives us an hour and a half to do the dinner Layla has catered and then plenty of time afterward to dance by the light of the twinkle lights and whatever lighting her uncle is bringing.

It is going to be beautiful.

Layla finishes her dinner and lies back on the blanket, looking up at the sun-streaked sky. "Jesus, please keep it from raining tomorrow."

"Amen." I nod.

"And please help Aunt Wendy to remember that it's a surprise party and not tell my parents, and please help her arrive sober so she won't hit on Peter and Tyler."

"Amen," both the boys say simultaneously.

I bite back a grin and lie back next to Layla. Layla's Aunt Wendy is one of those women who is ridiculously fun but also really needs Jesus and really doesn't get that.

We are all quiet for a few minutes. It is very peaceful in the park right now, lying on my back, the grass soft under the blanket, the sun slowly dipping behind the trees. A few birds are singing and I hear one early cicada whirring in the trees.

I could fall asleep right here.

I close my eyes and yawn. Today has been another good

day. I went to work, did some stuff on the banquet, and spent two hours talking to three people about the adoption process on the phone.

One lady ended up crying right before we hung up. "Thank you so much," she sniffled. "My husband and I have been trying to have children for six years. You are the first glimmer of hope I've had that maybe we'll someday have a baby."

I almost joined her in crying.

I open my eyes and look over at Layla. She is staring up at the sky, curling a tendril of hair around and around her finger.

It occurs to me then that all of us are waiting for something, just like that lady. I am waiting for life to calm down. Layla is waiting for this party to be over so she can then start waiting to marry Peter. And I'm sure the guys are waiting for something as well.

Tyler lies back on the blanket a foot away from me. "So," he says, staring up at the sky. "What are you thinking about?"

I look over at him. "What are you waiting for?"

"What?"

"In life. What are you waiting for?"

He looks up at the sky again, expression thoughtful. He has a slight blond fuzziness on his face from not shaving recently, and the sky makes his eyes very blue.

It suddenly hits me that Tyler is a very attractive guy.

"I don't know," he says slowly, a few minutes later, still looking at the sky. "A promotion. Marriage. Kids. Football season to start up again."

I smile at the last one.

"Why?" He turns his head to look at me.

I shrug. "Just a conversation I had with a lady today. She and her husband have been trying six years to have kids."

"Wow," Layla says. "That's a long time. Are they going to adopt?"

I nod. When we hung up, I scheduled her for an initial meeting with Peggy. "What are you waiting for, Layla?" I ask, even though I already know.

"Short term?" She turns her head toward me. "I'm waiting for the stars to come out. Long term? I'm waiting until I get married so I can cut my hair short with no regrets."

I laugh. Tyler grins.

"What are you waiting for, Peter?"

"Layla."

One word, which is typical of him, but I actually like his answer. I smile.

"How about you, Paige?" Tyler asks.

I look up at the sky. For a long time, I've been waiting for life to slow down, make sense, have a purpose. I am waiting to become a real counselor, not just a secretary. At some point I want to get married, but that thought scares me more than excites me at the moment. I am waiting for life to turn out like I always imagined it would as a little girl.

It strikes me while I lie there on the grass, staring up at the darkening sky, surrounded by my best friend, someone who is quickly becoming another great friend, and Peter, that I am completely happy. I'm not stressed. I'm not thinking about what my next ten minutes will hold.

Maybe I've been waiting for this.

"I don't know," I say, taking the easy way out rather than trying to put all my jumbled thoughts into words.

"Wimp." Tyler grins over at me.

"Wait, can I change my answer?" Layla asks.

"Sure," I say.

"I'm waiting for the new Panda Express entrée to be released. I've been seeing the little hints on their Facebook page for the last two months." She squints at the sky. "Chicken. Tangy. Spicy and sweet." She shakes her head. "I'm voting it's something with pineapple."

I start laughing.

"I'm waiting for home-cooked meals." Peter grins. I am fairly certain this is the first time I've ever heard him make a joke.

"Hello? Did you not hear how excited I am for Panda's new entrée?"

"I'm waiting for Starbucks to start a delivery service," I say.

"Pineapple. Tangy. Spicy," Layla repeats, ticking the points off on her fingers.

"I thought you were only guessing the pineapple."

"It's an educated guess, Peter," Layla says.

I look up. At some point, it got dark. I squint up at the sky and see a couple of stars starting to make their appearance.

"Tomorrow is going to be a crazy day," Layla says quietly a few minutes later.

"But tonight is nice." I smile over at her.

She grins at me and nods. "Tonight is perfect."

At ten o'clock, Layla and I finally stand up and say our good nights. "We'll be here first thing in the morning," Layla tells Peter. She gathers up the blanket we were lying on, and Peter walks her back to her car.

I pick up the leftover bread from dinner as Tyler grabs

the cooler I brought for the leftover meat and walks with me over to my car. "Well," I say, looking at Tyler. This is awkward. Peter and Layla are a couple. Tyler and I are just friends, but something about the starlight makes everything seem more romantic than it actually is.

"Well," he says, smiling at me. "I hope you sleep well."

"I hope *you* sleep well."

"Me too." He grins. "I think I'll be fine. I can usually sleep anywhere."

"Air mattresses?"

"Yeah."

"Backseats of cars?"

"Yes."

"Airplanes?" I ask.

"Yep."

I sigh. "I'm jealous."

"It's a gift." He shrugs. "With great sleeping talent comes great sleeping responsibility."

"You are very strange, do you know that?" I ask him with a smile.

He looks at me for a second, smiling, though it is dark and I can't really make out his expression very well. Then I feel his hand on mine, squeezing it gently, lightly rubbing his thumb along the back of my hand.

"Sweet dreams, Paige," he says softly. He drops my hand and waves, walking over to his truck, then opens the passenger door and pulls out a sleeping bag.

It is best if I ignore the ten million grasshoppers suddenly residing in my stomach. I wave at Layla. "I'll pick you up at six forty-five."

"Okay. Night, Paige."

I drive home, climb the stairs to my dark apartment, change into my pajamas, crawl into bed, and flick on my lamp on the bedside table, pulling my Bible over. I stare at my hand.

Surely Tyler held my hand tonight out of friendliness.

Surely.

Even so, the grasshoppers are still there.

I open my Bible to the Psalms. Psalm 40 catches my eye.

"I waited patiently for the LORD; *he turned to me and heard my cry. . . . He put a new song in my mouth, a hymn of praise to our God. Many will see and fear and put their trust in the* LORD.*"*

A new song.

I like the idea of a new song to God.

* * * * *

Six o'clock comes much too early. I squint at my alarm clock and groan. But then I stop groaning because at least I am waking up in a comfortable, warm bed and not in a sleeping bag on the hard ground.

I need to do something nice for Tyler to tell him thank you.

Since we are coming back to shower after we set up, I skip showering this morning and just yank my hair into a sloppy bun. I pull on jeans, a T-shirt, and sneakers, add a little bit of mascara, and grab my purse and the bag of stuff I'm thinking Layla will probably forget, like scissors, tape, twisty ties for securing the twinkle lights, and stuff like that.

I leave my apartment at 6:20 and go to Starbucks. I am fairly certain Caramel Frappucinos are a universal drink, and it is still pretty cold outside, so they'll stay semicold in the car for the next twenty minutes. I buy two venti Frappucinos for the boys, venti caramel macchiatos for Layla and me, a couple of apple fritters, and four of their bacon breakfast sandwiches.

My car smells like I imagine heaven will. I get to Layla's apartment, and she is already out front with six boxes of stuff on the curb next to her.

"Good morning!" she says all cheerfully when I pull up.

"Hi, Layla." I smile. Sometimes I hate that she looks so cute so effortlessly. She doesn't have any makeup on at all, her hair is in a long braid over her shoulder, and she is wearing jeans and a teal long-sleeve shirt.

"Trunk or backseat?" She points to the boxes.

"Probably both." I pop the trunk and help her load. She opens the back door and inhales deeply.

"Oh wow, I am moving into your car."

"You might get a little cramped after a while."

"What on earth did you buy?" She keeps sniffing. "Coffee? Caramel? Bacon?"

"Yes, yes, and yes. Goodness. You should start fighting crime with your nose." I grin at her over the box I am carrying as she slides another box in the backseat.

"I've been asked by the FBI a few times." She nods. "But you know, it's one of those mixing-business-and-pleasure things for me. I just like to smell recreationally too much to ever consider doing it for a job."

I laugh. "You are way too awake this morning. I'm debating whether I should give you this macchiato."

"This is totally adrenaline." Layla climbs into the passenger seat. I slide in behind the wheel and hand her the coffee cup. "I barely slept at all. Come tomorrow, I will be a zombie." She grins at me. "Thanks for the coffee, friend. And for everything you've done for this party. I owe you a million times over."

I wave a hand. "You'd do the same for me."

And she would.

We get to the park right at seven. It is completely bright outside, the birds are chirping, and there is not a cloud in sight.

Perfect day for a party.

Peter is awake, but Tyler, miracle of all miracles, is still in his sleeping bag. He has a pillow over his head to block the sun, so I imagine he is probably just dozing.

Layla carries one of the Frappucinos over to Peter, and I guess their talking wakes Tyler up for good because he pushes the pillow off his face and sits up, stretching. I hide my grin behind my coffee cup. His hair is a complete mess. His face is all scratchy, his eyes bleary.

I walk over and hand him the Frappucino. "Good morning."

"Morning, Paige," he says, his voice rough and an octave deeper than usual. He smiles at me and takes the Frappucino. "Thanks."

"How was it last night?"

"Good." He nods and sips the drink. "I really need to find a place to brush my teeth."

"That would probably be good. Y'all can head home now if you want."

"What are you guys going to do?" He slides out of his sleeping bag and stands up, stretching again.

"I'll need to check Layla's spreadsheet." I roll my eyes.

"I saw that, Paige. The spreadsheet is a brilliant idea."

Layla pulls it out of her back pocket and hands it to me.

I give her the bag of breakfast, and she digs through it to get an apple fritter. "Come to mama," she whispers to it.

"I have never understood that expression." I open the folded spreadsheet. "Kind of implies cannibalism. And not just cannibalism, but cannibalism of your own flesh and blood." I make a face.

"You think too much," Layla says.

Peter walks over, rubbing his short dark hair. "Hi, Paige."

"Hi, Peter."

"Thanks for the coffee."

"Thanks for spending the night here," I say.

Tyler pulls his phone out of his pocket and squints. "Seven fifteen. How about I run home, change clothes, brush my teeth, and I'll be back in about thirty minutes to help?"

"Nope." Layla shakes her head. "You can go home and take a nap and then come back around two."

"I don't need a nap, Layla."

"Yes, you do."

"Layla, I'm a big boy," Tyler says to her. "I think I can tell if I need a nap or not."

He doesn't say it meanly, just matter-of-factly. Layla looks at him for a minute and then hands him a bacon sandwich. "At least don't argue with me about eating."

"I never argue about eating bacon." He takes a huge bite.

Both of the guys end up leaving around nine and Layla turns to me, hands on her hips, sunglasses covering her eyes. "All right. Go time."

We unload all the boxes from my car, finish our Starbucks drinks, and have just started working on the lights in the gazebo again when Tyler pulls back into the parking lot.

Layla stands on one of the benches while I hold a huge mess of twinkle lights and slowly feed them to her. We watch as he unloads a ladder and a toolbox from the back of his truck. Then she nudges me with her foot.

"Um, ow." I rub my rib cage.

Layla nods to Tyler walking over. "Nice. Helpful. Pretty darn cute in the morning. And I guarantee he's not here for me."

I hate that I blush.

Layla laughs.

"What?" Tyler asks, walking up the gazebo steps with the ladder.

"Nothing," I say quickly before Layla opens her mouth. "You brought a ladder," I say, trying to distract them both.

"Yep." Tyler nods to the top of the gazebo. "We can string the lights all the way up now if you want to, Layla."

"Yes, please." She smiles sweetly at him. The second he looks down to step up on his ladder, she nudges me in the rib cage with her foot again.

"Will you stop that?" I hiss at her.

"What's that?" Tyler asks.

"Nothing," I say again. "What time are the tables getting here again, Layla?"

She looks at the clock on her cell phone. "Anytime between now and noon, I think."

We are just about finished with the gazebo when the people with the tables show up, and Peter arrives right after that. To be honest, I am amazed that there hasn't been anyone else at the park yet. The day is gorgeous, and while this park doesn't have a playground like a few of the other ones in the neighborhood, it has huge willow trees all around it, rustling in the slight breeze.

It is going to be a great party.

It takes the two men with the table company about forty-five minutes to set up the sixteen tables and all the chairs around the gazebo. Then they start in on the dance floor. That takes another hour because each piece has to be puzzled into the others. That and apparently they can only work one guy at a time on that while the other guy tries to talk to me.

"So, what's the party for?" both of them start the conversation with.

I finally make an excuse to walk back over to the boxes and try to dig through for the tablecloths.

"You have a yes face," Tyler says, coming over, backhanding his shiny forehead.

"What?"

"Your face. It's too nice."

It sounds like a compliment but not necessarily with the tone he is using. I mash my lips together for a minute. "Um. Thank you."

He grins. "No, I meant, you just have a friendly face." Then he frowns. "And a nice face. Don't get me wrong. It's nice and friendly."

Layla comes over and hefts one of the boxes holding sixteen lanterns on her hip, groaning slightly. "Oh my gosh," she mutters.

"I got it." Tyler takes the box from her and carries it to the gazebo.

"That was not what I was talking about," Layla says, rolling her eyes. "You two are ridiculously cute."

I ignore her comment and focus on the tablecloths. "All blue?"

"Blue on the bottom. White lace on the top."

"Pretty." I nod.

"They were Mom's wedding colors."

"Where do these go?" I look through a box with framed pictures of her parents through the years.

"I'm going to scatter them around. Think that would be too weird?"

Somehow I know that even if I think it is weird, it won't matter at all in what Layla ends up doing. So I shrug. "Nope."

"Good."

The table guys leave at noon, and we spend the next two hours getting the tablecloths and table settings done. The same florist I talked to from At First Sight shows up at one thirty with all of the centerpieces and two huge arrangements for the gazebo.

By the time three o'clock comes around, I am exhausted and I have no idea how all of us are going to make it through the party and then clean up afterward. Apparently, another stop at Starbucks is in my future.

Layla comes over and rubs her forehead. The day is unusually warm for the end of February.

"Ready for a shower?" she asks me, handing me a bottle of water.

"Are you?"

She squints at the park. Somehow between this morning and now, the plain white gazebo has been transformed into a stage. Yellow roses tumble out of different pots and huge white lanterns on the steps of the gazebo. The light blue tablecloths flutter gently in the soft breeze, small squares of white lace are turned so the corners barely fall over the edges of the tables. Layla has arranged different sizes and styles of white lanterns on the tables with the yellow roses, daisies, pictures of her parents in antique-looking frames, and lots of candles.

It is going to look like a spring fairyland tonight.

I start getting excited for her parents to see it.

Layla is smiling.

"Like it?" I ask her, elbowing her gently.

"Mmm," she says, still smiling. "It's exactly what I hoped for."

I sling my arm around her shoulders and give her a hug. "You realize that you are showing up every daughter on the planet tonight."

She nods. "As it should be."

I laugh.

"Shower time." She pats my hand. She waves to Tyler and Peter. "We're heading home for a bit. Back in an hour!"

They both nod, talking by the gazebo. I have never seen Peter talk to anyone as much as he's been talking to Tyler today.

Tyler is special.

I drive to Layla's apartment, drop her off, and drive straight to mine since I have to be back there in an hour and I am in desperate need of a shower and some makeup. I run up the stairs, lock the door behind me, jump in the shower, and start scrubbing.

I blow-dry my hair straight, add some curls with the curling iron, and take my time doing my makeup. Makeup has always been a challenge for me, unlike Layla who takes to it more naturally than milk chocolate takes to almonds.

I finally get my eye shadow looking the way I want it to. I am going for a slightly smoky look since it is a nighttime party. I found a dress a very long time ago that I've never had the occasion to wear, and tonight seems like a great night for it. It is a light gray dress, knee-length, sleeveless, fluttery, and super soft. The dress is maybe a little summery for the end of February, but I pull a white cardigan over it, which makes the dress look like a springtime outfit.

I am at Layla's apartment fifteen minutes later. She is again waiting for me by the curb, looking gorgeous as always in a blue gauzy dress with a brown belt and heels. She curled her long dark hair into ringlets.

"Wow," I say when she opens the door.

"Same to you. You clean up good, Alder." She grins. "I'll text Tyler and let him know he'll need an extra pair of socks tonight, seeing as how you're going to knock the ones he has on right off."

I roll my eyes but my cheeks warm. Again. All this blushing is not very characteristic of me.

Layla looks at the dashboard clock. "Four thirty. Perfect. The caterer should be showing up in thirty minutes, guests in an hour."

"Hopefully the boys have enough time to shower and get back to the park."

Layla waves a hand. "It seriously takes Peter fifteen minutes to go from absolutely disgusting to good-smelling and adorable. Sometimes I wish I were a man."

"No, you don't." I pull into the park's parking lot.

"Sure I do. No shaving the legs, no wearing makeup, no curling the hair."

I look over at her as I park. "No wearing makeup, no curling the hair," I echo her. "No wearing dresses, no good excuses once a month to binge on chocolate."

She looks down at her dress. "You win."

"Thank you."

We get out and head back over to the gazebo. Peter and Tyler are sitting on the steps, talking. They look up when we walk over.

"Wow," Peter says, smiling at Layla.

"Thank you." She grins.

Tyler just smiles at me, but it isn't a smile I've seen on him before. This one is softer, sweeter.

I'm pretty sure my toes are blushing.

This is getting old.

I quickly try to change the subject. "Y'all need to go shower so you can be here before Layla's parents get here."

They both nod. "We told off a group of little kids trying to have soccer practice," Tyler says.

"Oh, now I feel bad." Layla bites her bottom lip.

"Don't. They are fine. There's another park two minutes away. They just went over there."

While Tyler is talking, the band shows up. The guys say their good-byes and hurry out so they have time to be back before Layla's parents get here.

Layla booked an oldies swing band and I watch them set up and practice. They sound a little like Michael Bublé's music. Layla comes by with a huge stack of plates then, and I go to help.

"Nice band," I say, helping her set the plates and napkins on the table that will also hold the food. We are doing it buffet style but with assigned seating. Layla says it is so her mom doesn't have to sit next to someone who makes her nuts the whole night.

"Still like them?" Layla asks, listening to them practice for a minute. There are seven of them—a guy on a piano, two guitarists, a drummer, a bass player, a violinist, and a cellist. Only the guy on the piano and the girl guitarist do the singing.

They sound good. We chose the right band.

"My only criteria was that they sounded okay and knew songs that Mom and Dad know," Layla says. "Which right away eliminated 98 percent of the bands in the city."

I laugh.

The caterer shows up a little after five, right as some of the guests are arriving. We help her transfer hot serving dishes set over Sterno cans to the table, and then the lady nods once everything is out. "I'll be back around ten to get the dishes," she says to Layla. "Enjoy!"

"Thank you." Layla motions me over and lifts the lid on a steaming bowl. "The Burgundy sauce," she whispers, awe filling her voice. She arranges the food table a little more while she talks to some of her extended family who just arrived. I walk over to the tables to start lighting all the candles.

"Paige Alder." I am on my last table when I hear the voice behind me and bite the inside of my cheek, my chest squeezing tight. I turn around.

Luke Prestwick is standing there, all dressed up in a black suit and gray tie. He smiles at me, holding out his hand. "It has been a long time."

Chapter 19

Luke looks good, but then he always did. Same thick, straight dark hair. Same big smile. Same chocolate brown eyes.

Why didn't I figure on Luke coming? And why didn't Layla warn me?

I look around for her, but she is apparently in the middle of a big group of Prestwicks over by the stage.

I finally settle my gaze back on Luke and smile. "It's good to see you, Luke." I put my hand in his, aiming for a brief handshake.

He holds my hand with both of his. "You look beautiful, Paige."

This is just awkward. We broke up. He moved. I closed and shelved the book on Luke Prestwick, and as far as I'm concerned, on the shelf is a good place for him.

"Paige, do we need to set up anything else?"

Suddenly Tyler is standing beside me, looking from me to Luke and then down to my hand in both of his.

Awkwardness is just flowing tonight.

Somehow I ratchet my hand out of Luke's grasp and cross my arms over my chest. "I'll find Layla and ask, Tyler."

Tyler and Luke are just looking at each other, and I immediately feel like a bad hostess, even though I'm not the one hosting this party. "Tyler, Luke. Luke, Tyler. Luke is Layla's older brother, Tyler."

"Got it. Nice to meet you." Tyler holds out his hand.

I take the opportunity to hurry as fast as I can into the throng of Prestwicks and find Layla, laughing with one of her cousins.

"We need to talk." I grab Layla's arm and march her out of the family pack.

"Paige?"

I pull her over to the corner by the gazebo. "Why didn't you tell me Luke was coming?"

Layla brightens immediately. "He's here?" she asks excitedly. Then she sees my expression and sobers quickly. "Oh, Paige. I'm sorry. I didn't know he was coming, I swear."

I sigh. "It's fine. I should have figured."

"Why? He hasn't come to anything here in a long time." She is bouncing on her toes, looking over the growing crowd of people at him. I can tell she is trying to hold back her happiness, and I feel awful for feeling weird about it.

Too many conflicting feelings tonight.

I hear a buzz, and Layla pulls her phone out of the front pocket on her dress and grins. "Mom just texted to say thank you for the limo!" She cups her hands over her mouth. "Everyone! They're going to be here in ten minutes!"

A brief cheer goes up from the crowd. I turn around, amazed at how many people have come. The Prestwicks have a lot of friends and family.

The band starts playing something without vocals, a quiet, catchy song that people can still talk over. Layla disappears to go give Luke a hug.

"So." Tyler is suddenly standing beside me again, and I look up at him and smile.

"So," I echo. I realize that I wasn't really paying attention earlier. Tyler cleans up nicely. Khakis, a blue dress shirt over a white T-shirt, and brown shoes. His hair is curling in a blond mess. He doesn't have any resemblance to a logger tonight.

I grin. "You look nice."

"Occasionally I dress up." He winks at me.

"Everyone!" Layla shouts again over the noise. The band stops playing and motions for her to come up on the gazebo. She hurries up the steps and grabs one of the microphones. "Guys, they'll be here in five. If everyone can find their seats, I'd appreciate it. When they arrive, the band is going to play their first dance song and introduce them like they did at their wedding."

People start moving all around the tables, looking for their names. Tyler smiles at me. "I hope we're at the same table."

"We are." I nod. "We're at the back table so we can help do things if we need to." I point to the table, thankful it's about as far away from the Prestwicks' table as possible.

I need some perspective.

Jesus, help me out here!

I follow Tyler over to the table with our place cards on it and smile as he pulls out my chair for me. "Thanks."

This table isn't completely full. Layla's neighbors growing up and a man who works with Mr. Prestwick and his wife are already sitting there. We make our introductions, but I forget their names as soon as I hear them.

A few minutes later, a limo pulls up alongside the park and the driver opens the back door. Mrs. Prestwick climbs out, looking completely confused and absolutely beautiful in a simple black dress. The band starts playing "Up Where We Belong," and I force back a laugh.

Ah, the music of the eighties.

Mr. Prestwick climbs out then, and the guy playing the piano leans into the microphone. "Introducing Mr. and Mrs. Michael Prestwick!"

Mrs. Prestwick immediately starts crying as the crowd cheers and applauds. Layla hurries over to give her parents a hug, and I feel myself choking up for no reason at all except for the sweet scene in front of me and the ever-so-cheesy song the guy and girl are now singing together.

The three of them walk over to the front by the gazebo, and Layla is urging her parents to dance.

They finally agree and the crowd cheers again. I look over at Tyler, curious what he is thinking as pretty much the only person here who has never met Layla's parents.

He is grinning. He glances at me and his smile grows.

I smile back.

The band finishes the song, Mr. Prestwick kisses his wife, and we all clap again, a few people whistling. Layla is back on the stage and steals the microphone again.

"Mom, Dad, happy anniversary!" she says, and Mrs. Prestwick starts crying again.

Layla grins at her mom. "Well, I hope you're surprised. And I was actually planning on praying for our delicious food myself, but in another surprise, someone else flew in to say it for us." She waves to the side of the gazebo, and Luke walks up the steps.

There are really waterworks from Mrs. Prestwick now. I think Mr. Prestwick is even wiping away tears.

Luke grins his signature smile at his parents. "I love you guys," he says into the microphone. His gaze flickers over the tables until he meets my eyes. He smiles wider. "Let's pray. Lord, thank You for this evening, for Layla and Paige for arranging all of this, and most of all, for my parents. Lord, they are the biggest blessing in my life, and I know I owe everything—especially growing up learning to love You—to them. Bless them and keep them, Lord. And bless this food. Amen."

"Amen," the crowd mumbles.

Layla takes back the microphone. "We're going to let my parents get their food first, and then it's open eating!"

The crowd erupts into chatter, standing, getting in line, and moving around while the band plays "How Sweet It Is." I lean back in my chair, deciding to wait until the frenzy by the food tables has calmed down before heading over there. Tyler apparently has come to the same conclusion, because he doesn't move either, while both of the couples sitting at our table get up to get food.

"This looks great," Tyler says after a minute or two. "You guys did an amazing job."

"Thanks, Tyler. You helped a lot." The sun is just starting its descent, and I start worrying that we haven't put up enough lights. I frown at the candles on the table. "Think it's bright enough out here?"

He looks around. "Surely the five thousand Christmas lights on the gazebo will help a little." He grins. "I think it will be fine. Besides, I like dancing more when it's kind of dark so people don't notice how terrible I am at it."

I grin.

We get in line for the food just as Layla is bounding back up to the stage. "Now that some of you are done eating, I'm going to have Mom and Dad cut their cake, and then we'll open up the dance floor."

I hurry to put the Burgundy sauce on my steak and potatoes, add a scoop of salad, and grab a roll so I can be out of the way for the cake cutting. The caterer did her best to duplicate a picture of the Prestwicks' original wedding cake.

I carry my plate a few feet back and watch. Tyler already headed back to the table, but I want to see the cake cutting. Mrs. Prestwick is still teary eyed and going on and on about how beautiful the cake is and how it looks just like their wedding cake.

"You guys outdid yourselves."

I look up and Luke is right beside me.

"Layla outdid herself," I correct.

"You're too modest. She told me everything you did to help." He is smiling at me, but I make myself look back at the Prestwicks cutting their cake. They carefully feed a piece to each other, and the crowd cheers again as they kiss.

Luke is distracting.

"Want to dance?" he asks me.

"I need to eat." I hold my plate of food a few inches higher. "I'm starving." All I've eaten today is a bacon sandwich from Starbucks and a granola bar.

"After you eat then," Luke persists.

"Look, Luke." I take a deep breath and look at him for the first time since he came over.

"Paige," he interrupts, "I know what you're going to say."

"Really?"

He smiles gently at me. "Let's not talk here. Go eat. I'll come find you and we can talk later tonight." Then he leaves.

Great. I walk back to the table and sit beside Tyler with a huff, then grab my plastic utensils that look just like real silver.

Layla was ecstatic when she found those.

"So, I didn't even know Layla had a brother," Tyler says.

"Sometimes I wish I didn't know either."

Tyler apparently catches my not-so-subtle hint that I don't want to talk about Luke, because he quickly changes the subject. "Rick, Natalie, and Claire are here."

I nod. I saw them pull up, but I was trying to light the candles quickly so I just waved. Claire has doubled in size since I saw her last.

I finish my delicious dinner and sit back just as the sun dips completely behind the trees. "Layla is right to speak of that sauce in hushed tones."

Tyler laughs. "It was pretty good."

"Pretty? That went way beyond pretty."

I look around. The gazebo is lit up, and the rest of the park is glowing in the soft light. Candles and lanterns flicker all over the tables and on the steps of the gazebo.

It is a magical fairyland.

The band starts playing "Come Fly with Me," and Tyler smiles over at me. "Want to dance, Paige?" The dance floor is getting crowded with the sun setting. Apparently, there are a lot of people who like to dance in the semidarkness.

I look over at Tyler and smile. "Sure."

I follow him over to the dance floor, and he reaches for

my hands. The song is a little up-tempo and I'm not the greatest dancer, but we do the best we can. I am laughing a few minutes later as he spins me into another couple.

"I'm so sorry," I say.

The man shrugs. "It's dark," he says, being nice. It isn't *that* dark.

The band finishes the song, everyone applauds, and the band goes right into "Have I Told You Lately."

Tyler smiles sweetly at me, and a thousand gummy bears do a jig in my stomach when he slips a hand around my waist and pulls me close. "I don't think I ever got the chance to tell you how beautiful you look tonight," he says quietly.

I swallow. "Thank you."

I set my hand on his shoulder and we gently sway to the music. I love this song. This is my parents' song, so I heard it from the time I was a little girl. Preslee and I would sneak out of our rooms after bedtime some nights and see Mom and Dad dancing barefoot to this song in the kitchen. We would sit behind the couch and watch, and Preslee would whisper about how she wanted to sing music like that someday.

It is a good memory. Unlike a lot of the ones with Preslee in them.

I squeeze my eyes shut for a second to refocus on what is happening right now. Tyler holds me very gently, his right hand lightly skimming my back.

I look over and Layla is dancing with Peter, snuggled into his chest, eyes closed and smiling. I grin. She is happy. And honestly, Peter is quiet, but he isn't so bad.

Not so bad at all.

Mr. and Mrs. Prestwick come onto the dance floor and

he kisses his wife again, gently twirling her on the crowded dance floor.

Then I see Luke. He is sitting at his family's table, the one closest to the dance floor and the gazebo, watching his parents and then looking over at me. He smiles at me, but it isn't his usual cheerful, huge smile. This one is sad.

We need to talk, he mouths to me.

I shake my head slightly and look back up at Tyler. Tyler is sweet. Tyler seems to genuinely care about me. He doesn't mince words. If it weren't for him and Peggy and Candace, I'd still be running around like a crazy person, too stressed to see straight.

Tyler looks down right then, sees me studying him, and grins. "What?" He pulls me in a little closer.

"Nothing."

He leans down then and kisses my cheek.

My whole face warms.

I dip my head quickly so he can't see the way I am blushing. I squeeze my eyes shut briefly.

Lord, thank You for Tyler.

I sway with him to the music and think for a little bit. Aside from feeling like a fish in a fishbowl, thanks to Luke, I am happy. Relaxed even. I still have the banquet for the agency to do, but I'm not worried or stressing about it at all.

It is hard to be stressed when the stars are shining in the dark sky and the park is lit up with twinkle lights and candles. God has given us the perfect weather for tonight. It is a little chilly but nowhere near cold.

Tonight has gone perfectly. Next weekend will as well.

"So," Tyler says quietly, tightening his hold on me briefly.

"What do you say to maybe coming out to dinner with me on Friday?"

I look up at him, grinning. "I don't know. Is this a date?"

He smiles at me, blue eyes warm. "Most definitely a date."

"Then I say yes."

He kisses my cheek again, and again I blush, my knees shaking. We turn right then and Luke is still watching us.

It is a little unnerving.

The song ends and we all clap again. "I need a drink," I tell Tyler, even though I mostly just want to get away from Luke's prying stare.

I walk back over to the table and take a long sip from my glass of cranberry punch. Tyler is close behind me, also reaching for his glass.

I smile at him, feeling confused. I don't really feel like picking apart my emotions tonight, though. Tonight is about Layla and her parents. Not about Tyler, not about Luke. Tonight is about enjoying the calm, peaceful night.

There will be plenty of time this week for dissection of feelings.

I lean down and grab my purse from under the table for my lip balm. I check my phone too. There are two texts I haven't read. The first one is from my mom.

HOPE YOU ARE HAVING A GOOD TIME AT THE PARTY! WISH WE COULD HAVE COME. PLEASE CALL ME TOMORROW MORNING WHEN YOU GET UP.

Weird. I chew on my bottom lip, wondering what I need to call her about. Probably just a rundown of the party. Mom likes to know details like that.

Tyler smiles at me and nudges my shoulder, holding his

hand out. "Need more punch?"

I nod. "Sure, thank you." I give him my glass and he walks over toward the table. I check the last text quickly.

And stop.

Hi, Paige. I'm in town and I need to see you.

It's from Preslee.

"Paige, we really need to talk," Luke says, suddenly standing right beside me.

So much for peace and calm.

I look down at the text, back up at Luke, and then over at Tyler and Layla, who are talking by the food table.

A thought strikes me right then. What if this whole learning how to control my schedule isn't as much about my crazy life as it is about learning to give control over to God?

"A need does not constitute a call."

But God meets needs. And He gives calls.

I look at Luke, bite back a sigh, and nod. "Okay."

Don't miss out on the next chapter in Paige Alder's life
in *Paige Rewritten,* coming from NavPress's
THINK line October 8, 2013!

About the Author

Erynn Mangum is married to her best friend, Jon. They have one adorable toddler here on earth and one precious baby in heaven. Erynn loves to spend time with her family and friends, particularly if there is coffee or chocolate involved. She's the author of the LAUREN HOLBROOK and MAYA DAVIS series. Learn more at www.erynnmangum.com.

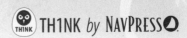

MY LIFE IS **TOUGHER** THAN **MOST** **PEOPLE REALIZE.**

I TRY TO
KEEP EVERYTHING
IN BALANCE:
FRIENDS, FAMILY, WORK,
SCHOOL, AND GOD.

IT'S NOT EASY.

I KNOW WHAT MY
PARENTS BELIEVE AND
WHAT MY PASTOR SAYS.

BUT IT'S NOT
ABOUT THEM.
IT'S ABOUT ME...

ISN'T IT TIME I
OWN MY FAITH?

THROUGH THICK AND THIN, KEEP YOUR HEARTS AT ATTENTION, IN
ADORATION BEFORE CHRIST, YOUR MASTER. BE READY TO SPEAK
UP AND TELL ANYONE WHO ASKS WHY YOU'RE LIVING THE WAY
YOU ARE, AND ALWAYS WITH THE UTMOST COURTESY. 1 PETER 3:15 (MSG)

www.navpress.com | 1-800-366-7788   THINK TH1NK *by* NAVPRESS